STEEL RAIN

Special Agent Vincent Piper of the London FBI Field Office is a newcomer to this vibrant city. There is anger simmering beneath its surface. He's only here to patch up his marriage ... But when his daughter Martha is murdered in a terrorist bomb attack in the city, Piper realises he's staying. He knows who planted the lethal device: all he has to do is find him ... Sarah, his daughter's tutor, and the mysterious Celeste, help him piece together his shattered life. Piper invests his trust in them, but what exactly are their motives? Before he can find out, he has a man to kill.

TOM NEALE

---◆---

STEEL RAIN

Complete and Unabridged

ULVERSCROFT
Leicester

First published in Great Britain in 2005 by
Headline Book Publishing
London

First Large Print Edition
published 2006
by arrangement with
Headline Book Publishing
a division of Hodder Headline
London

The moral right of the author has been asserted

British Library CIP Data

Neale, Tom
   Steel rain.—Large print ed.—
   Ulverscroft large print series: adventure & suspense
   1. Americans—England—London—Fiction
   2. Terrorism—England—London—Fiction
   3. Suspense fiction 4. Large type books
   I. Title
   823.9'2 [F]

   ISBN 1–84617–175–X

Published by
F. A. Thorpe (Publishing)
Anstey, Leicestershire

Set by Words & Graphics Ltd.
Anstey, Leicestershire
Printed and bound in Great Britain by
T. J. International Ltd., Padstow, Cornwall

This book is printed on acid-free paper

This is for Susan Cook

Author's Note

There is an FBI Field Office attached to the US Embassy in London, staffed by Legats, as depicted herein. However, at the request of the Bureau, and in the light of ongoing security concerns, certain operational procedures and personnel details have been changed.

Prologue

The last night of Christos Malacco's life begins much like any other. He finishes an afternoon minicab shift and hands his battered Vauxhall Vectra over to his brother, with whom he splits the overheads and the radio rental. After an early evening meal at home and reading his girls a bedtime story, he catches the bus from Green Lanes in North London, down to New Oxford Street. There, he alights and walks the three hundred yards to his firm's lock-up garages. He has less than a hundred minutes to live.

At one time horses were kept in the cobbled yard. Now it is home to tired and bruised steel carts, dozens of them, all showing the wear and tear of twenty or more years of being wheeled around the streets of the capital, and the jaundiced discolouration caused by a combination of propane flames and rivers of hot grease.

George, the site manager, is already there, his Ford Transit van reversed into the yard with the roller-back up, revealing stacks of buns, baps, burgers and hotdogs plus grey imports of Coca Cola and Fanta, many of

1

them with Arabic writing and overstamped 'sell by' dates to make them illegible.

This obscuring of the dates is purely for the Environmental Health Inspectors who, from time to time, marshall their meagre resources for a crack-down on the street vendors. This normally lasts a week or two before some high-profile story about rat infestations in Chinese takeaways or a plague of cockroaches in kebab shops sends them scurrying elsewhere.

Christos unlocks his favourite cart, checks that the full complement of condiments is all present and correct and that the gas cylinder is charged, and then he pushes it to the Transit. There, he helps himself to a series of plastic bags and cartons and stashes them in the multi-compartmented body of the stand. Finally, once he has restocked the cracked acrylic container on the side with paper napkins, he is handed a fist-sized bag of pills, which he puts in the utensil rack, covering it with his knives and spatulas.

He signs for the items he has taken — not for the tablets — and heaves the cart across the oily threadbare piece of carpet that George has laid down over the cobbles to muffle the sounds of the wheels. Christos propels his stand out onto New Oxford Street, crosses the road and heads for

Centrepoint. The streets are quiet. It is Tuesday, not his busiest night, and there is rain brooding in the air. Still, when the pubs kick out, he is fairly certain there will be enough people who want a dog 'with a little something extra', as the accepted street code goes, to make tonight worthwhile.

He yawns as he steers the cart. Minicab, hotdogs, minicab, hotdogs; it is a constant struggle just to pay the mortgage, and now his wife is insisting that nothing less than private schools will do for their two girls. Twenty thousand pounds a year he will need, just for the fees. He tries not to think how many hotdogs that is. 'A fuck of a lot,' he mumbles to himself.

Seventy-one minutes.

He sets up on the corner of Tottenham Court Road, where it intersects with Charing Cross Road; this has been his pitch since the 1980s, when he supplied mostly to the young people coming and going from the club in the YMCA basement in Great Russell Street, now long gone. It is a good position, because he can be seen clearly from several approaches, and he will catch the after-theatre crowd from the Queen musical that seems to have been on at the Dominion for ever.

Christos fires up the propane, filling the

broiling compartments of the cart with water, then heating up the grill plate. Within five minutes he has sold two veggies, one meat and four cans of soda. It is close to eleven by now, and he eyes up the small knots of wobbly-legged drinkers wandering round the West End. Pissed blokes, that's what he needs. Girls are no good. They rarely stop and buy, not unless it's a hen night or they are out of their minds on those fruit-flavoured vodka drinks. Nor does word seem to have got around to female clubbers that Christos, along with many of the other stall-holders, can serve something with your dogs to give you a bit of a lift.

'Hotdog.' It's a tourist, just out from the show. 'No onions. Chilli sauce.'

Christos barely looks up at the man, just throws the meat tube into the ready-cut bun, and takes the man's money, three pounds exactly. Another quid profit in the kitty for Channing School for Girls.

George strolls past at twenty after, and Christos asks him to mind the stand while he goes off for a quick slash in the darkness underneath the Centrepoint tower. As he is about to unzip himself, he sees his hotdog customer, leaning against the wall, his dog in his hand, untouched.

'How long you been selling this shit?' The

4

voice is low, a whisper almost. He is a big man, the bottom half of his face swathed in a scarf, and he has gloves on, Christos notes, something you rarely see on September days any longer.

'Is not shit. Is good stuff,' he protests.

'Right. How long have you been a purveyor of this fine product?'

'Fifteen, sixteen years.'

'Ah. Sorry to hear that. You ever heard of a restaurant called the Phoenix? In New Jersey?'

Christos's voice shakes as he answers the strange question. 'No.'

'It made the same mistake as you.'

'What mistake is that?'

The gun the man produces has a Centurion suppressor on it, the finest silencer in the world. The man raises the weapon and, before any words can escape Christos's constricted throat, fires two shots into his chest.

Christos flies backwards as the nine-millimetre slugs enter him and he lands heavily on the pavement, skidding through the dust and litter that has accumulated in this piss-stained corner. The customer walks over and forces open the dying man's mouth. Into the gaping hole, the man stuffs the untouched three pounds' worth of hot dog, and walks away, heading quickly off to St Giles High Street, the gun glowing warm in the inside pocket of his overcoat, right next to his heart.

Thirty seconds left. As his life fades, a strange thought plays around Christos's dying cerebrum: his life assurance should cover the girls' school fees.

1

When he enters the bar at the Stafford Hotel in St James's, Vincent Piper feels the eyes of the drinkers flick over him, then turn quickly away. He isn't a man worth lingering over. Piper doesn't blame them — he knows he isn't looking his best. Life is not running smoothly, and it shows in his face, which is grey, tired and drawn — with signs that even shaving is a task beyond him. Too much worry, too many arguments, an overload of what his wife calls 'unresolved issues'. Which is rich, because she is one of the main ones.

Piper slides onto a stool at the bar, almost orders a dry martini, stops himself and switches to a gin and tonic. He has tasted too many shitty martinis since he arrived in London three months previously to risk it. He looks up at the US baseball and football pennants and the caps that, by some old tradition, adorn the Stafford's ceiling and feels a stab of both homesickness and nostalgia. Houston Oilers, they've moved on, and the Brooklyn Dodgers . . . jeez, how old must that be? The Dodgers moved west thirty, no, forty years ago. He trawls through the names and places displayed on the garish triangles of embroidered material, checking off teams he has seen, cities visited, Superbowls watched, until his neck gets stiff and he looks down and glances across at the woman a few stools along from him, holding the stare a little more than is usually appropriate in this town.

His drink arrives and he sips, feeling it hit the spot immediately. The guilt spot. He is drinking too much. Not enough to become a problem at work, but along with his absences from the gym and the firm's softball team, he can feel his pants getting tight around the waist. Nothing there yet, but forty is almost his new best friend and he knows he is entering the danger zone: the stomach will grow, the belt will slip below the gut, the shoulders gradually round off and he'll be heading for his government pension. He saw it happen to his old man, but not till he was twenty years older than Vince is now.

He's been craving alcohol since lunchtime when he had watched the crowd at a reception in the wonderful drawing room of Winfield House, the US Ambassador's Residence in Regent's Park, slurp its way through ten or twenty cases of champagne. It was the launch of *America at Play*, a new travel portal designed to encourage foreign visitors back to the domestic US market in the wake of 9/11, the Iraq War and the immigration fiascoes, when tourists had to wait in line for two or three hours before they were allowed into the US to spend their dollars. Many had decided they might as well take their cash where there was a warmer welcome.

The journos drank and munched on the canapés as they waited and waited for Jack Sandler. Piper could feel the irritation building to breaking point when, with consummate timing, the Ambassador swept in, shaking hands and slapping backs, apologising profusely. In his striped shirt with rolled-up sleeves, he could have come from a poker school, but he assured them he had been 'woodshedding', as he put it, some fine details of the US-British road map for the new world order. This would be the version 9.0, Piper had thought cynically. They'd produced more maps in the past twelve months than Rand McNally.

Within thirty seconds at the lectern Sandler had disarmed the crowd. The man might be a Republican, thought Piper, but he had that easy, downhome manner that Clinton had once used so successfully. The kind of warmth that could make a man

President, no matter what his sexual peccadilloes. And, the word was, Sandler had none of those. One wife, three teenage kids, two dogs and no skeletons.

He had launched into a history of the Ambassador's grand house, from hunting lodge, in the days when the Park was countryside, to its time as a home for Woolworth's heiress Barbara Hutton, who fled when a German bomb fell in her garden, and later sold it to the US government for one dollar. It took half a million to fix it up. He pointed through the tall French doors to a coy statue of the troubled Woolworth's heiress. He indicated Chippendale mirrors and hand-painted Chinese wallpaper, laboriously stripped from an Irish castle and re-hung in the Green Room. Then, a few jokes about the importance of getting travellers to come to the US and spend their money, some schmaltzy words about the website, and he was gone. Piper, like most people in the room, would have voted him into the White House there and then.

During Sandler's speech, Brewster of the Secret Service had come over and told Piper that they were a man down for a 'five-five' security check over at the Fairmont Hotel in St James's for Gideon Klein. The guy had been one of Bush's security advisors, and was

10

here for a book tour. Being an architect and apologist for the Iraq invasion, he warranted a once over by the Secret Service. Could Piper lend a hand?

What about the DPG? Vince had asked, meaning the Brits. Brewster had curled a lip. He didn't rate the Diplomatic Protection Group. So Piper had agreed, just to get away from more speeches about tourism and dollar income, even though Federal Agents don't normally like doing the Service's work for them. Especially as the Treasury Department's guys get to carry weapons as a matter of routine, and the Feds don't — not in London anyway.

There has long been an FBI presence in London, just as there has been a CIA office in the Embassy, but both have expanded exponentially in the last few years. The FBI has grown from four agents to a minimum of a dozen, with that often doubling, stretching the office space to the limit. Some of the agents, who are linked into the Homeland Security International Task Force, are exclusively concerned with terrorism that poses a threat to US citizens, and forging links with MI5 and SIS.

Piper, though, is part of AAPL — Anglo-American Policing Liaison, usually known as APPLE — which means that he gets the cases involving his fellow countrymen, whether they are mixed up in drug running or computer fraud or murder or, as often as not, getting murdered, and he acts on such matters with Scotland Yard's Detective Chief Inspector Fletcher. It's good, interesting work, nicely varied and more satisfying, although possibly in the long run less essential, than chasing shadowy terrorist cells. All he misses is his gun. And his wife. And Martha, his daughter.

Piper watches the Stafford barman mix a Stoli martini for another customer and regrets not having one. The guy behind the bar knows what he is doing. The vodka and the gin are kept in the freezer, and they have a lovely oily consistency as they hit the frosted glass, like a near-frozen sea, when the viscous water can barely bring itself to form waves.

'Want to play a game?' says the woman next to him and it makes him start. In New York or Washington or LA, you speak to strangers in bars, it comes with the territory. You don't want to shoot the breeze, you sit down the end, or watch the TV. Otherwise you talk sports or politics or alcohol or divorce or the economy or Alan Greenspan or what-about-those-Nicks. In London, you don't. Not so he's noticed. Maybe he's been going to the wrong places.

He turns slightly to look at her more directly. He's already taken in the essentials on that first examination a couple of minutes previously. Thirty-ish. Redhead. Smart, very well-cut lightweight grey suit. Sparkly eyes, nice cheekbones. Beautifully manicured nails, something of a rarity in London. As far as he can tell, the voice is top drawer. He isn't too hot on British accents yet. He can get vague regions, broad brush-strokes — Welsh, Scots, West Country, his wife's Mancunian, DI Fletcher's Geordie — but the subtleties elude him. Hers, though, he knows, is right at home in these streets, St James's and Mayfair.

Piper swirls the ice in his drink and grins at her with what he hopes is his best winning smile, if he still has one. 'OK.'

'How many men in the room?' she asks. 'Without looking.'

'Seven.'

'Women?'

'Including you?'

A nod.

'One.'

'What about the man directly behind you?'

'Fifty. Thinning hair. Terrible suit. Looks bored. Probably not waiting for anyone. In town on business. Not English, but not French or Italian. Maybe Eastern European.'

13

'Latvian.'

'You know that for sure?'

'No. But to my mind he's a Latvian.' He looks puzzled. 'It's catch-all. I had a Latvian friend once. Ghastly dress sense.' She drains her glass.

'Can I get you a drink?' he finds himself saying, a little voice warning him this is the kind of place that serves fifteen-dollars-a-glass champagne and his *per diem* isn't up to it. London is an expensive posting.

'That would be nice,' she says, showing those perfect teeth. 'Champagne, please. The Clicquot.'

He signals the barman and then asks for a martini after all. *Probably twenty bucks.*

'Are you by any chance a policeman?' she asks demurely, as if she is suggesting that he has a second cup of tea.

He laughs. 'I'm American.'

'I know. So that would make you an American policeman.'

'Not necessarily. Why do you think that?'

'Just the way you walked into the room. Hyp-obs, isn't it called?'

Piper finds himself smiling. It is called exactly that. Hyper-observation. He's just come off the five-five sweep — so named because there are twenty-five essential checks to be made, in groups of five — at the

14

Fairmont down the road, and he's clearly still in the Zone, measuring distances to doors, sight-lines, hiding-places, scanning faces, checking hand positions. Especially the hands.

'I'm not a cop. Honest,' he says. Well, it is true, after a fashion. 'Vincent Piper.'

He holds out his hand and she takes it briefly, so fast he has but a fleeting impression of the warmth of her skin. 'Celeste Young. If you aren't a cop, you do a fine impersonation.'

He opens his mouth, not even sure of how much he is going to tell her, at the exact moment a tiny, almost plaintive beep sounds from her Tulita handbag. She lifts her mobile phone out, glances over the text message and flashes him what he hopes is a regretful smile. 'That's me. I have to go, Vincent.'

'Most people call me Vince.'

She drains her glass, the fastest disappearance of fifteen dollars since he'd last been in Vegas. 'Nice meeting you, Vince. Enjoy your stay.'

I'll try, he thinks. All two long years of it. The bill comes and he is suddenly glad that Martha has refused his offer of a blow-out dinner.

★ ★ ★

Piper walks up St James's Street back towards the Fairmont. London is hot for September, pushing into the eighties and clammy. He can feel the suit sticking to his shirt, which in turn adheres to the sheen of moisture on his skin. He wants to look and feel better for Martha, but running around the hotel checking for non-existent assassins for two hours has left him creased and crumpled, and the two drinks — especially that martini — means he is sweating pure alcohol. She'll smell it on him. He can just see that cute button nose twitching with disapproval.

On impulse Piper crosses the road into Jermyn Street to see if he can pick up a fresh shirt, but all the traditional stores with their flamboyant torsos in the window wearing bespoke numbers and fancy braces are closed.

There's a Gap at Piccadilly Circus; maybe he can get something more casual to soften the formal line of his regulation dark blue suit. He rips off his tie in anticipation, opening the collar to let some air in.

As he hits the main road he spots the familiar telltale green symbol of a Starbucks. He checks the time. Seven-thirty, she had said, at the Barnes & Noble café on the Charing Cross Road. That gives him time for a quick slug of caffeine, and he weaves through the stationary traffic, cursing a cycle messenger who is pedalling against the flow. Lycra Boy flashes him the finger, making him another Londoner lucky that Vince isn't allowed to pack a weapon 24-7, as was the norm at home. Always on duty, always armed, that was the FBI maxim. Unless you get a British posting. It doesn't figure: every UK airport has SWAT-like cops with sub-machine guns and they won't let him pack a lousy handgun off-duty.

In the Starbucks Piper orders a latte, sits down and stares out at the parade of passing humanity, feeling vaguely misanthropic. Outside is a river of commuters, heads down, powering on home, faces mostly etched with worry. It is a joyless crowd, trudging and tired. It could be the weather, but he has seen nothing in the city so far to make him think the natives do wild exuberance in the streets. Yet in a way he envies these people heading off for their suburban bolt-holes. He so wants to go home.

His daughter has seen his wife in the last two weeks, and she knows the state of play between them. Well, he knew the state, too: match postponed indefinitely. But she'd know if there had been any softening in the granite-face that Judy has presented to the world. She is up there, in that big house on

17

the outskirts of Manchester, repelling all comers. He'd gone up to see her — making the fundamental mistake of taking the dirty, unreliable train — but was rebuffed by her yard-dog of a mother without so much as a hello. 'Tell him to go away,' was all he heard.

Wasn't there a statute of limitations for this kind of thing? It was nearly two years now since the final split. He wasn't hoping for reconciliation, but surely civility wasn't out of the question. And it wasn't as if he had invented infidelity. It was a far from original sin. 'Have you never been tempted?' he had once asked her. 'What about that Portuguese gardener we had back in the States who looked like the flamenco dancer Joaquin Cortez? I saw how you spent three hours washing a coffee cup so you could admire him pruning.' At that point she'd slapped him. He guesses he was wrong about the gardener.

Martha, after an initial bout of frostiness that almost matched his wife's arctic chill, had begun to thaw a little. They had spoken on the phone, had an awkward dinner, even joked about her run of loser boyfriends. Perhaps he can salvage something from the wreck of his marriage to Judy, if only a decent relationship with his daughter,

He finishes the latte, takes a last lungful of

18

the store's chilled air and steps out onto the grimy sidewalk. The Gap store is open and he buys a standard Oxford, changes into it in the cubicle and walks out with his wet rag of a JC Penney number in the blue bag. He dumps it in an overflowing rubbish bin. He is running fifteen minutes late now, something he hates. Martha is always telling him to stop being so uptight, to chill a little, as she puts it. He'll remind her of that when she taps her G-Shock in irritation.

Here in Soho the people are livelier, no longer just ground-down commuters trudging towards the underground. He cuts up through the back streets, avoiding Shaftesbury Avenue, crossing Wardour Street and hurrying along Old Compton Street. He is beginning to learn short cuts now, resigned to the fact that his grid-pattern-trained brain is going to have to loosen up when it comes to street-plans. 'You can't pronounce 'em and you can't find 'em,' had been the Roth's summing up of the city's main thoroughfares. 'If you get lost, just ask a cabbie.' He'd tried that once: the driver told him to buy an *A to Z*.

Stanley Roth is the Assistant Legat, the Deputy Legal Attaché, and Piper's immediate superior. He has been in the city for twenty-seven months, and he likes it. Maybe it grows on you. Or maybe it helps, living with your wife and kids in Hampstead in a happy family, not scattered across the country, bound only by resentment and suspicion. Christ, snap out of it, Piper, he thinks. Nobody died. Sooner or later, the storm will subside, and reason will prevail.

Past the gay sex shops, the leather harnesses and tight shorts once so outré now barely registering on the crowd, many of whom have piercings and tattoos of their own. He tries not to feel his age or his upbringing — or the crushing conservatism of the FBI — and fails. He can hear his father's voice yapping in his ear about the youth of today. Well, Martha is part of that youth now. He has to be tolerant.

A familiar face swims into view. Fifty something and frowning. The name follows. Monroe. Henry Monroe.

'Hey,' Piper says, but Monroe hurries on. He raises his voice. 'Hey! Henry!'

Monroe stops and turns, but no smile lights up his face. He nods. 'Vince. How are you?'

Monroe is an old family friend. As a rookie he had worked with Piper's father on the infamous Wrecking Crew case — the last hurrah of the anarchist Weather Front group — in the early 1970s. Even when they were no longer partners, he always came over for Eddie Piper's Fourth of July barbecues.

'I'm OK,' Vince says.

Monroe is old school FBI. He is dressed in a dark suit, too heavy for the weather, white shirt and navy-blue tie. Little wonder he looks hot and bothered. He is screwing the magazine he has in his fists into a tube.

'What are you doing here, Henry?' Piper struggles for the wife's name. 'Is Kate with you?'

'What are *you* doing here?' Monroe shoots back.

'Associate Legat,' Piper says. 'I told you when I applied. Your old number. Two-year stint. Look, I have to meet Martha. Come along. She'd love to see you.'

'Martha? She's in London?'

'At college, yeah. I told you — ' The look of apprehension on Henry Monroe's face makes him stop.

'Do yourself a favour. Now. Get her out of here.'

'What do you mean? Henry?'

Henry pokes him in the chest with the rolled-up magazine to emphasise his point. 'It isn't safe.'

'What are you talking about?'

'Get her out.' Monroe pokes him again

21

and, irritated, Piper grabs the magazine from him.

'What do you mean, Monroe?'

But Henry is gone.

Piper watches his back disappear into the crowd, walking fast. What the hell was that all about? He shrugs the encounter away and resumes his walk. He unravels the magazine still in his hand, then ditches it. Jerk, he thinks.

He passes the uninviting budget restaurants — all you can eat for £3.99 in London was surely an invitation to some virulent strain of *E.coli* — and the licensed sex shops, and makes a left onto Charing Cross Road. The bookshop that is his destination is housed in a building a hundred yards or so up ahead on the corner. Piper checks his watch: twenty minutes late.

He sees Martha at the kerbside across the street, looking for him, head swivelling anxiously, searching the crowd. She is raising her mobile to her ear, shaking her hair aside as she does so. And then he doesn't see her any more.

★ ★ ★

It comes like a sudden blast of fog, as if all the water vapour in the air has turned to ice,

22

a giant's breath blown across the thirty feet from sidewalk to sidewalk. He feels that exhalation brush over him; the needle-sharp crystals prickle his skin, his eyes sting and water in the second before he can get his arms up to protect his face.

Then the noise comes, the dull crump that he has heard on countless training videos, seen at Quantico, tasted at Oklahoma and Cape Town and Riyadh and at Ground Zero, and with it the shockwave, a punch of super-heavy air, thudding his lungs flat and driving him back into the people behind, limbs flailing. He staggers and catches himself and remains upright. Others aren't so lucky.

Silence.

Just a hum, like a low generator, as the foul cloud starts to dissipate. Mouths are moving, but no sound comes; faces are contorted by pain and fear and shock, but there are no screams.

His ears start working again, and a howl rises up from the few hundred square yards in front of the ruined bookshop, mixed in with a chorus of shrill alarm bells. He can see dozens of prostrate bodies, and even more walking wounded, staggering around stiffly.

Cars are splayed across the road, windshields webbed where bodies have hit them. One vehicle has mounted the pavement outside Foyles, pinning an unknown number of pedestrians against the shattered plate window. It is the atomised windows that have created the fine mist, a deadly, lacerating dust. Now all that is left in the air are the shreds of dismembered books, swinging gently to earth.

Not again! his mind bellows.

Piper touches his own face and winces at the jolt of pain. He looks down at his fingertips. Blood. He checks himself in the sex-shop window. There are a few little globs of red, like bloody freckles, but his is a mere sideswipe.

Panic has gripped the bystanders now and bodies hurl into Piper, spinning him this way and that. But he runs towards the scene, not away from it.

He estimates where he had last seen Martha and tries to recall what she was wearing. She'd have been blown out of position, that was for sure.

'My face? How's my face?' a woman shouts at him, clutching at his leg.

He looks down at skin like hamburger and grabs her wrists. It is impossible to tell whether she is young or old. 'Fine,' he says, 'but there's some glass. Don't touch. I'll be a second. Don't touch.'

She nods obediently. Piper lets go and

picks his way across to the dazed boy standing outside the guitar shop, his jaw slack. A minute ago the teenager had been looking at Gibson guitars and Roland drum machines, now he is in the inner circle of hell, stunned at being left unscathed by a blast that had spread like a fan from the shop's frontage, into the street rather than along it.

'What's your name?' Piper demands.

'John,' he mumbles.

'John,' Piper says, pulling him into the road, kicking the broken-backed books out of his way, 'hold this woman's wrists. Here. Don't let her touch her face.'

'I'm going to be sick.'

Piper spins him away. 'Listen to me.' He takes a breath to calm himself down. 'Be sick. But be sick holding her wrists.' To the woman, he says, 'This is John. He's going to stay with you until help comes.'

'I can't see.'

'It's just dirt,' he lies. 'Stay calm, someone will be here soon. What's your name?'

'Emma.'

'OK, Emma, hang on to John. If it hurts, squeeze him.'

With a farewell pat of the kid's shoulder he steps over bodies, some moving, some not, checking each one, trying to find Martha. There are too many people, an overwhelming mass of tangled humanity. He wonders if London has a casevac plan, a system for evacuating mass casualties from a terrorism scene. *What, in a city where even the subway doesn't run properly?*

He looks back at the remains of the shop. There are flames on the ground and first floors. All that paper, pure kindling, he thinks. He can see sprinklers working, but fitfully. Where are the fire crews? Panic is starting to well up around him like a tangible presence.

He pulls out his mobile, speed-dials Martha's number and hears the tinkling tones to his left, the theme tune to some teen TV show, and he homes in on it until he can see her, one arm lying out at a strange angle, her blonde hair tarnished, the face masked by a splash of blood.

He gently moves the legs of a man whose trousers have been blown clean off, leaving his white hairy legs miraculously free of damage, so he can crouch down next to her.

'Martha. MARTHA. It's OK, darlin'. It's OK.'

He brushes her hair aside and gasps at the sight.

Two clear, sparkling eyes stare at him, a mouth trying to smile. A face in one piece. He moves his hand over her skull and she winces. There is glass in her scalp. Her hair is roped together with sticky blood in places, but the blast has missed her face.

He looks around for assistance. A small army of helpers has materialised — passers-by, shopkeepers, traffic wardens, a policeman, his white shirt already stained dark red. They are passing around water, clothes, bandages. Some are trained, he can tell they know what to do, taking pulses and doing the standard Glasgow Coma check, scoring the victims. Three to fifteen, where three means don't bother for now, that they are beyond immediate assistance.

Piper grabs a small Evian bottle off the Asian guy who appears with armfuls and pours some into Martha's mouth, then rubs away at the blood on her face. It is someone else's. He kisses her nose and wipes away his tears.

'Dad? Dad.'

'I love you,' he says. 'Just stay still. Help'll be here soon, baby.'

Where are the medics? He can hear the chuck-chuck and whoop-whoop of various sirens, a long way away, and car horns, growing ever more irate. The area is becoming grid-locked.

Piper stands up, looks around for a sign of organised action. There is none that he can discern. Martha's strangled voice makes him look down at her. Her eyes are fluttering.

Piper picks up his daughter, scoops her in his two arms, carefully supporting her head, not feeling a thing, because she is no weight at all. And he begins to walk away from the dead and the dying, as fast as he can.

2

Celeste Young leaves the American Bar at the Stafford and walks down King Street towards St James's Square. She still loves this part of London, with its gunshops (but, of course, no guns on show), old-fashioned clubs, chemists like apothecaries, Japanese restaurants that would shudder at the sight of a conveyor belt, and arcane premises such as the Dickensian Berry Brothers & Rudd wineshop, where the floors resemble the crazy house at a funfair.

All that is changing now. A Michiko Koshino jeans store is slated to open on Jermyn Street, with an FCUK across the street, both still cocooned behind hoardings for the moment. Youth is colonising the territory.

For the moment, though, it is still possible for her to feel she is in an older, more elegant London, frozen sometime in the 1950s, when shops closed prompt at five-thirty and the very best refused to open at all on Saturday, let alone Sunday. She is, of course, too young to remember such an era, but her father used to bring her to St James's to return books to the London Library, for his fitting at Hilditch

29

& Key or to pick up shoes at Lobb and headwear at Lock. They inevitably took tea at the Fountain Room and while they sat there in Fortnum's, sipping from fine china, his descriptions and recollections made her feel a connection to those times.

Dead now, of course, her father. A brain tumour took him. He had left them money, making them quite comfortable she had thought, but her brother Roddy had ripped through first his own inheritance, then hers.

He had his eyes on their mother's share, too, but it looked as though that would be swallowed by the care home she had opted to retire to, and very quickly at that. All that would be left was the Stables, a near-derelict property in the Cotswolds that might realise an income if the renovation was ever finished.

She crosses over the square, the flames outside the In and Out Club making her feel even hotter than she already is. The sober Rodriguez suit she is wearing had been a bad idea: she should have chosen something lighter. It was intended to undermine any preconceptions that DeVaughan might be harbouring, such as expecting her to turn up looking like a Footballer's Wife. It is too late to do anything about it. She locates his apartment on the corner of Charles II Street and looks up at the elegant stone-clad façade, wondering how much a flat in an area almost exclusively occupied by embassies and gentlemen's clubs is costing him.

She rings the bell and is buzzed up. She travels to the second floor by charming old-fashioned lift-cage and his door is right opposite the gates. He lets her in with a flurry, so the first view of him is his back as he issues the invitation to make herself at home. The living room is grand, if rather sparsely furnished, plain white, high ceiling, insipid landscapes on the wall, good view over the Square. The rental must be four or five grand a month, she decides. He enters from the bedroom, threading turk's-head links through his shirt-cuffs. Blue shirt, white collar and cuffs. Nasty. Mark him down a point. Tall, six foot at least, forty-ish, beginning to get a little jowly, but still attractive.

'Hello, Charles DeVaughan. Thanks for coming.' Then he stalls completely. 'Er . . . um.'

He is seconds from a flat spin, so she helps him out. 'Would I like a drink? Yes, please.'

'Yes. Sorry.' He runs a hand through his hair. 'Gosh. I'm sorry, it's just . . . '

'White wine?'

He takes a breath and pulls himself together. 'Right.'

She looks around while he is gone. A few nice modern pieces of furniture, an open fireplace — a big square hole in the wall where, she would guess, some ornate son-of-Adam had once stood — a fine quality leather sofa. No music of any kind.

DeVaughan reappears with two glasses and they sit. His eyes dart up and down, taking in her legs and hovering over the jacket. He is wondering how big her tits are. Difficult to tell, given the way Narciso had tailored the top. Let him wonder.

'So, Charles,' Celeste says, causing his gaze to snap back up. 'How long have you known Denis?'

Denis is the investment banker, someone who had been with her three years now, who knew she had a vacancy and had suggested she meet DeVaughan.

'Before I was sent to Paris we worked on the gilts desk at Bonnet and Roy. You know it?'

'I used to know John Roy,' Celeste told him. 'He was a friend of my father's.'

'Really? I met him once or twice. In his eighties. Bloody shrewd man,' DeVaughan says with heartfelt admiration.

'Yes.' She'd always felt Roy was a dreadful old lecher. 'How long are you back over for?'

'A year.'

'And your family?'

DeVaughan shifts uncomfortably. 'My . . . my wife didn't want to disrupt the children's schooling.'

'You have how many?'

'Two. Ten and fourteen. Quite bilingual now. Didn't want to lose that either.' He took a large gulp of wine. 'But a year . . . it's a long time and, well . . . I'll get over now and then, but you can't be certain how often . . . '

He is blushing. 'You don't have to explain,' she reassures him. 'How much did Denis tell you?'

'Well, the basics, I suppose.' He outlines the terms and she nods at each point, only having to clarify the payment arrangements. Denis had done well.

'One more thing,' she adds. 'I don't swallow and I don't do anal.'

★   ★   ★

Celeste drives along Shaftesbury Avenue and up Greek Street — they've changed the Soho one-way system yet again — heading for Roddy's place. Her brother had a suite of offices above one of the bars in the street, which this month has reverted to a Latin-American vibe, after an ill-advised stint as a vodka bar called Ossi, a retro-homage to all things East German. She just prays she can find a parking space on the square.

DeVaughan had excused himself after around ten minutes, saying he had a business dinner. She wondered which part of the deal didn't appeal to him. Celeste had done this enough times to know he wouldn't be calling back, could tell from the way he ushered her out. So what was it? He'd known about the money before he made contact, so it could only be her restrictions. Which one? Well, she could probably guess.

She crawls across the junction at Old Compton Street, past Roddy's office, with its garish *alphasport.com* logo on the doorway. Roddy seems to be the only one of the rash of late-twentieth-century dot-coms that is still breathing. He tore through millions of pounds a week with his sports-streaming service, but now he is shifting to online betting — focusing on anything but the horses, which Betfair has sewn up. Both he and his backers swear the corner is just ahead.

She really hopes so, for his sake.

The blast funnels itself down the alley to her right, smacking into the side of her M-Class Mercedes, causing it to rock on its suspension. She is flung halfway across the car before the seat belt bites. Her ears feel as though someone has slapped their hands over them, a sudden sharp stab of needle-like pain.

Celeste pulls over to the kerb, lowers the window and leans out to look up at the sky. A chopper is hovering, the rotors slashing at the air. A thin line of smoke begins to drift upwards. Bomb, she thinks. She'd been around when the Admiral Duncan public-house in Soho had gone up in that homophobic attack. In fact, Roddy had been in the pub the night before, and the impotent anger at that near-miss had burned for weeks. She could feel it again now, the sheer rage that anyone should think their pissy little cause — and they were all pissy little causes as far as she was concerned — was worth the taking of innocent human life.

The sirens from the fire station on Shaftesbury Avenue have started up. Ahead, other cars have stopped. Celeste looks back over her shoulder. No way out. She honks her horn furiously and there are a dozen answering calls.

'Bollocks,' she shouts to nobody in particular.

Then she sees him. The face from the bar, twisted into anger and pain, a girl's body draped across his arms.

She leaps out, trying to recall his name.

35

'Hey . . . hey, Mr Policeman,' she yells. 'Here! Come here!'

He stops and stares at her, uncomprehending.

'The bar,' she reminds him. 'We met in the Stafford American Bar.' The name comes to her. 'Vincent. Come here.'

He strides over. 'My daughter . . . a bomb . . . she's . . . I need to get her to hospital.'

'You shouldn't have moved her. Let's do this properly.' Celeste yanks open the rear door of the Mercedes. 'Look, slide her in — like this. Support her head. You're a bloody fool. OK, get in the back with her.'

She climbs behind the wheel and snaps the belt on. 'You ready for this? Hang on, better clip her in.' She undoes her seat belt again and strips off her jacket. 'And put that under her head.' She barely registers that it leaves her covered by just the silk camisole top underneath.

He does as he is told and she engages drive and grits her teeth as the M Class lurches forward and tears the door off a little Toyota abandoned in the street ahead and gobbles it under its big wheels.

'Shit,' he says.

'I've got good insurance.'

Martha groans and he lays a hand on her. Celeste works her way around Soho Square, cracking a few wing mirrors as she goes. Ignoring any one-way systems, she turns right on to Oxford Street then roars off up Tottenham Court Road.

'Where are you going?'

'UCH — University College Hospital. It's the closest Accident and Emergency department.'

He can hear the desperate wailings of ambulances now, a few streets across from where they are, heading south, as Celeste squeals the wrong way down Grafton Way, the big SUV narrowly missing a bus. And then they are at the grimy, tired exterior of the hospital and she is out, door open, engine still running.

A stretcher is at the side in a second, with Celeste urging the medics into action. Piper stands at one side, helpless. Just another dumbstruck, anguished father. He watches his daughter being wheeled off, waiting for the hand on his shoulder that will shake him awake.

Celeste turns and parks the battered and bruised Mercedes up on the pavement ten yards down the street. She returns to the hospital entrance and grabs Piper by the arm. He looks at her, vacant, puzzled. Well, she thinks, maybe even policemen go into shock. She hustles him in through the doors, and into the cramped space that is the A&E reception area.

A nurse intercepts them. 'Are you with the young lady? I need some details, Mr . . . '

'Piper,' he says, recovering his composure. 'Vincent Piper. Her name is Martha.'

'Is she a victim of the Soho blast?'

'Yes.'

'And you are?'

'Father.'

She looks at Celeste. 'Friend,' she replies to the unspoken question. A friend in her underwear, she realises, and crosses her arms.

'Can I see her?' Piper pleads.

The nurse glances back at the scratched, opaque doors leading to the treatment rooms and wards. People are running through them, grim-faced, many of them pushing equipment trolleys. Doctors are arriving, some pulling on their white coats as they come. Piper is aware that some kind of disaster plan has kicked in, something these people had drilled for, hoping never to use.

'You can see her soon,' the nurse assures him. 'There'll be others coming in any minute now. If you could just fill in an admission form . . . '

Celeste suspects it is simply a device by the nurse to shunt him to one side for a few precious minutes, give the staff time to take a beat before they are submerged in a cascade of the injured, their relatives and friends. 'Come on,' says Celeste. 'Thank you.'

The nurse gives a quick flash of a smile. 'And we'll get someone to see to you,' she says as she hurries back to the sharp end.

'Forget about me,' he shouts after her.

'Keep still.' Celeste reaches up and he feels a tug as a jagged edge snags on his skin. She holds up a glinting triangle of glass. 'That's the biggest. Here.' She dabs at the speck of blood. 'Come on, let's make it all official.'

Celeste steers him over to the desk, takes a form and sits them down, away from the blank-faced rows of the minor injured. She takes a pen from her bag, reckoning his shaking hands aren't really up to the job of writing, and begins to fill in the boxes for him.

'Name?'

'Vincent —'

'*Her* name.'

'Oh. Martha Piper. No, Saxton. Sorry, she's using my wife's maiden name.'

'Nationality?'

'American. No, no, dual citizenship. My wife's English.'

'Address?'

'She's at the American AIL Hostel in Regent's Park, that's the American Art

Institute in London.'

Outside, ambulances are screeching to a halt, sirens still blaring. More trolleys burst through the doors, with the attending medical staff calmly reeling off requests for plasma, drugs and equipment.

Piper sees the boy John, still holding on to the hand of Emma, the faceless woman, whispering in her ear, and he feels a catch in his throat. His insides feel raw. The situations he's been in — hostage negotiations, bank robberies, firefights with survivalists in Montana — all those taxpayers' dollars on training him and it all goes to shit when it hits close to home. Maybe it always does.

'You want a tea?'

'Coffee.'

'Have tea. It'll taste like coffee anyway from those machines,' Celeste says firmly.

She hands the registration card to the desk and crosses to a vending machine.

Piper stands up and stares towards the plastic double doors through which the trolleys are disappearing one by one.

Please be OK, he finds himself praying.

Celeste returns with the drink. He sips it and grimaces. 'I don't take sugar.'

'You do today.'

He nods and takes another sip. 'I saw it happen to her.'

'You weren't with her?'

He tells her the scene as he recalls it, one sequence in particular that is seared into his mind. Tossing her hair, looking this way and that, seeking him out. Using her mobile phone. She was there: then she wasn't.

'Why a bookshop?' Celeste asks. 'Why bomb a Barnes & Noble?'

'Why anywhere? You think these kind of people care? Maximum damage, that's the idea.'

'Who did it?'

He'd already been through that. The usual suspects, household names these days, rolled by like movie credits. Truth is, until someone put their hand up and said, 'It was me,' they probably wouldn't know. Even then, you couldn't always believe them. 'It's too soon. Look what happened in Madrid. You shouldn't jump to conclusions.'

It isn't safe. Who had said that?

Celeste is about to speak but the commotion at the door makes her spin round. 'Oh, Jesus!'

There are more victims, some with missing limbs, the glistening blood sickeningly bright next to pale skin. Now the room is echoing to the sound of hurrying feet, rubber-soled shoes flapping on linoleum tiles as resources

41

and people are switched from the main body of the hospital.

'What are you doing in London, Vincent?'

'Vince,' he reminds her. 'I'm with the Embassy. I'm a Federal Agent.'

A laugh escapes from her. 'A what?'

'FBI. Federal Bureau of Investigation. I'm with the London Legal Attaché. I'm an Associate Legat.'

'Christ. I've never met one of those before.'

He buries his face in her hair and onto her naked shoulder, covered only by the silken straps of her top and it feels good, reassuring, alive. He takes a deep breath and lets it out slow. 'Stay with me.'

She gently pushes him away, but not far. 'Of course. I've just got to call my brother, let him know I'm OK.' She stands, aware she'll have to go outside to use her mobile. 'Will you be all right for a second?'

'Sorry. I don't think this is how we Agents are meant to behave.' He runs a hand through his hair. 'I don't . . . I should be stronger than this.'

'Sssh. It's OK. I understand.'

'Look, Celeste, I have to see her. They think I've never seen blood before?'

She nods and watches him stand. As he walks briskly towards the opaque doors, Piper sees the young doctor emerge ahead of him,

42

his eyes scanning the room and alighting on Piper. As the doctor breathes in, readying himself to break the bad news, Vincent Piper feels himself begin to crumble. A fist grips his heart. She's gone. His little girl is gone.

3

Piper is wrong to underestimate the British response to the explosion. This is a city which has lived with terrorism for far longer than most, and certain well-practised mechanisms swing into place at airports, train stations and docks. The West End is sealed off, surveillance, both physical and electronic, stepped up to the maximum. Sources are quizzed, deep-cover agents asked for reports, terrorism experts recalled from leave, some arrests made where there is considered a danger of flight. Across London, interrogation centres are told to expect an influx of customers.

The Home Secretary has put in a request for a MACP standby. Military Aid to the Civil Power effectively deploys the Army as part of the police. He will proceed to full MACP if the sit-reps — the situation reports he will receive every two hours — look as though they demand it.

Preliminary reports are quickly drawn up for the Prime Minister and the Cabinet, the meagre amount of information fleshed out by the authors as best they can. Above all, meetings are called. The London Resilience

Liaison Organisation and the Emergency Planning Authority, which feature representatives of all the emergency services, convene a joint session in Vauxhall. At the Palace of Westminster, the Civil Contingencies Secretariat, composed of MPs and Cabinet Ministers, is put on alert, while the clumsily named DOP (IT) (T) and DOP (IT) (R) — concerned respectively with prevention of and responses to terrorism — are hurriedly called to the House.

At Downing Street, the PM is briefed by Sir David Omand, the Security and Intelligence Co-ordinator, a man who holds the spooks' purse-strings. He mostly cautions against naming names and pointing fingers before they have a clear idea of the bomb's provenance. He reminds the PM of mistakes made in the past, when such incidents have been used as cheap political capital, especially in Spain.

Probably the most significant meeting of the day, however, takes place at Thames House, the MI5 headquarters on the Embankment.

Here the Joint Terrorism Analysis Centre (JTAC) is convened in emergency session — more than a dozen members of MI5, MI6, GCHQ and senior officers from Scotland Yard, with 'observers' from the US State

Department sitting in. It takes place around the polished wooden table at the centre of Room 01, sometimes mockingly called the Situation Room, at other times *Das Bunker*. It is windowless, heavily screened against eavesdropping and has a complete Hostile Climate Pack — full air filtration for chemical and biological weapons, as well as the most up-to-date anti-radiation systems. Several doors lead off into anterooms, one of which contains enough provisions to last twenty men sixty days, another a series of bunk beds. There are nine such rooms in various buildings across London. If the security services and the government misjudge a terrorist attack, they intend to keep functioning in the aftermath, no matter how severe.

Right now, though, the worst thing about the atmosphere in Room 01 is the sense that the meeting could easily tip over into recriminations. The main purpose of this gathering, as far as each representative is concerned, is to make sure that his or her department does not carry the can for failure to prevent this atrocity. After so many recent successes against would-be bombers, from Operation Crevice onwards, which involved seven hundred officers and exemplary team-work between MI5, MI6, Special Branch and

GCHQ, being caught on the hop like this is a bitter pill to swallow.

Sir Jeremy Lazell of MI5 is the chair — the position rotates between the two security services every six months — and he calls for silence for the fifth time, on this occasion by slamming his hand on the table in frustration. Professional spooks my arse, he thinks. It's more like a convention of fishwives. He looks up at the corner camera and smiles. A live feed is being relayed directly to Eliza Manningham-Buller, his immediate superior and Director General of MI5, and the new head of the Special Intelligence Service, or MI6, a man known, as tradition dictates, simply as 'C'.

'Ladies and gentlemen,' he says pointedly, and feels all eyes swivel towards him. He helps himself to some water, his throat dried by the artificial climate. 'There is one thing I want to know as a matter of urgency. Am I going to read banner headlines in the *Guardian* any time soon telling me that MI5 ignored a terrorist threat? Or that MI6 knew the identity of the bomber? Or that our allies' — Sir Jeremy catches the eye of the CIA representative — 'failed to pass on a tip of a high-level threat to London?'

Heads shake around the table. Damned by both the UK's Butler Report and the US

47

Senate for their intelligence failures over Iraq, nobody wants to see any more accusations of incompetence.

'No?' He eyes up the GCHQ contingent, whose electronic intercepts have helped save the day half a dozen times in the past twelve months. They have nothing this time. 'I suggest we all go back and re-check everything for the past month. Every scrap of intelligence, human and electronic, to see if we missed this, because if we did ... ' He doesn't have to finish the sentence. 'Back here in twelve hours.'

As he watches them gather their Palms, papers and notebooks, Sir Jeremy feels that they are probably right. There was no warning, no intelligence and this attack is not part of an established campaign by familiar enemies. This is something altogether different. He wishes he knew what.

★ ★ ★

Piper has trouble sleeping. When he does, the dreams come. Not, as he hoped, Martha during the good times, the cute little girl nestled in his arms, playing on the beach, riding her first bike. He wishes he could recapture the round face with the dimpled cheeks, the gap-toothed smiles. He knows there were times when they were a happy family.

However, his memory insists on playing the immediate past, the rifts that erupted when he went and ruined his marriage. Martha, of course, sided with Judy, and he didn't blame her. There has never been any question about this: he was in the wrong. What he felt aggrieved about was, he was never really allowed to try and put things right.

So for a year, Martha shunned him, refused his calls or, if he did track her down, she stormed off, leaving him alone and distraught. It always came down to one final question, often yelled into his face: 'How could you do that to Mom?'

Things were changing though. In the past six months, that damning question was asked less often. They'd managed to meet without histrionics. She was growing up, accepting that the world, and the people in it, weren't perfect. She'd even experienced first-hand how relationships can founder.

Then a steel rain came and snatched her away, leaving just a gaping wound that could never be healed now. His daughter had died while they were still on the road to full reconciliation. He could see it, off in the distance, but they never quite made it.

Now, Piper knows, Judy will blame him for

putting their child in that place at that time. She had once told him what she'd told Martha, just before her sixteenth birthday: 'Daddy still loves us. He just doesn't want to live with us any more.' If it hurt him to hear it, how must Martha have felt?

At two-thirty on the second night after the explosion, he wakes from his fitful slumber, the pillow wet from his sweat, the sheets damp and wrinkled. His eyes might be gritty and sore, but he knows sleep has gone for the night.

Now he just has the long, empty hours until dawn to think about what might have been.

★   ★   ★

'I am sorry we have to do this again.'

'I understand.' This is the third interview, the one taken at a controlled pace, not snatched like the other two. This is the one where his mind is meant to be clearer, less emotional, where he will spill the crucial piece of information that will crack this monstrous act wide open. That's the theory anyway. At least two dozen other witnesses are going through the same process, and all the investigators need is a break from one of them.

'If there was any other way . . . '

'I'd do the same. Please.'

There are two of them facing Piper, one FBI, one Special Branch, interviewing him in the Legat office in Upper Brook Street. Simons, the Brit, is tense and nervy, but all Cardew, the Fed, shows is remorse and sadness. He's good at it. He's the one you would send to speak to grieving parents, thinks Piper. Too good. He'll be the one to watch.

Simons clears his throat. 'Can you tell us everything from the start?'

'The beginning of the day,' adds Cardew.

'Everything?'

'Vincent,' says Cardew, 'I don't have to tell you . . . '

'No. Anything could be significant,' he agrees.

'And you are the only law-enforcement professional who was a witness.'

'US professional,' corrects Simons. 'There were two British policemen and a former military policeman.'

'That's correct,' agrees Cardew, in a tone that is hard to read.

Piper can feel the numbness coming back. He doesn't feel like a pro of any nationality, he feels tired and light-headed.

Something must show in his face, because

51

Cardew asks: 'Have you seen a traumatologist?'

Piper shakes his head. He has recommended them himself to victims of crime and bereaved parents, they are good guys. Traumatologist is still a dumb-ass name, though. 'Several times,' Piper says. 'I'm OK. Really.'

The pair exchange glances which reveal they don't believe him, but the Brit says quietly: 'In your own time. Starting tape now at 10.20 a.m.'

So he begins, in a ragged monotone, from breakfast onwards, to the Embassy, the Fairmont, the Stafford. Hard to believe it was all just two days ago. But there are gaps, as if his memory has a short that sparks fitfully, throwing up scenes of appalling clarity, then fading to black. He thinks of all the times he questioned witnesses, wondering why they had such confused recall, why there were breaks in the narrative when the events happened right in front of them, his voice full of impatience. Now he understands. The brain recoils, it doesn't want to go back. You have to force it.

'You had arranged to meet at Barnes & Noble?'

'Yes. Barnes and Noble,' he says. 'The coffee-shop.'

'And who chose the venue?'

'Er, Martha did, I think. Yes, she was going bookshopping in the area.'

'Why was she outside? Did you arrange the rendezvous inside or out.'

'In.'

'But she was on the street.'

'Yes.'

'Why?' asks Cardew.

'I'm not sure. I was late. Perhaps she began to think . . . I don't know.'

'Are you OK?' Simons asks again.

'Yes,' he says stiffly.

'I'm sorry. But can you go through your progress to the . . . incident.'

He steels himself as he describes the walk through Soho, then the scene of the bomb, being as precise as he can, and tries to explain the impatience that led him to snatch up his daughter.

'This woman, Celeste Young — is she available for questioning?' asks Simons.

'I guess. I have a number.'

'Good. Carry on.'

His narrative gets slower, his words harder to formulate, as he finally takes them to the doctor, the news of her death, his identification of the body, and the detached, dream-like hours that followed.

'Can we just go back? You picked your

daughter up rather than wait for assistance,' Cardew says. 'Can you just clarify why, again?'

'Because she was my daughter,' he says tetchily. 'I didn't want to wait to see her die while the ambulances tried to get through, OK?'

'You wanna break?' asks Cardew.

'No.' Piper takes a sip of water. 'Let's finish.'

He takes them over the past few days, the phone call to Judy. How she blames him, even though there is nothing concrete she can pin on him.

Eventually, as the pauses grow longer, Simons says: 'I think we are about done. Nothing else?'

Yes, he thinks, there is Henry Monroe. Piper opens his mouth to describe the strange meeting, when the words come back to him.

It isn't safe.

He pictures Henry Monroe poking him in the chest with the magazine. He knew. Monroe knew something was about to go down. But that is crazy, surely? The man is FBI, his father's old partner. *Get her out of here.* They'll think him deranged if he starts making accusations like that. Won't they?

A cold sweat prickles on his forehead. A strange flickering starts in one corner of his

54

vision. A rare migraine is about to take hold. He feels a jolt of nausea.

'OK, Vince?'

'Yeah.' He rubs his temples and squeezes his eyes shut. 'Just . . . '

'We're nearly done,' says Cardew.

'We have the pathologist's report here, Vince. It seems the blast didn't kill her.'

'No,' he says, his voice a croak. 'I know.'

★ ★ ★

By the time he has left the interview and put himself in a cab, the migraine is in full effect, filling his world with iridescent flashes and long snakes of distortion. He flops back in the seat and concentrates on Monroe. While the real world is reduced to a light show, he rewinds back to the meeting in Soho, and the words Monroe spoke to him. He examines the scene frame by frame. The look on the face, the twisting of the magazine, the poke in the chest.

What had he done with the magazine? He'd glanced down at it, barely registered and dumped it in the trash. The masthead comes into focus, but the image swims away again as the driver makes a fast, jerky left turn, and Piper's head swims.

Then the logo leaps out at him. White on

black, sans serif block letters: the *Fourth Way*.

Then it's gone again. Piper leans forward, head between his knees, riding the sparkling waves of the migraine, waiting for them to subside.

★ ★ ★

Bereavement is like a stalker, waiting for the moment when his defences are down, when he has for a second forgotten why he has a hollow feeling inside, and then it pounces. When it does, it is all he can do to get out of the chair. He needs to work, he needs something else to focus on, other than his grief, otherwise he will succumb to this torpor.

'I want to come in,' he'd said to Roth, the Assistant Legat. 'To help.'

'No.'

'Are you giving me some kind of 'it's too personal shit'?'

'That's exactly what I'm giving you,' Roth had said.

'It's nonsense.'

'Yes? And say we get a lead that it's the Sons of Osama or some such crackpot group and you decide to go down to the Edgware Road and take out the juice bar where they meet?'

'You think I'd do that?'

'No,' says Roth, his voice softening with sympathy. 'I think you'd take out the whole Edgware Road, just to be sure. I know I would. Stay home. Get something from the Doc at the Embassy to help you sleep.'

He'd asked Roth for one favour. To find out about a magazine, self-published by the look of it, called the *Fourth Way*. His friend, although clearly thinking he'd lost his mind, said he'd get back to him.

Now he spends the days pacing the living room of the US Government apartment he has been given just off Warwick Way in Pimlico. Roth has taken his caseload, including liaising with Scotland Yard, the normal procedure when American citizens have been killed. They want to keep him away from that. Because Piper thinks they should just bring in a full incident team from Quantico and fuck the Brits. Everyone else wants to follow the protocols that are in place.

The TV is playing endless clips of Deputy Assistant Commissioner David Church, head of the Anti-Terrorist Unit, and his soundbite. According to him the explosion had been planned to maim and kill young people and was a 'calculated evil deed'. It just doesn't seem strong enough to get across what Piper

57

feels. Evil. Somehow, the over-used word has lost its power.

Roth calls him a couple of times a day, to check how he is and to give snippets of news. PERME, the Propellant, Explosive and Rocket Material Establishment, has produced some preliminary findings. It was not a homemade bomb, but a professional one. There were large traces of RDX, which suggested either C-4 or Semtex. This was different material from the ammonium-nitrate base often used by Al-Qaida and its acolytes — as in Bali and Istanbul — or from the explosives used in the Madrid bomb, the most recent outrage, which was Goma-2 Eco dynamite. Both Spain and London, however, used copper detonators, rather than the more sophisticated aluminium ones that some terrorist groups have moved on to. The bomb had been placed against the window on the first floor, probably behind the counter in the coffee-shop.

There was another difference in the Madrid incident. The death toll in London was, miraculously, just four, including Martha and the waitress at the drinks bar where it detonated. Seventy-two had been injured, five with lost limbs. One of those was a US citizen from Omaha, whose parents were being flown over. Seven were still critical but expected to pull through. It was tragic, but it wasn't in the hundreds. It was something to be grateful for, although he couldn't really manage that yet.

There had been no warning call. The JTAC committee has confirmed that there was zero intel to anticipate the event. Nobody knew anything. Not a single piece of chatter from GCHQ, not a suspicious movement by a monitored suspect.

The level of electronic surveillance in London is, next to Monaco, the most intense in the world. In this city, Big Brother watches all the time, twenty-four seven. Yet, the CCTV footage in the shop was damaged in the fire that broke out, then doused by water, and is being flown to the US for enhancement. That was something, at least, where the British accepted that the US was better equipped. The street cameras were working fine, but so far, nothing. Piper has to accept this is slow, painstaking work, the operators scanning each face in the crowd, hoping for the gesture, the expression, the exchange that will give them the break they need.

At least, thanks to the pills Doc Turner at the Embassy medical centre has sent over, he can sleep now.

The bell to his apartment buzzes and he feels a little stab of apprehension. It will be Judy, his wife. This will not be an easy meeting. He had expected them to have a truce for a while, at least, but she is clear she doesn't want any part of unity-in-adversity.

Perhaps she thinks Piper will use it as a conduit back to her affections. That isn't what he wants at all. Just some peace between them, for a little while. He guesses her anger is in the way. He presses the street-door release and says, 'Come on up,' into the speakerphone. He unlatches the apartment door, walks through to the small kitchen, plugs in the kettle, the coffee-machine, and is working on the cork of a bottle of wine, when there is a soft knocking.

'It's open.'

Another knock. Piper puts the wine down, crosses to the entrance and swings the door back. It is not Judy, but a woman who is younger, perhaps thirty, with shorter, finer, more delicate features. She looks like a blonde Audrey Hepburn.

'Mr Piper?' The accent is American.

'Yes?'

'I'm Sarah Nielsen, Martha's tutor. We spoke over the phone when she enrolled.' She holds up the black folder she has under her arm. 'This may not be the best time, but I've brought some of her work. Can I come in?'

Piper steps aside. 'Sure. Sorry. I'm . . . I was expecting someone else. Sit down.

Coffee? Tea? Wine?'

'Coffee would be great.'

He sets about making it, and speaks from the kitchen. 'Forgive me, but how did you get my address?'

'It was on Martha's admission card. I saw her mother was up in Manchester, so I thought . . . listen, I am so sorry about her. She was — '

'I know.' He heads her off quickly. Nobody really knows what to say or how to say it. He can see what they feel in their eyes, it doesn't need words. 'I don't know what to say to you, you don't know what to say to me. There's nothing to say.' He emerges from the kitchen and hands her the drink. 'Is there?'

'I guess not. But you gotta try.'

'Yeah. We got to try. Where are you from?'

'Toronto. But the accent is all over the place.'

'I worked there once.' He'd spent a few months in Canada as part of CANAL, the Combined North American Law Enforcement Initiative, a kind of police/Federal free-trade agreement, which meant fugitives could no longer treat the Canadian border as a get-out-of-jail free card. 'Nice place.'

'It's a great place to leave,' she says.

'I didn't think it was too bad.'

'You spend a winter there?'

'No,' he says truthfully.

'My family are originally from Utah, way back. We haven't got the genes for cold. One or other of us would lose a body part to frostbite every January.'

He laughs at this. 'Can I see?' He points to the folder.

'Sure.' She puts down her coffee, unwraps the ribbon and flips open the cardboard top, revealing a dozen or so thick sheets of cartridge paper. 'This is just a fraction of what we have. These were studies for something she was going to cast next semester.'

It is a figure, reaching for the sky, its influence startlingly obvious to anyone who had ever seen Giacometti. Piper moves to sit next to Sarah and flicks through the pages, watching the figure take shape from different angles, grow in strength with each charcoal outline, losing its debt to the Italian sculptor.

'Lovely,' he says.

There is a moment's silence before Sarah asks quietly: 'Is it true the blast didn't kill her?'

He nods, the little worm of guilt in his soul turning once more, sending sparks of pain through his chest. 'Yes.' He recalls listening with growing incomprehension to the explanation, feeling doubly cheated of his daughter.

'It was Sudden Arrhythmia Death. That's what she died of.'

'Oh.' Sarah shakes her head. 'What is it?'

'An electrical storm in the heart. Triggered by shock. I mean, that's what they told me. In layman's terms.'

'At her age?'

'It only affects young people. It's genetic.'

Ed Turner, the Embassy's chief physician, had sat him down and gone through it, stage by stage. Long QT syndrome is caused by two mutant genes which affect the ion-pumps in the heart. Had Martha ever complained of chest pains, palpitations, panic attacks? No. Had she ever fainted? No. *Yes*. But when she was nine, in a school parade, when it was baking hot. 'Is it genetic?' Piper had asked him, meaning, 'Could we, Judy and I, could we have it?' The answer came: it was unlikely. Truth is, if they were affected, they'd be dead by now. But one or both of them could be carrying the faulty genes. Both Vince reckoned. It was the final, poisonous twist to their marriage.

'The bomb did kill her, not directly, but by triggering the attack.'

'How terrible,' said Sarah, dabbing at her eyes, overcome. 'Look, I'm going to leave these with you.'

He examines the drawings once more.

'These are very good, aren't they?'

'Yes. Even better in 3-D. Her bronzes . . . well, I'd have brought them but they're a little heavy to carry across London on the Tube.'

'Right.'

'I should be getting back. But if you'd like to see her other work, maybe even collect it, you're welcome any time.'

'Thanks.'

'When is the funeral?'

'It'll be in America. We live . . . lived in Washington. It was where she was brought up. Most of her friends are there. Listen, Miss . . . what was it? I'm sorry, it's very rude of me.' God, even his memory for names has gone.

'No problem. Nielsen. But Sarah'll do.'

'Sarah. Thank you for coming over. I'm sorry if I'm a bit fuzzy. But I really appreciate it.'

'Don't worry. Look, here's my card. Call me. I don't think I can get over for the funeral, but I'd love to do something — a gesture of some sort. So would some of her fellow students, I'm sure. Something to remember her by.'

He looks down at the Art Institute of America in London card and runs his thumb over the embossing. 'That would be nice. I'll

64

let you know what's happening. For sure. Thanks again.'

After she has gone he sits down and carefully closes the folder, retying the ribbon and quickly sliding the drawings under his bed.

The downstairs buzzer again. Piper straightens up, runs his fingers through his hair and goes to let her in. Judy. Time to do battle.

★　★　★

Judy is a tall, rangy woman with lovely long legs, now wrapped in a pencil skirt that keeps her stride short as she paces up and down the room, her heels leaving a scattershot of depressions in the carpet. Piper, on the sofa, listens mostly in silence, watching his wife, trying to remember how it once was between them. It doesn't work. Today, her clothes are black, her hair is black and her heart is black too.

She stops walking and turns to face him, hands on hips. 'So you thought you'd go ahead with all the arrangements and just have her shipped back to the States without a by your leave, did you? Washington? How the bloody hell am I meant to visit my daughter in Washington? Or is that the idea? You'll be in control, then. Waiting for me to come back

65

over. Well, fook you.' Her Mancunian roots come out when she swears.

It was Judy's voice, and the spunky attitude behind it, that first attracted him. He'd met her skiing in Denver, both of them on vacation with a party of college friends. The two groups, the rumbustious Yankee boys and the cute-sounding Brit girls, with the sort of accents eventually made popular by Daphne in *Frasier*, had more or less paired off, but Vince'n' Judy's coupling lasted a lot longer than the others. Mainly because when she got back to England, she was pregnant with Martha.

He was barely in his twenties, but he did the honourable thing, became a husband and father. Normally the Bureau would have dumped him — it liked its young Agents unencumbered — but The Wolf, his father, smoothed the way for him to continue. Almost twenty years ago, it had gone so fast.

These days, Judy's once cute English vernacular now grated terribly. He hadn't been able to watch a re-run of *Frasier* since the bust-up.

'She can be buried in Didsbury. So you can tell your State Department chums that, thanks very much, but she won't be going in the belly of any jumbo. And you can tell your Dr bloody Turner that it is a bit late for us to take ECG tests, isn't it? It's not likely we'll be having any more children after this, is it?'

No, he has to admit, that's not likely at all.

* * *

Once she's made her point she calms down. She sits and accepts a glass of the wine. He sits on the floor opposite, the bottle between his crossed legs. Eventually, she asks: 'How are you, Vince?'

He shrugs. Everything is written on his face, there is no need to answer. He is lost and he is lonely. 'I'm sorry about what happened, you know. Really sorry.'

'Which part?'

He drains his glass, refills it and tops up Judy's. 'All of it. But let's start with the thing with Rachel.'

The 'thing' is his infidelity, the straw that apparently broke the marriage's back.

'I know. But you never, ever understood how it felt from my end. Once you destroy that trust, it can never be the same again.'

These are well-rehearsed arguments, except this time they are being aired at a far lower volume than in the past. It is getting dark outside, the street lamps are fizzing fitfully to life.

The wine has blunted the edges of his sorrow.

'We know people whose marriages survived worse.'

'Survived,' she agreed. 'Never thrived. And often the women had to make accommodations I would find impossible.' Judy shakes her head. 'This is old ground, Vince.'

The phone rings, but Piper lets it take a message.

'I'm looking at it from a different perspective, now.'

She smiles at him. 'Aren't we all, love. This is uncharted waters for me, too. No good asking me for a map and compass.'

'No. I guess not.'

She finished her drink and left. At the door, he thought of offering a kiss on the cheek, and then reconsidered. He sat back on the floor in the same position, a second bottle between his knees, dreading the long night ahead.

★　★　★

The chosen soundtrack to the wee small hours is comprised of languid, smoky singers. He doesn't care who it is, as long as the music reeks of cigarette smoke and bourbon stains on the piano lid. While he is listening to a particularly sultry 'My Funny Valentine', he finally faces up to the fact that he has been less than honest, both with himself, and with the various interrogators in this case.

Or with Roth. He plays back the message on the answerphone. 'Sorry to get back to you so late, Vince. You OK? You there? Pick up if you are . . . It's just about the Fourth Way. It's a kind of Greenpeace movement. It gets a grade three surveillance note. Pretty low. Is this something to do with Martha? Let me know.'

Yes and no, he thinks. Why would an FBI man be carrying the magazine from eco-warriors? The Bureau wasn't renowned for supporting green campaigns. Unless Monroe was infiltrating them. But equally, the Bureau doesn't send retired Agents in worsted suits to merge in with lefty pressure groups.

Why hasn't he come clean with the investigating teams? Because he wants this one. He wants to track down whoever or whatever killed Martha. Roth is right: it's personal. People find it hard to accept that sometimes that's a good thing. It's the engine that can drive an investigation where those less deeply involved will stall. What's wrong with that?

In the end, his brain decides enough is enough. Piper falls asleep on the floor just as dawn breaks, and Tierney Sutton sings her last few tracks to an audience of none.

4

Mothers are nearly always awarded custody, even in death, and the plans to fly Martha home to the US are scrapped. Piper doesn't object. Part of him thinks Judy is right, that their daughter would be better tended in her care. What grieves him is that there was no way The Wolf, his father, could make the trip over the Pond. Which meant a no-show from his mom, too.

They were upset, but in truth his parents didn't miss much. The burial of a young person, especially a funeral so sparsely attended, has no redeeming features. There is only pain. The images are all fading fast, thank God. It is another day Piper is blocking from his mind, for his sanity's sake. Even the short eulogy he gave is decaying, no longer playing over and over in his head.

He has spoken to his old man on the telephone, listening to the crinkly breaths as he gasped out his condolences through fibrous lungs. The Wolf. He remembered as a kid how he thought his dad had the coolest nickname. It was a while before he realised that it was a partly ironic take on Wolfgang, his old man's middle name, and didn't refer to his cunning, lycanthropic methods of capturing the bad guys.

Piper used to relish hearing the clean-cut Agents who came round for barbecues in the yard every summer calling his old man Wolf, Wolfie, The Wolfman. Every few minutes one of his old chums holding court with the young recruits would yell across the yard: '*Remember when you made that jump off the freeway, Wolf?*' That was when he was up against the Weather Front, one of those misguided gangs of middle-class white kids who robbed banks and dealt drugs for their hipper black brothers and their political struggles. But there were lots of other cases.

It is fashionable now to find fault with your childhood, to seek the cause of your fuck-ups in bad parenting. Certainly, his dad was away a lot, Mom did all the cooking, washing and shopping, even when the old man was home. When he was there, he had his favourite Laz-E-Boy chair in front of the big old Zenith TV, and a brew in his hand, issuing orders and putting the world to rights. Had Feminism or Gay Rights raised their ugly heads in the Piper house, The Wolf would have put a .38 right between each of their eyes.

His views were a generation out of date, but he was an FBI man and, beneath the curled lip Vince Piper affected around his folks for a couple of years, he dug that. The other kids got tattoos and nose rings and smoked dope and snorted coke and listened to English punk bands, while Piper carried on looking like someone from a Gap ad. He couldn't play The Clash within two miles of home and it was made clear what would happen if he packed a phony ID like the others. Most of his pals understood, though. His dad was a Fed, it was a tough call, but he was no ordinary G-Man, he was The Wolf. It was like having a superhero for a dad.

Now, the superhero had inhaled a fatal dose of kryptonite. Something had been set off inside him, compromising his auto-immune system, which meant that his body was attacking the lining of his lungs, scarring the alveoli, replacing the soft, pliant tissue with rough, fibrous scars, reducing his capacity to take in oxygen a little more each day. Like a pillow slowly being forced over the face.

Piper could have understood this if The Wolf had smoked forty Marlboro a day or had a sideline in asbestos mining or spray-painting cars. But no, it was idiopathic, the doctors said. Causes unknown. Treatment, more or less pointless. A year at most until he gasped, coughed and choked his way out of this life.

A daughter and a dad, both with genetic defects. Bad luck? Just an unfortunate roll on the DNA craps table? If so, what did *he* have hidden inside him, ticking away, waiting to explode?

★　★　★

The phone snaps him out of it. He shakes his head. Once more, it has grown dark in his apartment while he has chewed over memory after memory, until they are all dog-eared. An empty glass of wine is in his hand. A Guigal Côte Rotie. On the table, the bottle, half of it gone. He can't even remember the taste.

'Yeah?'

'Vince?'

It's an English voice, but not Judy. 'Who's this?'

'Celeste — Celeste Young. Remember me?'

'Oh, I'm sorry. Celeste, hi.' The woman who had provided the soft shoulder for him to cry on. 'How are you?'

'Well, I was wondering how *you* were.'

'I'm fine.'

'It's just . . . It sounds so silly. Look — I feel involved.'

'Well, don't be.' It is an ungracious thing to say. 'No, no, what I mean is, please don't feel obligated, because . . . No, obligated is

73

wrong. You know, I feel like there ought to be a whole new language for this. Bereaved-speak. Because the vocabulary we got just ain't up to the job.'

The laugh is the best, warmest sound he has heard in days. He realises that people are tiptoeing around him, like funeral ushers, and he is living life at half-volume.

'Can I treat you to dinner?' she asks next.

Piper runs the phrase past himself again, just to check he's heard properly.

'I bet you could do with a good feed,' Celeste goes on. 'A steak, perhaps?'

'I'm not sure about the you treating me bit.' That's The Wolf in him speaking. 'But . . . well, the concept is sound enough. When?'

'Tonight?'

'Tonight?'

'As in, now.'

He touches his face, feels the stubble, can smell the sourness of his breath and armpits. He wonders whether he even has a clean shirt.

'Yeah, OK. Shall we say . . . ' He struggles for the name of a restaurant. What was the one near the Ritz that Roth had pointed out as suitably swanky? Something to do with Chevrolets, he recalls. *Caprice*. 'The Caprice. In an hour, say? You know it?'

'Of course I know it, but . . . ' That tingling laugh again, and a sparkle in the voice that suggests she is amused at something he has said. 'You'd better let me make the booking. And dinner is on me.'

The line goes dead before he can argue.

★　★　★

The last time Piper has been up on designer labels was during a knock-off scam in New Jersey, when some two-bit outfit were making Ralph Lauren shirts, Prada bowling bags and Matrix-style Armani leather coats (in low-grade plastic) and selling them in New York and Philly street markets. They also did mail order, which made the counterfeiting a Federal offence. But he is fairly sure that the sleek, form-hugging green dress Celeste has on is the real thing, by a designer with an exotic name and an equally exotic price tag.

Her red hair has been cut since he last saw her, and she looks great. A lot of other people in the restaurant think so too. The guys, mostly affluent and corpulent, certainly sit up and take notice. Piper isn't sure that grieving fathers are meant to feel quite so proprietorial about having a beautiful woman on their arm, but walking in and sitting down with Celeste certainly gives him a lift.

As they study the menus, a slightly awkward silence separating them, she breaks it with: 'You can't let it define you, you know.'

'What?' he asks.

'Martha's death. The bomb. Somehow it becomes the main focus of your life — '

'It's only been a couple of weeks. The shit-hot Special Branch still don't know — '

'Do you mind!' He looks around at the woman to his left who has the kind of wide-eyed stare left by the surgeon's knife, and mouths an apology for his language.

'I know how long it has been,' Celeste goes on, gently. 'I was there, remember? Look, I don't wish to sound callous, but if you're not careful, you'll dwell on it until it becomes your sole topic of conversation and anything else will seem frivolous. Without gravity. And living will seem equally pointless. Everything — food, music, love, sex . . . ' She sees something in his eyes. 'And that's wrong?'

'Is this your 'the show must go on' routine?'

She smiles. 'I suppose it is. Listen, I have a friend, Davina. She does bereavement ceremonies — '

'Whoa, whoa.'

'What?'

'Ceremonies. Like, New Age kind of ceremonies?'

She hesitates, and shakes her head. What had she been thinking? 'I expect you aren't a ceremony kind of guy.'

'Not if it involves going naked into the woods with a drum and a sheep's foetus.'

'So you *have* done one?' It is a moment before he realises she is joking and laughs with her. 'OK, subject closed,' Celeste says firmly. 'What would you like to eat?'

'Something simple. A steak. Fries.'

She orders a Caesar salad without croutons from a waiter who calls her Miss Young as frequently as he can, possibly to hammer home to her coarse guest that she is a regular and, without consulting him, she chooses a Californian Merlot that has found its way onto a particularly Francophile wine list. 'Sorry. It's my treat, so I thought you might enjoy it. I have an American friend who is crazy about that winery. But I shouldn't suppose that all you Americans are shaped out of the same mould . . . '

'Just our teeth,' he says, and she laughs and he realises he would have to try and make her do that again. It is even better in person than on the telephone. 'You were just saying I am becoming a dull, maudlin obsessive.'

'No, I wasn't. I said you *could* become a dull, maudlin obsessive. Right now, you're just maudlin. Understandably so. Has anyone any ideas at all about the bomb?'

'I don't know. They are kind of keeping me at arm's length. You know, all that 'it's-too-personal' shit.' He turns to his neighbour, 'Excuse me.'

'Don't mind me.'

'So until I go in and sit them down and make them tell me, I mean really tell me, I know as much as you do.' Well, that wasn't strictly true, but Roth's information flow has dried to a trickle. Piper has tried wheedling information out of every contact he has, but still gets the 'enquiries pending' response.

'Which is nothing much?' she suggests.

'Roughly, yes.'

The wine arrives, she sniffs, tastes and nods her approval. 'I find Merlot a little boring as a varietal, but that's not bad.'

He takes a larger slug than is polite. In contrast to most of his colleagues in the Bureau, he prefers French wines, but he figures she chose New World on his behalf. 'Nice.'

'It should touch the sides first. Just to give it a chance.'

'Yeah. Look — maybe I am not the best dinner-date a girl could have tonight.'

'Do you want to talk about her?'

'Martha?'

'Yes.'

'I — not yet. If you don't mind. It's like . . . ' he puts a fist to his chest ' . . . I start and all this tightens up. Even more so because we have . . . we had some things to resolve, Martha and I. About me. And Judy. I told you . . . my wife.'

'Well, not all of it. As I recall it went: 'We aren't together any longer.' So you want to tell me about Judy, then?' He looks into her eyes to see if she is joking. She isn't. 'Go on. Tell me how it went wrong. I'm all ears.'

Not from where I'm sitting, he thinks. Maybe it is OK to notice a woman again.

'Judy.' He takes a sip, deliberately letting the wine roll around his mouth until he has extracted every nuance from it, as if he is also neutralising the name. 'Judy's end begins with a mail fraud.'

5

In a woodland clearing thick with birdsong
and fallen autumnal leaves, Vincent Piper
zipped up his bulletproof vest and slipped
the raid jacket over the top, the one with
FBI in letters two feet high on the back. He
looked around at the other Federal agencies,
the Department of Transportation, Alcohol,
Tobacco and Firearms and the Treasury, a
dozen people in all, standing next to their
operation vans, their breath forming clouds in
the early morning air, rubber-soled boots
being stomped, fingers and hands blown on
before being slipped into gloves.

'Piper?'

It was the big, moustachioed guy from
Transportation. He held out a hand. 'Thanks
for coming. Jim O'Rourke. I'm RC on this.'

Piper pointed at his driver and back-up
man. 'This is Dermot Denham. Call him DD.'

'Dermot? Irish?'

'A ways back. Dublin.'

'Right. I'm a Limerick man.'

Piper doubted the Raid Co-ordinator had
ever been to Limerick in his life. What he
meant was, some distant relative came from

there, which gave him an excuse to paint his driveway green and sink a few tins of that disgusting black stuff every 17 March. 'What have we got?' Piper asked quickly before the pair burst into a few verses of 'The Wild Rover'.

'OK, the house is through the woods along that path. It's at the end of a small development. Maybe a dozen other properties. We have traced twenty-four packages mailed here in the last three weeks. From Amazon, Fedex, UPS, everyone. Same pattern as in six other places. All ordered on gash credit cards. Some of it electrical stuff, but also enough ammo and weapons to get these guys,' he indicated the ATF Agents, 'very interested. We reckon one, maybe two more days and they'll pull out and burn their traces to set up somewhere else. So we hit them this morning. Then you got time to get home and vote. You'll all be Gore guys, right?'

There is a ripple of laughter and a few shakes of the head. It was election day, 2000, and ninety per cent of the guys around him were going to vote for Bush.

'Warrant?' Piper asked.

O'Rourke tapped his top pocket. 'All in order, thanks for reminding me.' Piper knew that it wasn't sarcasm. You had to check and double-check each and every legal stage these days, otherwise some wise-ass lawyer walked straight in and shat all over you while the perps left with a wave and a smile.

O'Rourke pulled the group into a tight circle. He ran through the raid sequence. He and two other agents were going straight in the front door, opening it up with a ram. One agent would cover the rear — there was no exit there, just a door at the side — three would form an intermediary circle, and the rest would group into an outer, staggered ring for covering fire. It was what was known at the Academy as a Fan IV, designed so every man and woman had a clear line of fire, without the risk of hitting a fellow Agent.

They loaded up with weapons from the armoury van. The usual shortened M-16s, mace launchers, a couple of heavy-duty FN Minimis, gas masks, radios, grenades, flares. A quick check on magazines and actions, then they shouldered their weapons and walked from the car park through the woods, the frosted leaves crunching loudly. They were sweating already in their heavy nylon fatigues and Kevlar padding, although the ambient temperature was barely above zero. Piper looked at Dermot. 'You OK, DD?'

'Yeah. I love raids. It's why we joined, isn't it?'

'What, to turn up in some goddamn

commuter town at six in the morning and blow it apart? Right,' came a sardonic voice from behind them.

They spun round and looked at the speaker. 'Rachel Stanok? Treasury?' she announced with a rising inflection that suggested she was from the West Coast originally.

They introduced themselves.

'OK, quiet back there. Let's keep it down, people.' O'Rourke stood to one side and counted them over the boundary fence with a good luck squeeze to each shoulder. The team were into the felons' property now.

'How'd you get this gig?' Piper whispered to the female Agent.

'I tracked the nine-mil shipments in. Thought I ought to finish it up. You?'

'Temporary assignment to the local RA. My name was on the raid rota,' he replied.

Rachel nodded. Your name came round once in a while so you ended up putting on the big-lettered jacket. It was designed to keep you connected to Field Operations, even if you were mostly a desk jockey. 'I just hope O'Rourke isn't of the let's talk-'em-out-variety, eh?' she said with a wink. 'Gas 'em and cuff 'em, I say.'

They walked on in silence until the woods began to thin and they could see the house, a faceless modern ranch-style property, sitting on maybe three acres. Other identical versions of it, albeit on smaller plots of land, stretched off into the distance towards the suburban sprawl that marked the beginning of the outer tendrils of Philadelphia.

Another year and this wood would be gone, the land regraded, covered in houses that would all be sitting in yards of a few hundred square feet, and it'd be just another dorm town.

'Have a good one,' said Piper as he moved to take up his position. Rachel pointed a finger at him and made a clicking noise and moved off into the ferns and bracken, shushing through the waist-high growth to take up a covering position.

Just where the booby trap was, and what triggered it, nobody could say afterwards, but they had barely lined themselves up along the treeline when the firecrackers detonated in the canopy above their heads, snapping and cracking like the Fourth of July. Most of the raiding party leaped back for cover, weapons spinning madly, trying to locate the source of the firing. But there was no firing. Just the explosive warning of intruders.

'Shit,' shouted O'Rourke when he realised what they had triggered. They had a four-hundred-yard sprint to the front door. No cover, just ankle-high grass. But the chances were the inhabitants were still disoriented. They'd have heard the crackers, but they'd be rolling out of bed, pulling on their pants. There was maybe a two-minute window for an assault.

O'Rourke spent it vacillating.

Piper said, 'Time to pull it. Call for back-up.'

'No. We go.'

'I don't think — '

'Let's have that ram,' O'Rourke yelled. 'Come on! OK, cover us. Positions as agreed.' He pointed at Piper. 'OK?'

Against his better judgment, Piper nodded and flicked the safety off the short-barrelled M-16.

The three of them, O'Rourke and his two sidemen, started to run, crouched well down, weapons clanking, followed by the second wave, sprinting a little slower, weapons levelled at the house, ready to return fire, fanning to create the middle ring of firepower. Piper, DD and Rachel were in the last line, plugging the gaps left by the others, so the house could be decimated if need be with minimum risk of collateral damage to the raid party. Piper checked his automatic pistol was loose in the holster, just in case things got hairy.

O'Rourke made it to the door. The ram splintered it off its hinges and they were in.

The muffled cry of, 'Federal Agents!' hung in the morning air.

It was yelled a second time.

Piper knew what that meant. They'd gone, flown the coop. It happened. You were left standing there with your dick in your hand, all that adrenaline pumping around with nowhere left to go.

In confirmation O'Rourke came out and waved them in. Piper put the safety back on, slung the assault weapon over his shoulder and joined the others strolling down the hillside, already anticipating breakfast and coffee. Inside, the house was empty. No furniture in the big living area, just a recently unpacked hi-fi and a pile of rap CDs from Amazon and a stack of Coke cans and candy wrappers.

In one corner of a bedroom was an ant's nest of wrappings from all the parcels that had been dropped off in the last few weeks.

Piper said to DD: 'You know a good diner round here?'

DD shook his head. 'About three miles is the closest. I got some coffee in the car.'

Piper wandered into the kitchen, aware that he wouldn't be allowed to touch anything in the crime scene. Three mugs were lined up on the counter top. Some instinct made him take off a woollen glove and reach out to the kettle. It was hot. 'O'Rourke!' he shouted.

The first spray of bullets caught DD. They came straight through the open door and blew his insides out. Piper ran out and watched his colleague sink to the floor. Rachel was standing next to him, rooted to the spot. He grabbed her and dragged her back into the kitchen. They knelt down behind the units, as high velocity rounds chinked through the window and embedded itself in the wall.

The house began to fill with smoke as the Feds' M-16s from the other rooms opened up. Another volley of shots came from the forest, big thudding rounds. Someone had outflanked the Feds. There came a scream and an explosion as a Mace canister went up.

'I'm hit, I'm hit!'

'Masks!' shouted O'Rourke. 'Get me back-up.'

Half a dozen radios crackled into life. They'd be asking for medics as well, but he knew DD was dead. And he'd have to tell Susan, his wife. As the burning smoke from the pierced can rolled into the kitchen area, Rachel unclipped the breathing mask from her belt and pulled it over her head. She jabbed Piper, indicating he should do the same. He worked it on, recoiling at the sharp smell of synthetic rubber.

She said something and he indicated the radio mike button. She pressed it, and her voice crackled in his ear. 'How the hell did they get out there without us seeing?'

The window of the kitchen shuddered and fell into the sink.

He stood up and let half a magazine rattle towards the greenery, the cases chinking on the tiled floor as they bounced away, then ducked back down.

'Good point.'

'There's no rear entrance. Just the side door.'

Piper shouldered the M-16 and, keeping low, moved into the hall, where, across from DD, half-slumped in a doorway, an ATF Agent lay on the floor, not moving. Rachel followed as he made for the rear of the house, feeling the air whistle and crack close to his ear as a bullet zipped by. It was not a place to linger. Why not be a lawyer, The Wolf had suggested. It seemed good advice right now.

Piper found the door to the basement, pulled it open and threw the gas canister down, waiting for the choking cloud to erupt and settle. He switched on his vest light. 'I'll go point, OK?' he asked.

Rachel gave him the thumbs-up.

He heard the rumble of more detonations. The big Minimis were firing now, the noise reverberating around the house, rocking it on its shallow foundations. He could imagine the trees being blown to pulp, bark stripping, leaves shredding. How long to back-up? Ten, fifteen minutes?

He stepped onto the stairs, the M-16 pointing down, found the light switch and descended into a large, brick-lined room. This was where they lived. Four camp beds, the once-white sheets smudged grey from unwashed bodies, clothes left on the floor where they had stepped out of them, ash trays and the butts of joints. Coke wraps. Fried chicken and Chinese takeaway boxes.

Rachel saw it before he did. A wooden panel in one wall, still half-open. With the barrel of the gun he pulled it back, aware of the reassuring muzzle of Rachel's M-16 at his shoulder, ready to blaze away. She gave good back-up. The panel swung out, revealing the subterranean passage, barely large enough for a man to crawl through, disappearing into darkness.

They exchanged looks. They both knew a deathtrap when they saw it. Stuck in a tunnel with no room to turn around. Anyone waiting at the far end could pop you like shooting Feds in a barrel.

Rachel's voice rasped in his ear. 'I'm smaller.'

'I'm senior.'

'Fuck you.'

'Only if we live.'

It was a good thirty seconds before he realised what he had said. Sexual harassment, tribunal, reprimand, maybe dismissal. He could see it in an instant. He pulled his mask off and clipped it back on his belt, holding his breath until he was well into the tunnel, away from the swirling mace remnants in the room. His eyes began to sting and he ran an arm across them before going down on all fours and plunging in, feeling his back scrape along the roof.

The passage ran for maybe twenty feet, and he could see daylight at the end almost immediately. That meant no big fucker was leaning over, ready to let rip with a Mac 10 into his face. It was difficult to know who had cut this, but it didn't look like the work of felons. It was too neat, as if created by a machine. Maybe it was some sort of conduit, for electricity or water, that had never been used.

No, he realised as he felt the knees of his fatigue trousers soak through from the damp soil, it was a drainage tunnel. With the houses located at the bottom of a hill, the basements would be prone to flooding. This was a way to run a pumpline in.

Behind him he was aware of Rachel, her smaller frame making her faster, pushing at him, literally snapping at his heels.

Then he was into fresh air, into a drainage gully that ran straight as a ley line for the forest. He helped Rachel out and she shook him off, irritably. Oh shit. Piper allowed himself half a dozen deep lungfuls of fresh air, tainted with the smell of firing.

He peeked over the top of the earth and jerked back down. Someone was there. Rachel followed suit and hesitated, then pushed on ahead. She parted the long, coarse grass.

'Piper.'

A DoT Agent lay there, the one sent to cover the rear, part of his face missing. Shot at close range. He must have stumbled upon the fleeing occupants of the basement. How come they hadn't heard the shot? A suppressor, perhaps.

Along the gulley they went, keeping low, waiting for the inevitable shots. The fugitives were bound to have posted someone to take out anyone following. He poked his head up. Now they were well past the house and could see the muzzle flashes from the rooms as the trapped men returned fire. He wondered if he

91

and Rachel had been missed back at the house yet.

'O'Rourke? Piper? Do you copy?' The throat mikes had very limited range, and there was no reply.

Piper slipped off his garish raid jacket and discarded it. Rachel did the same. Now they were clothed in green, head-to-toe. They just had to hope no sharp-eyed Fed got a bead on them and figured, without the jackets, they must be black hats.

They moved into the treeline where the gulley petered out and slipped into the undergrowth, aware of the firing up close. The vegetation hissed and rustled as they moved, and Piper hesitated. They were making too much noise, even over the rattle of gunfire.

The figure stood up from behind the bush, raising the gun as he came and Piper would like to think it was his trained reactions that took over, but he would always suspect it was blind, life-saving panic. He heaved the butt of the assault rifle round and into the guy's jaw, watched the figure lift off the ground and crash into the undergrowth.

Another four steps and he was through to their firing positions, three of them, armed with big guns, BARs and even an NSV, a Russian tank gun, the chosen fetishist weapons of the survivalist and gun buff. All being fired by what looked like fourteen-year-old kids.

'Federal Officers, put up your weapons,' shouted Rachel.

The first one spun round; Piper saw the suppressed pistol next to him and without hesitating shot him in the calf. The nine-millimetre round punched straight through and into the leaf litter, leaving a spreading mist of blood as the kid shrieked in agony.

'Federal Officers,' repeated Piper. 'Stand up, away from your weapons, hands behind your heads. NOW.'

The others did as they were told.

* * *

The rest of the day was paperwork. Two Federal Officers had died. One ATF man was seriously injured, one Treasury Agent suffering from Mace inhalation. A boy had a fractured jaw, another a nasty bullet wound and a fibula that resembled granulated sugar for four inches of its length. There was a debacle to answer for. And, Piper figured, a charge of 'inappropriate sexual innuendo' waiting to be filed.

Except it wasn't. He and Rachel met up for a drink at Thornton's, a Philly bar that wasn't popular with cops or Feds. Too expensive, too many suits. She told him all about her life and he told her all about his. Including about Judy. And Martha.

She didn't care. She'd had quite a day and she wanted to get laid and he was a reasonable body close at hand. That's the way he figured it. A kind of Fed booty call. And for him? He was drunk. That's all he could say. Drunk and just a little wild, like someone had taken the regulator off his moral senses, drunk because he'd watched a man die, not a friend exactly, but someone that could have been him, and the next day, in the tradition of the Service, he would have to go and see the widow and tell her how DD died a brave man. It was that old sex and death thing.

So in the meantime he explained to Rachel all the places he wanted to put his fingers and his tongue and in between she leaned over the table and they kissed in that hungry way that new lovers do and the waitress had to come and tell them to keep it down, they were embarrassing the other customers. So they staggered to the Express Inn down the street, giggling at the name, hoping it didn't apply to them, and they stumbled into bed and no, it didn't apply to them.

6

Piper is halfway through the steak by the time he has finished the story. 'It was probably a little more detail than I actually needed,' says Celeste.

He feels himself redden. 'Ah. Sorry, I was just trying to tell you how I got carried away — '

'Not that part. The part about DD's chest opening up. Anyway, I would think that your reaction falls into what actors call DCOL.'

'DCOL?'

'Doesn't Count on Location. You know, the thrill of the chase, the near-death experience, the life-affirming one-night stand.' She watches him take a big bite of the perfectly cooked meat, wondering if he is appreciating it, or if it is just fuel. 'It was a one-night stand, wasn't it?'

His mouth is too full for him to attempt anything other than a raised eyebrow. Yes . . . and no. He doesn't bother saying anything more, about how Rachel became a difficult habit to break, about how he never discovered who it was who called Judy and told her that her starched-shirt husband was a liar and a cheat, or about Judy taking it about as hard as any woman can. He doesn't have to. She is way ahead of him.

'Ah.'

He pushes the plate away, orders a second bottle of wine which he will insist on paying for and admits, 'It's hard to explain.'

'Not to me it isn't.'

A tiny spark of anger flares up at what he perceives as her being judgmental. 'Well, it was to Judy.' He'd expected a rough ride, but he was engulfed by a hurricane of recrimination. He was hardly the first husband to stray, but that didn't help. What was left smouldering was the remains of his marriage.

Celeste touches his hand and he feels that little crackle you get when strange, unfamiliar flesh touches yours.

Habituation, that's what biologists call it, the way a man's sensory system can become used to any stimulus, even that of the woman he loves. That's why touching someone you don't really feel for, a person you just met, can sometimes make you feel alive again. You've just had a neurological jump-start. It was part of his justification for Rachel. Wasn't there some famous sex therapist who said cheating every once in a while was the only way to keep a relationship fresh? That wouldn't have played with Judy either.

'That's not what I meant,' she says softly. 'I'm not surprised by anyone's sexual behaviour any more. It's as if, beneath our calm, civilised exteriors, each of us has some sort of storm raging, some need to fulfil. Often we go to extraordinary lengths to do it.'

The weight in his chest is back. For a short time, he has pushed what happened to Martha to some dusty place at the back of his mind. He has forgotten he isn't meant to have a good time. 'Listen, I'm sorry,' he says.

She shrugs her shoulders in puzzlement. 'What for?'

'We have been here,' he glances at his watch, 'an hour. More. And not once have we talked about you.'

'Well, I didn't really want to get onto the subject of the storm raging inside me just yet,' she says with a smile that dimples one of her cheeks. 'Anyway, that's why we are here. So you can talk.'

'Is it?'

'Of course.'

'Then thanks. But I think we should switch. Tell me about you. Not the storm. Just you.'

'In a while. Can you excuse me?' She nods towards the rest rooms.

He stands as she gets up, and the waiter rushes over to fold her napkin.

'I'll get the dessert menu,' he says.

She has been gone less than a minute when he is aware of the hand on his shoulder. He half-rises but the voice slurs in his ear, 'Don't get up, old son. Just wanted to say — lovely lady.'

The touch has made Piper tense, ready for something to go down, but he looks up and relaxes. This guy, about his age plus three or four years, but heavier, greyer, he's no threat. I must be getting paranoid, he thinks. It's just a drunk. What's going to happen in an upscale West End restaurant? 'Yeah, she is. But what, exactly, has that got to do with you?'

'Nothing. No, nothing. Don't get me wrong. Just a bit of friendly advice. Friendly *male* advice, if you get my drift.' His breath is so laden with booze it must be close to inflammable.

Keep this calm and easy, Piper tells himself. The lush just needs a little discouragement. 'I'm not sure I do,' he says softly, and then allows his voice to rise, emphasising the last words. 'Or want to. Can you leave me alone now?'

Piper shrugs the hand from his shoulder and the man backs off, raising his palms in full submissive mode. 'Of course. I just wanted to say, in case you were wondering,' he leans forward conspiratorially, 'she won't

98

take it up the arse.'

The short punch to the windpipe is one of Piper's favourites. He jabs hard, fast and then drops his arm. The man clutches at his collar and staggers backwards, his face reddening. Now Piper is on his feet, looking concerned, and reaches over as if trying to support the guy. The staff are around him in seconds. Piper says: 'Sorry, he seems to have had some sort of attack.'

A creaking noise comes from the man's mouth.

'Maybe you'd best call a doctor.'

Two of the guy's companions appear, equally drunk and a tad confused. Along with the maître d', they help their pal towards the door and fresh air, while another member of staff dials 999. It is all over in a minute, and the diners now have a bit of excitement to relate about their evening. The man eating alone in the corner, Piper is fairly certain, saw what happened. Piper glares at him, but the man raises his glass and smiles. The woman with the surgery-tight face is staring at him, but Piper is sure that is just some kind of general animosity towards profane Americans.

Celeste has returned. As she sits she gives him a puzzled look.

'What was that?' she asks, wariness in her voice. She can only have seen the finale, not the opening titles.

'You know him?'

'I've met him. His name is DeVaughan. He's some sort of banker.' Her jaw drops as realisation dawns. 'My God, did you do that to him?'

'Kind of. I think we'd better get the bill before he regains the power of speech.'

He raises his arm to attract a waiter and she grabs it. 'No, you don't. It's taken care of. I have a tab here.' She repeats, 'You did that?'

'Yes.'

'I don't know what to say.'

'Thanks?'

She walks across to retrieve her coat at the front of the restaurant and he can feel the heat of her disapproval. She thinks he is out of line. He catches up with her and puts a hand on her shoulder.

'I did it for you.'

'I can fight my own battles.'

'I'm sure. You just weren't there at the time.'

'Next time, wait till I get back.'

He doesn't want the evening to end like this. 'How about a nightcap?' There is a pause while she considers. 'Please? You can explain to me what I did wrong.'

The pause lengthens then she gives a little nod, thank God.

★　★　★

'So what did he say exactly?' she asks once they have managed to slip unnoticed past the knot of people attending to the choking banker outside Le Caprice and have found a place in the corner of the basement bar underneath Caviar House on Piccadilly. 'That poor man you maimed — DeVaughan. Will he ever speak again?'

'Yes. But maybe not for a few hours. It'll just feel like he's swallowed a basketball.'

'So what did he say?'

'He said I shouldn't bother because you didn't take it up the ass.'

Piper suddenly realises how loudly he has spoken, just at the moment when, with a bizarre synchronicity, every other conversation has stopped on a dime, as has the background jazz track. There are two heartbeats, a giggle, and the rhythm of the bar resumes with a track from Koop.

Celeste bursts out laughing and corrects him. 'I think you mean *arse*.'

'I figured he must be an old boyfriend. Speaking from experience, or lack of it.'

Her only answer is to raise an eyebrow. She isn't going there, not now.

'OK, none of my business.'

'That's right.'

'I'll get some more drinks.'

'No, I'm fine. I'd best be going soon. Early start tomorrow.'

'Work?'

'Pleasure. Horse-riding. I have a regular date with a girlfriend.'

'You never did tell me what you do for a living.'

'I'm a woman of independent means.'

He senses the evasion in her answer and asks: 'You forgiven me? For the banker?'

She can't help a smile. 'It probably served him right.'

As they are leaving, the Nokia in his jacket pocket vibrates. He pulls it out and answers it as surreptitiously as he can. It is Roth.

'Vince. Where are you?'

'Look on your screen,' he says. The Embassy's PPT system on the computers, which link to his mobile phone's chip, can tell Roth exactly where Piper is, to within two hundred yards.

'I'm not in the office.'

'Piccadilly. Just getting a drink.'

The Assistant Legat says: 'OK. Vince, I thought you ought to know before you see the first editions. There's been another bomb attack. And it's got our name on it again.'

7

Stanley Roth is a jowly man in his forties, with a narrow beard that follows the line where his jaw should be and a healthy shock of still-brown hair. The conspicuous bags under his eyes lend him a hangdog look at the best of times, even when he is enjoying himself, and he isn't having any kind of fun right now. He is looking at another shattered shopfront, at streets littered with debris, at British techs combing through wreckage. He is looking at another poke in the eye for London, one she neither needs nor deserves.

Piper meets him just across the Police-Do-Not-Cross barrier near the targeted store on Covent Garden's Long Acre, a Banana Republic whose chinos and baggy Ts now lie scattered across the road, arranged into bizarre patterns that suggest their wearers have been vaporised. Police cars blockade either end of the street, their blue lights flicking back from every shop window. The fire crews have also arrived and the black van that rolls into the street is, Roth knows, the Bomb Squad. They have picked up speed since the Barnes & Noble event, he thinks bitterly.

The acrid smell of scorched material and wood causes him to flash back to the day of Martha's death, but he shakes his head and refuses to let the timeslip happen. He has to stay in the here and now.

Roth indicates Piper should follow him, and they walk away from the scene.

'What's the damage?' asks Piper, as they head towards the chain coffee-shop on the corner, pushing through the gathering crowd, who are being warned by loudhailer to stay away in case there is a second device.

'The Banana Republic was closed. The only damage was to property, some flying glass, a driver who crashed into a pole with shock. No US citizens were involved, so we're off the hook.'

Piper nods. 'But you think they'll find the same explosives.'

'Yeah.'

'Was there a warning?'

'Nope.'

'So why make the connection?'

'Bombs are like the buses here. You go two years without one, then two or three come along at once. They're normally related.' Inside the coffee-shop Roth orders two double espressos. 'You OK?' Roth can smell the booze on him. 'I interrupt something?'

'Counselling.'

'I thought you'd turned that down.'

'I did.'

'What changed your mind?'

'The counsellor.'

Roth looks suspicious. 'You sure you OK?'

Piper nods. 'Never better.'

'Like I believe that.' They take the drinks to a small metal table at the rear and sit. 'Fletcher says hi.'

'Thanks.' He's missed the weekly liaison meeting at the APPLE office at Scotland Yard with the Chief Inspector. Roth had stood in for him. 'Anything on the slate?'

'Not much that concerns us. Dog wars.'

'What kind of dogs?'

Roth knocks back his coffee and indicates he'd like a second. 'Hotdogs. Frankfurters. Seems that some of the stands do a little drug dealing on the side — pills mostly, ecstasy, speed. There's a turf war. We are to warn US citizens not to frequent the vendors in case they get caught in the crossfire. I'm having an advisory posted.'

'I think I should come back, Stan. I've worn a big enough hole in the carpet at the apartment.'

'I ain't sure, Vince. You look like shit. Why not go home — I mean real home. See The Wolf.'

Yes, he should see his father soon. It had been too long. The idea of the London assignment was to try and patch up his marriage, and his relationship with Martha, and then take compassionate leave and go home. However, now he has buried Martha, he has unfinished business that will keep him here a little longer.

'Barnes & Noble and Banana Republic — what do they have in common?' Piper asks.

'They are the latest of the US chains to come here, we already got that. That's what I meant when I said it had our name on it.' Roth hesitates. 'Sorry if you thought it was more than that. But we do have a partial print from the B&N scene, you know. From part of the casing.'

'No, I didn't know,' he says irritably. 'Nobody tells me anything.'

'I'm telling you now,' Roth snaps back. 'OK? I'm telling you now. Jesus, Vince, you're lucky we didn't ship you back home. Be thankful for small mercies.'

'Yeah. That's the only kind I got right now. Small ones.' He hears the self-pity in his voice, and softens. 'But thanks for keepin' me in the loop, Stan. Any match on that print?'

Roth starts on his second coffee. He won't be sleeping much tonight, thinks Piper. 'Nope. Not yet. It's gone Stateside, see what they come up with. Meanwhile, we will check every anti-global organisation as well as the regular bomb merchants.'

'There is the possibility it's the start of an AZF-type campaign.' This was the outfit which had used the modus operandi of terrorism — planting bombs on railways — to blackmail damage the French government and force it towards what the group considered a more Utopian regime.

'It's a thought,' said Roth. 'Although I can't see the Brits paying five million bucks or whatever the demand was.'

'Six. Or the US coughing up if it is American shops that are being hit.'

'Or the US,' Roth agrees. 'I'm curious about that Fourth Way you asked me about.'

'Yeah?'

'Yeah. Given this shit.' Roth indicates the explosion. 'On the face of it they are pretty harmless. It's about formulating a more ethical, caring society, blah-di-blah. But when I ran the numbers on them, turns out the CSIS,' the Canadian Security Intelligence Service, 'were checking activists who might disrupt an Organisation of American States summit in Quebec and it thinks there might be links, by some members of the Fourth Way, to Black Bloc. You know them?'

Piper dug into his memory. 'Out of

Eugene, Oregon. Preach civil disobedience.'

'Right. And CSIS also suspect World Action, the guys who ripped up Seattle and Gothenburg. And RALF, the Radical Animal Liberation Front — the people who like to burn down labs. So — why did you ask about them?'

Another chance to come clean goes by without him flagging it down. 'I was doing the APPLE backlog paperwork, keep myself busy. Came across it there,' he lied.

'Nothing to do with Martha? She wasn't mixed up in that kind of crap?'

'No,' he says firmly. 'Not at all, Stan.'

'Nothing to do with what happened?'

Piper swallowed hard. 'No. Absolutely. Coincidence. I'll show you the reference — '

Roth raises his hand. The last thing he needs is more paperwork flying across his desk. 'No need.' He sees the faraway look in Piper's eyes. 'There's something else on your mind, isn't there?'

'I'm just tired, Stan. That's all,' he says eventually.

'Right. Anything I can do, Vin, you know that.'

He nods, but there is nothing Roth can do. All Piper wants is to find the deranged maniacs who killed Martha, who ripped her from his life. He has one slim lead: Henry

Monroe, and the possibility that he is tied into something radical. But he isn't going to hand that to Stanley Roth, who'll pass the Monroe hunch to the Brits tomorrow, leave it to them and their antique legal system to handle. The best way to build on the slither of information is to use the Bureau's eyes and ears. Outside, he is floundering. So he says: 'You can let me back in.'

Roth pushes away the empty coffee cup. His jowls sag even further and they wobble as he shakes his head. 'Anything but that, Vince. Anything but that.'

Fine, Piper thinks. Then I'll do it without you.

8

'Have you told him yet?' asks Roddy.

'Told him what?'

Celeste's brother rolls his eyes. 'That you are a Sagittarius. What do you think?'

It is three days since her evening with Piper, and they are in Zagora, a members' club just off Regent Street, popular with the Vogue House crew. Although Celeste thinks that the mock-harem decor is passé, Roddy insists that after a day at the crumbling dot.com coalface he needs to feel like a sultan. Roddy is two years older than her, but the gap has never mattered. For as long as she can remember, they have held no secrets back. He is well aware of what she does, and neither approves nor disapproves. It's just a line of business.

'I'm not sure he needs to know,' she says.

'Ha. What about when he wants sex? What about your vow of celibacy? No, not celibacy. Monogamy? Trigamy, whatever you call it.'

She almost tells him that it is about to become a duogamy, since DeVaughan never worked out, but she thinks better of it. 'He's just a friend; sex won't enter into it.'

Roddy's choice of drinks arrives, lurid and over-complicated or stylish and adventurous, depending on your take. She sips hers, a Grey Goose strawberry martini, and has to admit it isn't as disgusting as the description on the card suggested.

Roddy smacks his lips and brushes back his mane of inky hair with one hand. For a long time she'd envied him the colour of his hair, self-conscious about her own ginger locks, but after the age of eighteen hers had gradually thickened and darkened until she no longer has to dye it to get the required auburn shade.

Roddy leans forward. 'Celeste, my love, he's a man. Sex will always enter into it. You of all people should know that.'

Celeste recognises the truth of what he is saying, even as she refuses to face up to it. There is a bond between her and Piper now which, she hopes, goes beyond all that. She really had been playing a game at the Stafford, teasing him because he was so obviously in some kind of security service. One of her Three used to be a spook, so for two years he drip fed her tricks of the trade, although never, as far as she knew, anything classified. However, he was always pointing out things that civilians would miss, and some of it stuck. Besides, she'd enjoyed

111

showing off a little.

She sighs and admits: 'I do realise. My life just doesn't need to be any more complicated.'

'I'm off to the Mills' at the weekend,' says Roddy, changing tack. 'Do you want to come? Bit of shooting, eating, drinking.'

The Mills are a new-money couple with an estate in Hertfordshire, which includes the usual vast swimming pools, a garage housing more cars than you could drive in a month, a state-of-the-art six-launcher skeet course and a five-hundred-acre beat. Roddy is probably going to use the houseparty as a fundraiser for his various ventures. He has found that shooting and golf are two excellent venues for a little surreptitious business.

Unfortunately, his golf handicap is an inability to hit the ball without cricking his neck. He has invested in a shotgun, though, and a set of tweeds, and taken up clay-pigeon shooting and slaughtering dumb, slow birds. She is suspicious of why he wants her along. 'I don't think so, Roddy. I'm busy. Besides, last time we shot together, you were all huffy because I was better than you.'

'Define better.'

'I hit more clays.'

He shrugs, as if that were only one way of

keeping score. 'You can bring your tame Yank.'

'Take him yourself if you want. He needs the break.' She nods to show Piper has arrived and Roddy turns.

He is coming down the stairs, looking smarter than she's ever seen him. She gets the feeling she's about to meet a previous incarnation of Piper. He spots them and comes over and introductions are made.

'You look good,' she says.

'Thanks. I feel it.' Resolution and direction suit him, he knows.

Roddy tries to make some appropriate noise of regret. 'Look, er, Vince. Terribly sorry to hear about . . . I mean, Cel told me about . . . Terrible business.'

'Things would have been worse without your sister.'

Roddy smiles as he glances at her. 'Things usually are. Look,' he says, gulping his drink, 'I'll leave you two to it.'

'There's really no need,' Piper protests feebly.

'Fulham are playing,' Roddy explains. 'On the box — upstairs. Have fun. Lennie already got us the seats.' Lennie is one of his new partners, a man who to Celeste's mind is something of a unreconstituted East End bruiser. However, he has money, and knows

113

his dogs apparently, so Roddy likes him. He pecks Celeste on the cheek, shakes hands with Piper again and is off, weaving his way through his fellow members and taking the stairs up to the club room.

'He seems like a nice guy,' says Piper.

'He is.'

One of the waitresses in the diaphanous pantaloons that look like a fire hazard considering all the candles around, wafts over to take his order.

'Coke,' he says. Celeste's eyebrows rise, before he adds, 'With a shot of Myers.'

'You've changed,' she offers tentatively. 'You're different somehow.'

'Yes. I took your advice about not letting it corrode my life. I'm no longer the grieving father. Not exclusively, anyhow. Had a medical today, passed with flying colours. Well, he could feel my liver, the doc said. I told him, 'I feel *for* my liver sometimes.' Did some blood work, says I gotta cut back on the booze. But when do they never say that?'

'When you're teetotal.'

'Right. OK. Miracles aside, then, I had a psychological, too. Scored eighty-eight per cent on the Global Assessment of Function.'

'Is that good?'

'You kiddin'? Over ninety-two and you're Batman.' He takes the rum and Coke from

114

the proffered tray. 'To be honest, the shrink said there is obviously some stress, but he was of the opinion that getting back to work would help. So here I am, Vincent Piper, Associate Legat, FBI London Office, here to apologise for screwing up our dinner-date the other night.'

She thinks of telling him that he's done a better job than he knows at screwing her up. The Caprice have called and suggested she bring a different companion in future, with a possible hint of perhaps she'd like to frequent the Wolseley around the corner more often from now on. DeVaughan has clearly got his voice back. She decides not to bring it up, he'll just feel bad, and she doesn't want to dent his new optimism.

'So, can we eat tonight?'

She shakes her head. Denis is in town and she has a ten o'clock with him. Business must come before pleasure. 'I'm afraid not.'

'No?' He considers for a second. 'Washing your hair?'

'I've already done that.'

'Oh. Yeah. Looks great.' Piper can feel his ebullient mood hissing away. His shoulders are already down. 'Is there someone else?'

She holds down a laugh, but feels herself tense inside, as she answers honestly. 'No. There's not someone else, Vin.' She makes sure the relief in his eyes is shortlived. 'There are three someone elses.'

* * *

The first one had been a friend of her father. In retrospect, he wasn't the old man she thought at the time, perhaps in his mid-forties. To an eighteen year old though, he seemed like a man whose testosterone would have run its course and she agreed to escort him to various functions while he was in Town by himself. He then suggested she might as well use the apartment full-time, as it stood empty for most of the year.

The second was a friend of his, younger, richer, sexier, and she had no doubt that bedding her was part of the deal, but she didn't mind; she was enjoying herself.

So by the time a third was added, a career was formulating. While her friends and contemporaries were globe-trotting in search of an elusive blissed-out Babylon, she was honing her taste for the good life. By her mid-twenties the game plan was pretty much in place. She would have no more than three 'friends' on a long-term contract, with stipulations as to who got precedence (a matter of seniority), and with final approval of when the relationship started and, just as

116

importantly, when it stopped. The fees were paid twice-yearly into an account in the Turks and Caicos Islands, in the West Indies, set up by Roddy's accountant and described as fees for financial consulting and tax advice.

It works well for her. She has at least three holidays a year: skiing, usually in the US, and trips to a tropical beach — Cocoa Island in the Maldives last winter, North Island in the Seychelles coming up soon — and a city or two. She earns twice what most of her friends make, except for a few fund managers in the City, and her only big financial blunder has been investing in Roddy's dot.com, which had lost her a hundred grand. That and letting him near her share of their father's money.

And boyfriends, the regular business of dating and marriage? That seems a different road, one that runs parallel to hers but never intersects. As far as Celeste is concerned there is no moral dimension to this. She does not threaten the stability of marriages, nor does she go fishing for new clients. She is happy with what she does, she doesn't need saving or rescuing. There is no pimp, no one to call the shots but her. Her father told her she should cut her own niche in the world. Well, she has. And it is up to others to deal with it, Vincent Piper included.

★   ★   ★

By the time she finishes, Piper has gulped through another rum and Coke, trying to get his head around this, his uptight East Coast upbringing battling with his under-developed sense of libertarianism.

'So,' he says at last, knowing he shouldn't, 'what do you call yourself?'

'How do you mean?'

'Well, you're not a prostitute, are you? You're too upmarket for that.'

'Thank you.'

He feels his glass frosting and the ice cubes in it stop melting as she says it. He knows he should call it a day, but the rum is goading him on. That and his crushing sense of disappointment. 'Call girl?'

'Companion.'

'Companion,' he repeats. 'That's nice and neutral. Like 'escort', I suppose.'

A silence grows. Piper knows this isn't her problem, it's his, but even so he feels his neck glowing red.

'Well,' he says at last. 'Thank you for being so . . . forthright. So you have one of the three tonight?'

'Yes.'

'Which is why you can't have dinner.'

'Yes. I'm sorry if I've upset you.'

118

'Upset me? Why should I be upset?'

'There is no reason why you should be upset.'

'None at all,' he agrees.

'So why are you upset?'

'Because . . . ' Piper stops himself. *Because I want to be with you so, so bad* is probably not the best answer. 'I don't like surprises. You have to give me time to adjust.'

'It's not as sordid as it sounds.'

'It doesn't sound sordid.' He knows his voice is less than convincing.

'Look, I have to go.' She stands and puts a hand on his shoulder. 'Vince, I do like you, but I thought it was best to be honest. That side of my life is taken care of. There are other parts still available, though.'

'Like being friends?'

'Yes. If you wish it.'

'I do.'

'Good.'

'Celeste?'

'Yes?'

'How much would it cost me to get you to blow this guy out tonight?'

Celeste Young shakes her head, turns and leaves without a backward glance.

9

George Tavos sits in the back of his Transit van among the buns and burgers, watching the sheets of rain fall onto the cobbles. Six carts are out, twenty-three left sitting idle. He leans back against the catering packs of baps and feels them hardly give. They are turning so hard and crispy that even the punters would notice now. He'll have to dump them.

It is eleven o'clock on a Saturday night, and the yard should be all but empty of carts, even in this rain. The weekend ten till three shift is the one that his vendors really wanted. Fights used to break out over the allocation up until three weeks ago, when what the *Evening Standard* calls the Dog Wars started.

His brother Terry had acted quickly following the murder of Christos. He knew who was behind it, and a couple of days later a car had mounted a pavement and ploughed into one of the French brothers' carts, maiming the vendor, smashing the stall to pieces. Same thing at a pitch in Paddington, the next night, although the seller died in that one.

George and Terry had lost two more since

then, one a shooting, the other a machete attack, the French brothers' trademark. Old Stefan bled to death while they waited for the ambulance. George had arrived just in time to see him shudder the last of his life away. The sight has haunted his dreams ever since.

People are scared. Pitches are being chosen more carefully now. No dark alleys or building overhangs, plenty of bright light, set well away from the kerbside. Those near police stations are particularly cherished. Terry has had enough, George knows. The Frenches want to control the pills this bad, then let them. Overtures have already been made about a meeting, to take place somewhere neutral, somewhere safe. They must be able to come to some arrangement.

He hears footsteps coming down the alley from New Oxford Street, splashing through the puddles; turning his collar up, he slides off the rear of the Transit. Better late than never, he thinks. Eleven to one are the peak hours, so whoever it is can still make a good few quid if they shift their arse.

George peers into the blurred light bleeding from the main road, and is just aware that the man has stopped, when the left side of his body slumps and he stumbles. Shock ripples through his body, followed by the agony of a shattered kneecap.

George rolls on his side, scrabbling in his inside pocket for his mobile phone and this time he hears the hiss of the silencer and a .22 slug shatters all the bones in his right hand. He bites his tongue, and his mouth fills with the metallic taste of blood. He squeezes his eyes shut, trying to blank out the waves of pain. George decides the best option, his only option, is to lie very, very still, and hope the pain — and the man — go away.

Through the storm apparently raging in his ears, George is aware of the raincoated figure entering the yard and searching through the carts, clattering them against each other until he finds the one he wants. It is a Carlson Royale, the king of all hotdog stands, the only one they have. Double-sized broiler, big grill, even a kebab spit.

The man grunts as he untangles it from the lesser carts and pulls it over the cobbles towards George, whose breathing is very shallow now. The man opens the side and turns on the propane and lights the flame to heat the water in the big square aluminium container on the top.

After five minutes the man tests the water and tuts. It seems to be too slow for him. He bends down and looks George in his dim eyes. 'What does it take to make you people stop?'

George doesn't answer. However, it becomes clear an answer is expected, so he manages to gasp, 'We'll stop. Promise. Tell French. We'll stop.'

'You certainly will. So will the Frenches.'

Is there a third party trying to squeeze both of them out? Have they been fighting the wrong enemy these last few weeks?

His assailant stands, puts his finger in the water and curses as it scalds him. 'That's about ready,' he says, as if he is talking about a barbecue. George hears a metallic whirring sound. He has set the kebab rotisserie turning. Now another noise. The edge of a knife hissing across a steel sharpener.

Now the man kneels again, closer this time. He sucks his burned finger noisily for a second before he speaks. 'Now, you know about these things, chef,' he says sarcastically. 'Do you think a human head will broil better if attached to or removed from the body?'

Mercifully, George faints.

10

The FBI was astonishingly slow to embrace the computer age. It still used typing pools to compile reports well after they became obsolete elsewhere, and it wasn't until the early 1990s that it set up comprehensive databases, available to all Field Offices.

Now, it is making up for lost time. The much-delayed and over-budget Virtual Case File system is finally online. Based at the Regional Computer Support Centers at Pocatello, Idaho and Fort Monmouth, New Jersey, the programme sorts through incoming data from fifty-six US Field Offices which issue two DUs, the daily updates. It also has to process input from each of the thirty-three Foreign Liaison Offices, including London, which file a nightly status report or SR.

This vast quantity of words disappears into the VCF's circuits, waiting for recall by EDGAR, the less than respectful nickname for the FBI search engine or PATTERN, which can be used by agents to flag similarities in disparate cases and reports. So if you enter 'pilot training', every DU or SR that mentions suspicious individuals asking

124

about flying courses will be collated. The idea is that PATTERN might have prevented 9/11, but nobody, not even its designers, can be certain of that.

Piper, however, does not want to access the DUs or the SRs or PATTERN, but the ALERT archives of COINTELPRO, the FBI's Counter Intelligence Programme. This lists all organisations across the globe considered to be a threat to US citizens. It includes the myriad of anti-globalisation organisations, like the Fourth Way. It will not tell him which of these are actively infiltrated — only COINTELPRO itself has such sensitive details — but that's OK. He just wants some idea of who he might be up against.

He sits down at the table in his apartment and sets up the Apple laptop and printer he has bought in Tottenham Court Road. Just as the salesman had promised, this two-thousand-pound piece of shiny metal has him on the Internet in five minutes. Within ten it is flashing a sullen *Access Denied* at him. His personal clearance to the FBI files is updated daily. By not entering either of the Legat offices and swiping his ID card, his ability to log on has been suspended. He can't get in. But he knows a man who can.

★ ★ ★

'Dad. It's Vincent.'

'Vincent. Hi. How y'doing?'

'OK. You know. Yeah.'

'Thanks for the photos. It looked like a nice service.'

'Yeah. It was. There's a video, too.'

'Sorry I couldn't — '

'I know, Dad. We've been through that.'

'Hold on, I gotta . . . take some oxygen here.'

'Go ahead.'

'OK . . . Better. You there?'

'Yup.'

'What time is it in London?'

'It's five after ten, Dad, so I guess about the same after five where you are.'

'Yeah. Your mother's just gone next door . . . you want me to get her?'

'No, Dad, I need to talk to you.'

'Right. Shoot.'

'Your memoirs.'

The Wolf laughs. 'I don't think you can call 'em that, son. Just a ragbag of ideas.'

'But you got clearance to write them.'

'Of course.' All former Agents must clear their manuscripts with the FBI's OGC, the Office of General Counsel, and the OPR, Office of Professional Responsibility, to

126

ensure there is nothing that might compromise Agents past or present or impinge on national security.

'So you got a computer clearance?'

'Only to level two.'

That was enough. It would give him the ALERT files. 'Can I have it?'

'It's lapsed.'

Piper puts his hand over the receiver and swears. He removes it and says slowly, 'But once you have approval, you can get another clearance.'

'I guess.'

'Can you get a PIN code for me?'

'Vin, what are you doing?'

'Trying not to lose my mind, Dad.'

There is a pause at the other end, before his father says: 'I'll call you back.'

'Wait.' It's time for a little fishing. 'I saw Henry Monroe just before . . . I saw him a while back, not that long ago.'

'Where?'

'Here.'

'Oh. You certain?'

'Hundred and ten per cent.'

'Oh.' Piper can tell he is conserving his breath. 'How did he seem?'

'Kinda odd.'

'Yeah. He's got problems of his own,' he wheezes.

127

Vince can tell his father is running out of steam and he says: 'Tell me later, Dad. When you call with the number.'

★   ★   ★

Piper sits in his darkened apartment, an untouched glass of wine on the table before him, Chet Baker on the CD. Roth would kill him if he knew what he was doing. His father would understand, though. He had always worked on hunches, always looked in the margins for clues. It was why he was so good. He'd appreciate that if something about Monroe smells funny, you have to check out what it is.

The phone makes him jump. 'Dad?'

'No.'

A woman.

'Celeste?'

'Three strikes and you are out, isn't that what they say?'

'It's what they say. Sarah. Sarah Nielsen.'

Martha's American tutor giggles, and he realises she is drunk or well on the way. 'Home run. I'm sorry it's so late.'

'That's OK.'

'And that I'm not your dad.'

Get on with it, he thinks. The old man is probably trying to get through.

128

'It's OK. How can I help?'

'Well, I've just been with some of Martha's fellow students and they've been thinking how best to commemorate her and her life.'

'That's nice.'

'Yes. So I wondered if we could meet with you to discuss it — what we have in mind.'

'Sure. When?'

'Perhaps you could come to school? How about Friday, at two o'clock?'

'Yes.'

'You know where it is?'

'I do.'

'I'll see you then. Room eight.'

He puts the phone down. In the darkness his mind begins to work, playing on themes he would rather ignore.

What is Celeste doing now? Dinner over? Brandy and coffee? Are they in his apartment yet? Is she going down on —

The phone rings again. This time it is The Wolf.

His words come in a rush: 'I have a PIN number. You got a pen?' He rattles it off.

'Thanks, Dad.'

'Vin, don't do anything you'll regret.'

'That's not the idea.'

'It never is.'

Piper changes the subject. 'What about Henry? You were saying he had problems.

129

Have you seen him lately?'

'No, not for a while. Not since his boy got sick.'

'Eric? Eric's sick?'

'Cancer.'

'Jesus. He can't be . . . '

'Thirty-five.'

'Jesus.'

'Yeah. Henry took it bad. I spoke to Kate.' Monroe's wife. 'He's just taken off. Can't face it.'

Piper knows the feeling. 'Yeah. Thanks, Dad. Thanks for the PIN.'

'You take it easy, Vin.'

'I will. Take care. Say hi to Mom.' And he adds some words he only recently included in his vocabulary where his father is concerned. 'I love you, Dad.' His father grunts, embarrassed but, he hopes, pleased.

Piper sits down, brings up the FBI entry screen and taps in the PIN number. *Access Granted.*

★ ★ ★

An hour later and his head is swirling with acronyms such as GOG, GAG, AGAIN, STOP, EGG, FUGG and RED. Just typing in Anti-Globalisation on EDGAR the search engine had given over 27,000 hits. Adding the word 'violence' had taken it down by half. When he put in UK, it reduced further. Then he linked in the Fourth Way, and it cut drastically. Even so, in the last sixty minutes he has ploughed through several hundred organisations which hate US companies, capitalism and coffee-shop chains. AGA, the Anti-Global Alliance, looked promising, and it had healthy links to the Fourth Way but also Greenpeace and Oxfam, and was unlikely to go rogue. Similarly, Greenworld might be a self-styled 'radical' splinter group of Friends of the Earth, but its strategy seems to be boring its opponents into submission with endless manifestos, the crux of which are about paying decent money to tea and banana growers. Piper has no problem with that.

Finally he is down to five UK-based organisations which are loosely affiliated to the Fourth Way but which also seem to believe that the ends justifies the means; they quote the Irish struggle, the ANC (in its early days) or FARC or Action Directe as role models. He looks at them critically again, trying to trust instincts blunted by grief. If he was the old Vincent Piper, would he have marked up DAGGER as a candidate? Direct Action Against Global Erosion of Regionalism. That's two As, guys, not two Gs, but as he's discovered, people take terrible liberties to make their acronyms fit something they perceive as cool or threatening or clever. He is fairly sure DAGGER is one guy in a rented room in Liverpool, Dartford or Gateshead — some such Godforsaken place — but that doesn't make him, or her, any less dangerous. On the contrary, some of the worst outrages are perpetrated by sad fuckers trying to get noticed.

And Monroe? Where did he fit in with these fruitcakes?

Perhaps nowhere. In which case, why did he say: '*Do yourself a favour. Get her out of here.*' And why was he carrying a soft-radical mag, if he hadn't undergone some kind of Road to Damascus conversion?

But what was Monroe's motive? Money? Maybe 'they' had hired him for his expertise. Perhaps he was trying to fund a cure for cancer, or at least some decent treatment for his boy.

Vincent picks up the phone to dial again and then lets it drop. He has troubled his father enough. Next time, though, he will ask a simple question: did Monroe ever do the Quantico Bomb Technology course, a ten-week primer, as it were, in all things explosive?

In the meantime, what does he do now

about the outfits he has found on ALERT? Cross-check with Roth, see if any of the names matched with their or the Brits' enquiries? He can't do that. Although Roth is letting him resume his APPLE work, unauthorised access to ALERT means instant dismissal. No, he has to follow any lead himself, to run down each of the five if need be. The chances of it being any one of them are slim, but just by making a start, he might stir something up. And it'll keep him busy. But let's be honest, he tells himself. Right now, you feel naked: an FBI man without a gun. He knows how to solve that, though.

Vincent Piper looks at his watch. Now would be a good time to check who was on duty at the Fairmont.

11

A steady drizzle falls outside, turning the London streets slick and shiny. Autumn is in the air now, and overcoats are out of the cupboard. So it is no surprise when one man walks into the hotel lobby, holding his umbrella up just a fraction longer than is really necessary, enough so that the only image on the doorway's CCTV will be of two legs behind a black nylon dome.

He makes his way through to the rear, skirting the bar area, ignoring the lift, strips off the overcoat then swerves through a service door into the dank concrete staircase, unpainted for many years, the sort of dilapidated underbelly that all hotels have. This is the part the guests will never normally see.

He loses the coat in the scuffed grey plastic wheelie bin. Underneath, he has on a smart Calvin Klein suit, of the kind all the Fairmont London staff wear. From his attaché case he removes a round black lacquered tray, and then the case joins the overcoat in the bin. Both were cheap and disposable.

He pulls the flesh-coloured surgical gloves

134

tight to smooth out any telltale wrinkles and looks for cameras on the stairwell. None. Nice to know that well-meaning and urgent advice is so readily ignored in this country. He moves quietly up the stairs.

On the fourth floor he opens the door a crack. There are guests, a few late revellers with slurred voices, shoes off, wedged in the doorway while they try and make the fiddly electronic key turn the light green. They are in, and silence descends.

A door slams in the stairwell. Someone is on the floor below, and footsteps ring on the concrete stairs. He cocks an ear. They are going down. He breathes easier.

He partially opens the umbrella and steps through the door onto the landing, his footsteps muffled by the new thick-piled red carpet. As he does so the umbrella snaps to fully extended and he hooks it over the CCTV camera that glares down the corridor.

Twenty steps to go now. The suite he wants is set back from the corridor, down a little side extension, and he waits until he is a few feet away before he takes the tray and frisbees it past, watching it bounce off the framed picture of an English hunting scene and scrape down the wall.

As he should do, the duty officer steps out from his position to see what all the fuss is

135

about. His left hand is up to his mouth, and he's ready to speak into the cuff mike. There are two options here. The guy can come out looking the right way, or the wrong way.

He looks the wrong way.

Piper puts a hand onto the guy's wrist, covering the mike, and pulls the arm up and over, popping the shoulder; two blows, the old Fairbairn stiff-fingered punches, and his legs sag. He is a big guy, though, so just for a finale, Vincent rams his head into the wall, and keeps on the pressure points while he reaches in and snaps the gun out of the holster. Then he lets him slide.

He lays him down on the floor, checks the pulse. Still alive. In fact, even now the eyelids are fluttering. He turns and retraces his steps, ignoring the sound of a door opening. Soon there will be screams. The Congressman will be wakened, just to check he is not dead. Police will be here. It doesn't matter. There will be trouble, especially for Kubilos, the Secret Service man now kissing the carpet.

Too bad. Mission accomplished.

Now Piper has a gun.

12

Catherine Deneuve. That's who DCI Fletcher reminds him of, Piper thinks. She is in her late thirties, or maybe she has slid past forty, and she is probably as attractive as she is going to get. He can imagine she was a gawky teenager, a rather plain twenty year old, but somehow she fits into her current age perfectly. He bets her fresh-faced contemporaries have not fared as well, but Detective Chief Inspector Jacqueline Fletcher looks pretty damn good from where he is sitting. Catherine Deneuve, albeit in a severe police uniform with a broad Geordie accent.

He is sitting in the APPLE office, looking down towards Broadway Buildings — the old MI6 HQ — and St James's Park station at a catch-up session for all the liaison briefings he has missed. She sent flowers for the funeral and, later, a note offering all the support she could give. He likes her, even if she does chew his ass off now and then. Somehow, the news that the United States is always the dominant half of this transatlantic partnership has not filtered through to the Chief Inspector. She thinks being on home turf gives her some kind of advantage. As if.

Today, however, she is a pussycat. Most people still tiptoe around Piper, fearing a misplaced word will cause him to collapse in tears, and she seems to have got the habit. He doesn't like it. Social interaction, without the cut and thrust, the odd traded insult, is like an anodyne business transaction.

'I haven't got much for you, Vincent,' she says.

'A few scraps would be nice. I've had enough of being shunted to one side.'

'Two muggings?' she offers. 'Not worth your while.'

'Anyone hurt?'

'Scared, but not hurt. I can email you the reports.'

'Fine.'

APPLE was set up in the aftermath of three high-profile attacks on US citizens: the murder of a female jogger early one morning in a park in East London, the discovery of a sixty-year-old tourist from Idaho floating in the Thames, minus his credit cards and various cameras, and the gang rape in Camden Town of a Mormon girl from Salt Lake City. The idea was straightforward enough — never again to have to say 'an investigating team is on its way over from Washington'. Piper's role is to be that US presence. At least, when he is on game.

'We have a credit-card fraud,' says Fletcher.

'Straightforward?'

She looks down at her notes. 'Yes. Two men in their twenties using dummies made in New Jersey, which they bought in a bar in Manhattan. We've sent details across to the relevant bodies on your side. Nothing organised at this end — just a couple of kids who thought they could take London on a weekend with a fistful of bent plastic.'

'They'll be tried here?'

'I'd imagine so, yes. Unless any of your boys have a previous on them they want to hit them with. Again, I'll let you know.'

'Nothing else?'

'Oh, I've got tons, love, but nothing that would interest you, Vincent. Hotdogs wars?'

'I heard about that.'

'Six dead.'

'Six? Jesus.'

'It's moved up to tit-for-tat. You know you can't get a burger on the streets of London after six at night now. The vendors are getting too scared to come out.'

'Is that a bad thing?'

'Probably not. Keeps the incidence of food poisoning down.' She grimaces. 'You heard about the boiled head?'

He nods and also pulls a face. 'Sick.'

She stands and smooths down her skirt. She is in uniform because the Met has a funeral of its own, a DC shot by drug dealers. She knew him, so she will speak — something she isn't looking forward to. She helped propose the operation that got him murdered. Even worse, they have nobody for the shooting right now.

'There is still the Fairmont. That was a bloody mess, wasn't it? I thought you blokes were meant to be good at that sort of thing. We offered him DPG.' The Diplomatic Protection Group, SO16, consists of five hundred authorised firearms officers used to protect a variety of targets. 'Not good enough for you?'

'He was a congressman on a fact-finding mission to look at tourism incentives. He got a Secret Service man because he was worried after the two bombs and felt happier with a homegrown — '

'He didn't get very good homegrown, did he?' she interrupts, laying on the sarcasm.

'No.' Piper feels bad about Kubilos, but Fletcher is right, he was too easy to take. He'd checked up on the roster at the Embassy, and Kubilos had leaped out as the one to go for. Piper knew he wasn't one of the best. Piper also knew the Fairmont layout, was aware that it needed security upgrading from when he did the five-five for the Secret Service: there were too many holes in its camera coverage. He was also certain nothing would have happened to close those holes in the interim. Well, it would now.

Kubilos wasn't badly hurt, but he was suspended from duty pending an enquiry. He'd be shipped back to the States for retraining, no doubt. It didn't matter. With the Brits' stiff-necked approach to weapons, Piper could check a gun out from the Embassy armoury only when it was deemed essential to an operation. It needed an affidavit signed by both Roth and Beckett. Every round had to be accounted for, forms filled in, in triplicate, each and every time a weapon was fired.

A Secret Service man is embarrassed and maybe disgraced, and has a very sore neck. Piper doesn't care. Now he has a 9mm Sig Sauer pistol that is untraceable to him.

'You going to tell me?' he asks at last.

'Tell you what?' she retorts.

'Where they are on the bombs.'

'Oh, fuck off, Vin,' she says with a sudden vehemence that presses him back in his seat. 'I'm not in the mood for games. Not today. Ask your own people.'

'You think they'll tell me?'

'Do you think they're wrong not to?'

'Yes.'

A raised eyebrow.

'No,' he admits.

Fletcher sits on the desk and makes herself relax. 'Sorry. I've got this.' She points to her uniform.

'I understand.'

'Look, I know as much as you do.' When he makes to protest she stamps back in hard. 'You know we are not routinely in that loop, Vin. All we've got is a request for any further information on a couple of dozen organisations.'

'Can I see it?'

'No.' He seems to sag in his seat and a wave of sympathy hits her. Vince Piper is not a bad man by any means. Just a human being, as they all are. It is easy to forget that, in a job overloaded with ranks and organisations to hide behind. He does not deserve the hand dealt to him. Fletcher reaches over and presses some of the keys on her computer. 'You want a coffee?'

'Sure.'

'Black, right?'

'Right.'

When she leaves he looks at the screen. There are the names. From his pocket he pulls his folded piece of paper. Of the five on the sheet, two are onscreen in front of him, including, towards the end, DAGGER, the agitprop brainchild of one Patrick Grey. It is where he will start.

13

She climbs on top of Piper, hand splayed on his chest, holding him still while she straddles him. He is about to burst, to lose control, and she knows that. She rises up, positions herself and lets her weight drop, causing her to shudder as he slides in. He utters a little gasp when she throws her head back and shoves her hips forward, her right hand reaching behind her to squeeze his balls. Then he comes, pumping away inside her, one big contraction after another and she tells him it feels like a river of silk, and he sits up to take a nipple in his mouth and that seems to be enough to bring her along too. He feels her muscles pulse round him, like bands of steel, so intense it almost hurts.

Sarah Nielsen looks down at him, licks her dry lips and smiles. 'Well, that was a turn-up for the books.'

Piper says: 'That's one way of putting it.' He runs a hand up her body, following the dip of her waist, the little rough patch of skin his palm finds, an anomaly on such a perfectly textured surface.

It is early evening, and the sun is low in the

granite sky. Beyond the window of her apartment he can see Regent's Park gathering the gloom around itself, watches the lights on the cars flick on, sees them stacked up around the Outer Circle as the Friday-evening rush hour kicks in.

She rolls off him and lies back, her chest rising and falling. The evening had started innocently enough, in the college, with a group of six students, contemporaries of Martha, all nice young American girls who, unwittingly, made his heart ache the longer they stayed in the room.

Martha should have been one of these, looking forward to a weekend, wondering, as he heard them discussing, whether to go to Soho or Hoxton, Clerkenwell or Camden, and who to ask along. Fabric or Herbal, they twittered, Lovebox or Underdog. They sat there, pierced navels proudly displayed, a mass of camouflage tops and cargo pants and bra straps and cascading hair, causing an ache, a physical pain in Piper's side, wishing that it was Martha explaining why DJ Trama sucks and Carl Cox rocks, rather than these young surrogates.

He had tried to hang on to their every word, as they were gently prodded and prompted by Sarah, explaining their drawing and projections. They would all chip in for

145

the cost, they explained — there were various fundraising schemes in the college mooted — all they needed was to think of a suitable site. He'd thanked the girls, they had scattered to hit the town, and Sarah suggested she and Piper discuss the concept further over a drink.

The one drink led to several. He supposes he had become maudlin, but the memory of that part of the evening is hazy. At some point an invitation back for coffee had segued into something more physical, until now they lay, post-coitally happy, or at least, as happy as he ever feels capable of being again.

She sits up on the bed, one leg thrown up and he admires her body. How old are you? he wants to ask, but the time isn't right for that sort of question. She could be a couple of years either side of thirty. Younger than him, for sure. In better shape, too.

Sarah turns and faces him and she must see something in his face because she reaches over and runs a finger across his forehead. 'Just remember. In the midst of death, we are in life. You know what I'm saying?'

He nods and smiles. He watches as she gets up, enjoying the movements of her naked body. She pads across the room, and presses play on the CD. An opera he is unfamiliar with, although that is hardly an exclusive

146

category, starts up.

'Bizet,' Sarah explains. '*Les pecheurs de perles*. The Pearl Fishers. You like opera?'

'I like this.'

'Not the same.'

'Jazz,' he admits cautiously, 'is more my thing.'

She wrinkles her nose.

'Is that a ye-chhh?'

'More a ho-hum. I had a boyfriend once in Toronto who was a jazz fan. All those concerts with endless noodling and you know, the sax does a solo, and you clap, and then the trumpet takes a solo, and you clap . . . '

He laughs. 'You either get it, or you don't. Like opera.'

'Do you play an instrument?'

Piper shakes his head. 'I tried guitar when I was a kid. I could do Neil Young howls of feedback and that was about it. You?'

'Piano. I'm OK, I guess.'

'Was Martha really any good?' he asks softly, daring only to whisper her name in such circumstances.

'As a sculptor? Maybe.' Sarah pauses. 'As a human being? Yes. I liked her. A lot.' She considers her answer further. 'The thing is, she would have been good, once the consistency came, and that piece is excellent.

I honestly mean that. I'll miss her.'

He nods. Words are still failing him sometimes. 'Thanks for doing this.'

'The sex?' An impish grin splits her face.

'The statue.'

The idea is that the class will cast Martha's most ambitious project in bronze, and they want to place it somewhere in London as a permanent memorial. One of the girls has come up with the idea that the figure, which is a sinuous female form, reaching up to the sky, with something that might be a child in her arms, be offered to the Embassy in Grosvenor Square. Piper has agreed to pursue it, even though he isn't sure they really need the headache of what to do with a six-feet-high piece of metal.

'It's not wrong, Vince. It's the most natural thing in the world. To prove you still can feel.'

'Like therapy?'

'Yeah,' Sarah laughs. 'My bill's in the post.'

Piper's mobile phone rings and he has trouble finding it in the tangle of their clothes that litter the once spartan, Kelly Hoppen-like bedroom.

He manages to catch it before it clicks through to message. 'Yeah?'

'Vince?'

'Hi.'

'It's Celeste.'

'I know. How's it going?'

'Oh, fine. You?'

'I'm good.'

'Is this a bad time, Vin?'

Sarah takes a wrap from the cupboard and says softly, 'You want that coffee now?'

But not softly enough. 'It's a bad time, isn't it?'

'No. I'm with Martha's tutor. We're talking about Martha's work. There's an idea for a memorial from her fellow students and friends.'

'That'll be nice. Is that Bizet playing?'

'Yes. At least, so they tell me.'

'Look, I feel guilty about the other night. I didn't explain properly.'

'I feel bad, too. I behaved like a schmuck.'

'It's not uncommon. People sometimes have problems with me. About what I do.'

'I can see that.'

'It's just not — '

'Conventional,' he suggests.

'Yes. It's acceptable for men to have mistresses or screw around, but ... sorry, don't want to give you my justification speech.'

'Is it well rehearsed?'

She laughs quietly. 'I give it a polish most days.'

Sarah puts her head around the door and

interrupts. 'How do you take it?'

'Excuse me.' He puts a hand over the tiny mouthpiece. 'Black, no sugar. Thanks. Celeste? Hey!'

'You free later?' she asks.

Sarah walks in, the wrap open, a coffee in each hand. He works hard at keeping his voice level. 'No, I gotta work. Some intel about the bombs. Probably nothin', but . . . '

'But some other time?'

'Yeah.'

'Do you want there to be some other time, Vince? Knowing what you know?'

'I do. Yes.' I think I do anyway. I did, he says to himself. Now things are a little more complicated. 'Can I call you?'

'Of course.' He feels bad, sitting naked on the floor, his desire for Sarah already stirring once more, when at the other end of the phone is a woman who put herself on the line for him that night, to help a stranger she'd met for five minutes, and he is giving her the brush-off. Despite her unorthodox way of making a living, he knows Celeste deserves better.

'Great. See you.' The line goes dead.

'Your wife?' asked Sarah. 'Don't worry if it's — '

'No. Anyway, that's ex-wife, remember? And it was a friend.'

'You sounded very cagey for a friend.'

'We had words the other night . . . it's no big deal. Forget about it.'

She hands him the coffee. 'Do you really have to work tonight?'

'No. Not really. No work to do.'

Sarah rolls back onto the bed and grins. 'I wouldn't be too sure about that, Vincent.'

★ ★ ★

'Dad?'

'Yeah?'

'Vincent.'

It is gone midnight and Piper is back at his apartment, still a little drunk, a little sore, feeling that life isn't quite as bleak as he had imagined earlier in the day, yet fighting the nagging feeling that he has done something despicable. He takes a moment to reassure himself, to underline that this time there is no wife to be hurt, and it was just two people having a good time.

Now, though, he has threads to pick up. He mustn't let Sarah or her project for commemorating Martha distract him from his mission to find Monroe. There is a time limit, too. At the moment his colleagues are indulgent, not surprised that he isn't focused. That won't last forever. He has to move.

151

'You OK?' asks his dad eventually.

'Yeah. I just wanted to talk.'

'You sound better.'

'Yeah, I am. A little.' He knows he will never really be 'better', but he wants to get back to what he once was. A good Agent.

'You find what you were looking for?'

'On the computer? Yes. Thanks for that. Dad, about Henry . . . '

'Yup?'

'You know if he ever did the Quantico Bomb thing?'

'The ten-week module? I dunno. After we split as partners, I didn't keep up with everything. Maybe. Why?'

'No reason.'

'No reason?' Piper listens to the rattle of air down the end of the line. 'I can't get this idea out of my head.'

'Which one, Dad?'

'That you are going to do something stupid.'

Piper hoots in derision. 'This just in from a man who once leaped off a freeway bridge onto a moving truck to try and stop a robbery.'

The laughter that follows makes them both feel good.

★ ★ ★

152

Scotland Yard are kept in the dark about the war chest. It is located in the original FBI offices inside the Embassy on Grosvenor Square, one of the most secure buildings in the world, and not in the overspill suite in Upper Brook Street, established after the office expanded post-9/11. The war chest contains documents and tipsheets to enable FBI Agents to impersonate various officials, from Customs Officers to tax inspectors and even policemen. It is illegal and has to be used sparingly. Breaking the laws of a friendly country is not to be undertaken lightly. It isn't difficult to access the war chest, which is actually a large metal cabinet, the keys kept by Marion, one of the secretaries.

It may seem an ungrateful way to behave, but then so is bugging the offices of the UN, and that was down to MI6. And there are those in the building who enjoy the idea of operating covertly under the ever-watchful eyes of the Brits. Marion is one of them. She hands him the keys with a wink.

Piper is rummaging through the files when he hears Roth behind him. 'Vin.'

'Yeah?'

'What you doing?'

'I need some information on British Customs and Excise. We got a kid from New Orleans busted at Stansted.'

'Drugs?'

'Crawfish and muffulettas. Says he doesn't trust the food here.'

'Kid's right.'

Piper turns and closes the cupboard door. 'They're talking about sending him back, which is a tad extreme, I think. But it can wait. What can I do for you?'

'We got a note. At least, the Brits did — from the bomber. I thought you might be interested. I had a copy sent over from E Squad.' Piper knew this was the arm of the Special Branch which dealt with non-Irish terrorist threats to London. 'Interested?'

'You kiddin'? Be right along.'

He waits a few minutes before he re-opens the war chest, extracting a tipsheet on Customs and Excise procedures but also leaving with a warrant card in his inside pocket suggesting that he is Detective Inspector Cox of the Metropolitan Police.

★ ★ ★

'It was found with an intact bomb placed outside the rest room of a Starbucks in Regent Street. The bomb had everything except a timer.'

They are in Roth's office and Piper is holding a photocopy of a sheet of A5 paper

154

with a few typed lines on it. No signature or organisation name.

'Who has the bomb?'

'SO13 and PERME.'

'I suppose they've checked . . . '

'Prints, paper type, CCTV footage — the whole works. I know you have some doubts about our allies here, but the Bomb boys are the real deal, Vince.' Piper nods his acceptance of this fact. 'We know it was printed on a laser printer, so it was probably written on a computer. Somewhere, on a hard disk, is a copy of this. You OK?'

He realises he has been scowling. The note is succinct. Any American-owned businesses in London would be a target, unless they packed up and left immediately. This wasn't exactly unsuspected. Since Gulf War 2, what had been presented by a hostile media as America's swaggering, belligerent attitude towards the rest of the world had managed to alienate large swathes of it. The US policy was caricatured as: like it or not, we are the only superpower on this earth, and if you knock us, we will strike back with ten times the force. Piper generally supported his country's stance, thought it was right not to be cowed or bullied by ethnic or religious groups, but he had to admit that mistakes

155

had been made. They didn't deserve this response, though.

'This outfit can't be serious. They can't blow them all up,' he says at last.

'They don't have to. Look, this gets out, and my guess is it'll pop up on a bulletin board or in a newspaper's email cache very soon, then who is going to feel safe going into a Gap or a Starbucks or a Ralph Lauren in this city? This is a blow against the American economy abroad. Which means anti-globalisation, which means . . . '

'London could just be the start.'

Roth nods with some certainty. 'London was just the start.'

And Henry, where did he fit in? It is just possible that Piper has got this all wrong, that the man really was an innocent party. Well, the only way to solve that one is to get to Monroe and ask him, straight out. Which is why he got himself a gun in the first place.

14

The Ockford Polo Club is just south of Dorking, in what used to be called the stockbroker belt, although these days footballers, ageing rock stars and comedians have been added to the roster. The club is owned by a bass player with the sort of 1960s outfit that re-groups every three years to tour stadiums in America, giving the surviving members enough cash to indulge their hobbies of polo, motor racing and art collecting for a while longer.

As they draw up next to the VIP marquee and Roddy squeezes his BMW Z4 between a Maserati and a Rolls-Royce, Celeste gasps at the size of the field. 'My God, how big is that pitch?'

'It's one-fifty yards wide by three hundred yards long. The goals are twenty-four feet wide,' says Lennie, Roddy's partner, in his heavy East End accent.

She stops and stares at him, all tarted up in his best Prince of Wales check suit.

'I did some boning up,' he explains. 'On the Internet. Don't like to be caught short on these occasions.'

Roddy escorts her to the open-sided tent, where lunch has already started. The three of them are placed on a table next to the Jamaican Minister of Tourism — the day's polo being sponsored by a travel company — and Roddy tucks into the complimentary food and wine.

He checks the form of the players, pointing out the rock star who has a handicap of four, and Tim Brogan, the man they are here to see, who has what Lennie reckons is a very 'useful' ten. Prince Charles has a two next to his name, and a female model, a regular in *OK!* and *Hello!*, has a minus one. Brogan is the number three man, which means he is the team's strongest player, Lennie informs her loftily. There was a Chilean player with a thirteen on the opposing team, however.

'So did you run his other numbers?' she asks Roddy.

After DeVaughan, she has decided to do a more thorough background check on each prospective client, and Tim Brogan is the latest candidate. Roddy had agreed to use his computer team to do some delving, which meant that Brogan would be traced back to the cradle, everything from education to credit rating to driving record. Roddy always said that if people knew how much was on computer and how easy it was to access, they would be very worried indeed. Every time you buy coffee, or groceries, or pay a tax bill, or eat out, that information is being logged somewhere. It can be used to create a very detailed snap-shot of your life. Which is why he and Lennie liked to pay cash wherever possible.

'I did,' he says.

'And?'

'I have a thirty-page dossier being prepared. Be ready tomorrow.'

'Can you give me a synopsis? No, thanks,' she adds to a waiter, who is trying to fill her glass with white wine. 'Just water.' Roddy's eyes are already glazed by alcohol, so she adds, 'I'll drive back.'

'The short version is: lots of money. Likes his sports. Fiancée out East. No scandal. Well liked. Young. Be nice for you to have a young 'un, Miss Young.'

As the jerk chicken is removed and replaced with ice cream and baked fruits, an auction of various trips is presented by an oldtime quiz-show host, cajoling close to fifty thousand pounds out of the audience. Lennie bids for two tickets to the next season's Monaco Grand Prix, but drops out at four thousand. 'It's a fuckin' borin' race anyway,' he complains.

The match begins at three prompt, and

Celeste wanders over to the fence to watch. A city girl at heart, she still loves the country, enjoyed shooting and riding with her father on the odd houseparty weekend, and still rides when she can, although that is difficult in London. She certainly thinks the sight of well-toned muscles in tight shirts and jodhpurs, and the hot horseflesh of the ponies is mesmerising, even if she can't quite follow the flow of the play. They all seem to chase the tiny ball back and forth, like boys playing soccer in the park. A slightly hysterical commentator, who can't decide whether to address the royal player as Prince Charles or Charles, settles on using his number.

In the interval — with Brogan's team in the lead — the crowd are invited onto the pitch to press down the divots that have been thrown up, a tradition that Celeste thinks more than a little patronising: we'll let the common people repair the field for us, permit them a few minutes on our hallowed turf.

However, as the competitors troop off to allow this, she gets her first clear sighting of Tim Brogan as he takes off his helmet and wipes his brow. He slaps his Chilean opponent on the back and smiles, the big, confident smile of a man who is used to winning.

She puts the binoculars down and grins to

herself. Roddy is right, it is nice to see some solid youthful flesh for a change, jowls that have yet to sag, a chest that is tight and hard. Tim Brogan will do very nicely indeed.

★ ★ ★

Piper is wrong. DAGGER isn't based in Dartford or Liverpool, but Blackheath. This suburb, it seems to him, is a lone, struggling green lung in the grey, dispiriting south of the city, a part he has never visited before and, after driving down the Rotherhithe Road, has little wish to do so ever again. According to the State Department database on London, the name comes from Bleak Heath. This was where Henry V was welcomed with the equivalent of a tickertape parade after Agincourt. He guesses it has all been downhill ever since.

The village itself, though, with its church and cluster of shops, is pretty enough, with a sense of community which, he surmises, comes from being besieged by drabness on nearly all sides. He spends an afternoon in and around the village, firstly going to every estate agent, showing his warrant card, and then the blurred picture of Patrick Grey he has lifted off the computer at the FBI office. Grey is the prime mover — maybe the only mover — behind DAGGER. At the Stockholm riots, where the picture was taken, he told one of his Swedish anti-globalisation colleagues — a US Government implant — that he lived in Blackheath. Nobody, so far, had bothered to be more specific. However, the agent had noted that Grey thought it would be 'a fucking good idea to start blowing up every Starbucks this side of the Atlantic'. That earned him a little red flag and a mention in dispatches. Why hadn't anyone done more? Like getting a full address?

He shows the mugshot around, but nobody has rented a house or apartment — flats as they call them — to this man. Nor have they seen him around. Piper is careful to keep his speech to a minimum, but also not to try and slip into any impersonation of a cockney. He'd end up sounding like Dick van Dyke in *Mary Poppins*. His Scots is closer to that engineer on the original *Star Trek* than the genuine article, so in the end he settles on a soft, tight-lipped staccato that, he hopes, won't pin him down as a Yank.

Next he tries all the local pubs, from the hole-in-the-wall Railway Tavern to the grander coaching inns. Again, he draws a blank. Now, as the afternoon moves into evening, he is sitting outside a pub on the edge of the heath, nursing a Scotch, watching a pick-up game of soccer on the green in front of him, trying to make sense of all this. Surely he is wasting his time, chancing spectres and hunches. He should leave it to those officially assigned.

Trying to be a one-man band, not telling anyone else about his suspicions, a vigilante, a lone wolf, that was just dumb. Mugging Secret Service agents for their guns, impersonating a British police officer? Madness. Just give it up.

He will tell everything to Roth, come clean. Even as he formulates the plan, though, part of him knows he will never carry it out. Whoever did this has to pay for Martha in a way no court — British or, he suspects, even American — will be prepared to countenance. He has to suffer. Mere revenge is not enough.

* * *

The envelope is waiting for him at home when he finally gets back from the outlands of South London. He pours himself a drink, puts on a Kenny Dorham Blue Note CD and opens the envelope.

It has grown to seven feet high, cast in bronze. The figure is clearly female, long,

163

graceful lines as she stretches on tiptoe towards the sky. There are details on other pages, a close-up of the hands with their elegant fingers holding . . . what? It could be a baby, but if you are being cruel you might say it was an oversized American football. Whatever it is, it is being offered to the heavens, perhaps in thanks.

He sniffs back the tears and rings Sarah. 'Hey.'

'Hey, Vince. Howyadoin'?'

'I'm OK.'

'You get it?'

'Yup.'

'What do you think? Be honest, now.'

Piper takes a breath. 'I think I'd like to be with you tonight.'

'That shouldn't be a problem. What about the sketches?'

'They're beautiful. I mean, I think they are. I'm no judge but — '

She interrupts him. 'You're right. It's going to be beautiful.'

'There is one thing missing,' he says.

'What?'

'A title. You don't say anywhere what it is called.'

'No, that's deliberate.'

'Why?'

'I thought it might upset you. But I don't

164

feel qualified to change it.'

'What's it called?'

A pause, the sound of her breathing carries down the line. He really does want to be with her, wants to regain that feeling which warmed him through for hours after the last time. 'It's called *Stripped*.'

15

'Hell of a thing, Vincent. Hell of a thing.' Jack Sandler, United States Ambassador to the Court of St James, leans back in his sumptuous leather chair, tossing the Tiffany paperweight globe from hand to hand. He looks much more drawn than when Vincent saw him at the tourism reception, as if he had aged a decade in less than a month.

'Yes, sir.'

'Sir.' An aide pokes his head into the office. 'You have the meeting with the Chamber of Commerce in three . . . no, two minutes.'

'I know, I know.' Sandler waves an arm. 'This is important, too.' The head disappears. 'Why us, Vincent, why us? We are just trying to . . . well, I don't have to tell you the arguments. You know this quote? 'What can be the Grounds of Malice of so many against America?' Ring any bells?'

'No, sir.'

'John Adams wrote those words in his diary in 1781. Not much has changed, eh?'

'No, sir.'

Sandler points at the document Piper has placed before him. 'So, is this the drawing?'

166

Vincent pushes the envelope across the vast desk. Sandler slips on reading glasses, eases the A4 sheet out and lays it on the desk. 'You know how many requests we receive for this sort of thing?'

'I can imagine, sir,' Piper says, his heart sinking.

'No, you can't. Oh, you can get the obvious ones: Vietnam, Korea, Kosovo, Somalia, Gulf One, Gulf Two, Nairobi, Lockerbie . . . ' He pauses as if not realising himself how long the list is going to be. 'But every time a US citizen dies on British soil, the parents want a statue put up on Whitehall.' He gives a heartfelt sigh. 'Sorry, that sounded callous.'

'No, sir. It sounded overwhelmed.'

'Do you like this country, Vincent?'

'The US?'

'Great Britain.'

'It has its moments,' he says.

'My father was stationed here during the war. He was flying Lockheed Lightnings. You know those?'

Piper shakes his head.

'Twin tail boom. One on the wall over there. Two Allison engines. Strange shape, tricky planes but fast and long-range. They used them for bomber escort. So my old man flew into Germany, took on the Focke-Wulfs and so on while the B-17s did their job. Only thing was, those engines were temperamental. On his last mission over Germany one of them, the port, cut out. OK, so it can fly on one engine, but the problem was the electric fuel pumps worked off that engine. So he had to use the battery to pump the fuel from one wing tank to another, to feed the good engine. Which meant sooner or later, it would flatten and bang goes his radio. The mechanical pump would feed the good unit, but whatever fuel was left in the port wing, forget it.'

Sandler puts the globe down and takes a sip of water. 'Two other P-38s nursed him home, half of it in silence. Imagine how alone he felt. So he makes it, turns for a landing on an 8th Air Force satellite strip, lowers the gear and out goes the other engine. Now he is flying a brick. The wheels add sixty per cent drag to the plane. He has no choice but to go down, and below is a town. He tries to land it on the main street, and pretty much succeeds till a wing catches a lamppost and flips it. Off go the engines in all directions; the prop blades sheer off and spin through the butcher's. One of the engines crushes the post office; the other the local garage. Still in the cockpit, Dad ends up in the blacksmith's, alive. But fuel is everywhere, and it's about to go up. He can't get out, because the fuselage has pinched his leg. The blacksmith and the butcher and the garage owner come and start heaving him out. Dad screams. The leg is broken.'

'Shit.'

'Yeah. I guess he said that. So, the butcher goes to get his best boning knife. The district nurse is called. Dad sits there waiting for the amputation, when part of the fuel ignites. It's hot now, dangerous, and the butcher can't get near. Dad thinks about shooting himself. Just then, in comes the blacksmith with a pole. He leans in with the bar and bends the fuselage back, pressing against the trapped leg. It hurts so much, Dad passes out. Next thing he knows, he's outside, having tea poured down his throat. The blacksmith has second-degree burns, and the butcher and mechanic are banged up because they beat the flames back while the smithy dragged my father out. But they are all alive. Nobody even hurt by the debris in the town. See? Miracles do happen in this country.' He bangs the drawing. 'How about we put this beautiful thing in the garden of the Residence?'

'Sir?'

'Winfield House. In the garden, where every visitor here can see what the country lost that day. It'll also be secure from those who wish us harm. How would that be? We'll have a ceremony. Show these motherfuckers who want to blow us up, just how we celebrate the fallen. Because that is what your daughter is, Vincent, one of the fallen, like my father almost was, but for the good people of Marsham. What say we give her that as a memorial?'

The door snicks open again. 'Sir, you have that — ' begins the aide.

'Shut up!'

'Yes,' says Piper. 'I'd like that.'

'Good. Talk to Geoffrey here about what you will need and we'll get the ball rolling. If he grumbles, tell him we have twelve goddamn acres over there. The only bigger garden in London is Buckingham Palace. We got room.' He picks up a Mont Blanc pen and fiddles with the cap for a second. 'One last thing, Vincent. Don't blame this country for your daughter's death. There were several thousand people who felt safe in their offices in New York one September morning a couple of years back, hundreds travelling to work on a regular March day in Madrid. You can't blame the country. OK?'

'OK. Thank you, sir.'

The Ambassador stands, shakes Piper's hand, and as he strides out, Vincent has to suppress the urge to salute.

Sarah's face lights up at the news. 'In the garden of the house? My God, Vincent . . . ' then it dims again. 'Will we be able to see it?'

They are in a Greek restaurant in Primrose Hill, full of families and noise, eating an excellent meze that Sarah has ordered, drinking too much wine because it is Sunday afternoon, and the day is theirs, to do with as they wish. They can walk the alcohol off across the Park. He'd managed to hold onto the news about Sandler's suggestion until he could tell Sarah in person, although God knows how. He feared it would explode out of him while they spoke on the phone.

'There will be a ceremony. Me, you, the class.' Then it hits him. 'And Judy. Of course.'

She sees the look on his face and cups his hand with her own. 'That'll be OK,' she says softly. 'I'm cool.'

'Suppose she isn't.' He pops a piece of spicy sausage in his mouth.

She touches his other hand. 'Vince. It'll be just fine. What we are doing, it's . . . '

'It's pretty good, isn't it?' He can't help the lopsided, half-a-bottle-inside-him grin.

'It's better than pretty good, Vince. The thing is, it's between you and me. Nobody has to know. Not Judy, not my class, nobody.

We aren't breaking any laws. I'm not your tutor, for God's sake. We didn't plan it. It's not dishonouring Martha. And you shouldn't be expected to wear widow's threads. Widower's threads, I guess I mean. It's what happens to people, all over the world, every day. They get laid, they have a good time, they want to do it some more. That's us. So sue me.'

He nods sagely, and if he hadn't made to signal for more wine, he wouldn't have seen Celeste and the well-built guy with the dark curly hair enter, then turn and leave the restaurant in a hurry as soon as she spotted him.

★ ★ ★

Monday morning. Piper is having coffee in the Parlour of Sketch on Conduit Street, a slightly surreal take on a French patisserie, with more than a hint of the velvet-soaked brothel about it. The coffee is excellent, though, and the pastries and cakes lined up behind glass are exquisite, albeit, he thinks, about a tenth of the size they'd need to be in the US. And why can't they just have menus, rather than pasting them into antique books? Anything to be different, he guesses.

Opposite him, across the faux-Louis XIV

table is Celeste. The meeting was her suggestion — she had avoided the Fountain Room, too close to where they first met on that day — after he had called her the previous night to ask if she had turned heel in the Greek restaurant because of him.

'She seems nice,' she says.

'You can only have glimpsed her,' he replies.

'Short blonde hair, blue eyes, nice blouse, could be a Chloe, could be a Zara knock-off, lipstick one shade too pale, but OK, thirty-ish, give or take — '

'I thought I was the cop.'

'I said. She seems nice.'

'You didn't have to leave.'

'He's new — Tim. He might not have understood if you'd come over. No, that's a lie. He knows the score. I just didn't want to interrupt.'

He wonders if she was really worried that he'd pull the same stunt as he did on DeVaughan. Although this new guy would be a tougher prospect to take out, judging by his build. Six two, maybe a hundred and seventy pounds, in good shape.

He fixes her with a disbelieving stare and she smiles. 'OK, I couldn't stand watching you slobber over each other.'

'We weren't.'

'I could virtually hear it as I walked in the door.'

'Jealous?'

'No, embarrassed for you,' she says, and regrets it instantly.

'Embarrassed? How very British,' he sneers.

'That's unfair.'

'Hey, you are hardly the most demonstrative nation on God's earth. A handshake is an over-the-top display of public affection.'

The kiss is so unexpected he jerks in his chair and a coffee cup flies off the table, spilling its contents onto the carpet. They sit in silence as the mess is cleared up by stony-faced staff. Celeste asks for the bill.

'I don't know where that came from,' she says, flustered by her own uncharacteristic impetuousness.

'Nope.' Piper wipes his brow. He is suddenly hot.

'Sorry.'

'No need. I enjoyed it. Kind of.'

'It won't happen again.'

'I'm a tad confused now,' he says.

'It was meant to show we British can demonstrate affection.'

Just affection? he wants to ask, before he remembers he is spoken for now. The bill arrives. 'I'll get this.'

'No.' She pulls out a twenty-pound note and leaves it. 'I really am sorry, because I don't want you to think . . . Oh, Lord.'

'It's not a problem,' he says with a grin, pleased by her discomfort.

'I mean — '

'It's not a problem,' he repeats firmly. 'Forget about it.'

'I know what you must think of me.'

'I don't. I don't think of you. I mean, not about what you do. Not much, anyway,' he admits ruefully. 'Mostly I think about that day, and what you — '

'Shush.' She squeezes his hand. 'Anyone would have done the same.'

Anyone in a million perhaps, he thinks, but just nods. They are back on an even keel.

They walk outside, past the sultry receptionist with her seen-it-all-before eyes, and out into the street, where the first of the shoppers are slipping in and out of the garish boutiques opposite. Piper switches on his mobile phone.

'Listen, one thing. It may be nothing, but just stay out of American chainstores. Clothes, coffee, books . . . ' He lets it tail off, realising his error. 'I would imagine you don't shop in The Gap too often.'

She grins. 'It's been known. But thanks for the warning. Is that what this is all about?

175

The bombs? Anti-globalisation, or whatever it is called these days?'

'Maybe,' he says cautiously. 'I'll see you around.'

This kiss is a chaste peck on the cheek.

As he turns to leave there is a peep from his phone. Four missed calls, but only one with a listed number. The office. He dials in and he hears Stacey, one of the Bureau assistants, tell him that his mother has been trying to get in touch. It is four in the morning back where she is. Piper slowly closes the phone and looks back at Celeste who is still hovering.

He doesn't have to return the call to the US to know what it means. Monroe will have to wait. DAGGER can be put on ice. Martha is in no hurry for her revenge. There is the dying to attend to.

'I have to go home,' he says.

'Can I give you a lift?' she asks, pointing up to Bond Street, where her car is parked on a meter.

It takes a second for him to realise she means a ride. 'No,' he explains slowly. 'The other home.'

16

He isn't expecting the culture shock. Not on his home turf. Piper is driving from John Dulles airport in his rental car, heading south towards his parents' place. To the regular freeway users, this looks like any other arterial strip mall, rows of car dealerships and electrical outlets. To him, it looks like space and sky, a sky he feels he hasn't really seen for months, and the sense of a road that goes on forever. Part of him wants to just get onto the Blue Ridge Parkway and keep on till he hits the Smokey Mountains. The part of him that wants to avoid the next twenty-four hours, that is. The same head-in-the-sand section of the brain that means he hasn't bothered to call ahead. Piper doesn't want to hear over the telephone that he's too late. For much of the flight he has been chanting a little mantra: *Please God, let him hold on a little longer.*

He pulls off the freeway and he's edging into the Virginia countryside now, the first paddocks and rolling fields like a hyper-real version of the English landscape, albeit one littered with signs to Civil War battlefields. The towns have started to space like beads on a string, discreet commuter nuclei, as opposed to the continuous sprawl he has been travelling through for the last thirty minutes. Flashes of his old life appear. The once decrepit drive-in, now a vast Wal-Mart, his high school and its football field, where he tried and failed to live up to The Wolf's expectations, Fleming's Farm, where they would make out in the orchard, although the trees seem to have gone. He can still smell them, though.

He cracks the window and the late-afternoon warmth bleeds in, and for a dangerous second he wants to close his eyes and just drift into it. He realises he is beyond tired, that there is a weariness deep in his marrow, and that it might never, ever go away. He opens his mouth to feed more oxygen to his brain and puts on the radio.

Fifteen minutes later, he is in the street, twenty once-identical suburban houses, customised over the years with additions, extensions, new sidings, double glazing, lofts. In the driveways, American sedans have given way to domestic and foreign SUVs. He pulls in front of his parents' home and gets out.

There is the smell of barbecue in the air, and for a moment he thinks it is coming from his parents' yard, that it has all been a terrible mistake and The Wolf is out there turning steaks, but the hickory-infused smoke is blowing from next door, the Walshes'. They are a nice couple, but newcomers, moved in five or six years ago, after his time. Across the street, old Mr Samson is mowing his lawn. He raises a hand and Piper does the same in return. He remembers games of touch football with his two boys, Ralph and . . . For a second the name is gone, then comes back. Jerry. Ralph and Jerry, both moved away now.

He's heard that the only kid left on the block from when he was growing up was little Max Turner, who stopped developing mentally and physically when he was about twelve. It was as if someone had pulled a switch. He is pretty scary to see now, his ageing skin loose on a child's body. He wonders what happened to Susie Carolli, whose house at the end of the street was now painted egg-shell blue. Susie had been the neighbourhood's good-time girl, vilified by all the parents, including her own. In retrospect, she was just trying to bust the stays of this claustrophobic life. Piper hopes she succeeded.

Piper examines his own house, wondering what those kids thought of him, when they came back here to the traces of their own childhood. The FBI-Kid was probably all that would stick in their minds. He notes the repairs and additions his folks have made, like the re-roofed porch and the antique bell-pull. He is brought up short when he looks at the garage, and a petulant voice fills his head: *Damn, they took away my hoop.*

He pulls the iron handle of the chimes. His mother opens the door and he hugs her, smelling the same Elizabeth Arden perfume she has worn for decades, looking down at the top of her head, wondering when she got to be so short. When Maggie Piper looks up at his pallid, drawn face she sees him glance at the space above the garage, where all that remains are four rust-streaked holes. 'You took away my hoop.'

'You weren't planning on shooting some baskets, were you?'

He shakes his head. 'I guess not. Just a shock to see another bit of your childhood gone.'

'I thought you might phone.'

'I . . . wanted to just get here.'

'He's not dead, Vin.'

Piper nods.

'Coffee?' she asks, as he slides his suitcase into the hallway and closes the door behind him.

'Extra-black.'

In the living room, he walks over and stands behind his father's chair, noting that the Zenith is now a Sony, and sees his life flash by him in the photographs on display on the low side-table next to it. Martha leaps out at him as a sticky-faced one year old, her features hidden under a layer of milkfat, a year or so later at Cape Cod, then five, kite-flying at Kitty Hawk on Hatteras . . . and there is Judy, always at his or Martha's side. She looks stunning, and he feels the old warmth towards her stir inside him, a faint echo of the first time he saw her on the ski slopes.

He picks up a picture of Martha, aged sixteen, and is examining it when his mother comes with the coffee. 'You remember how you fussed when she had her ears pierced?' she asks.

'And the first time she wore this top.' She is wearing a skimpy halter-neck.

'But look at her there. The prom. What does she look like?'

'She looks beautiful.'

'She will always be beautiful.'

It's another platitude. He has heard them all, from her being in a better place to him being lucky to have had such a light in his life, no matter how briefly. 'Yes,' he always wanted to reply to the last one, 'and some motherfucker blew it out and he's going to pay.' However, all he does is smile and ask:

181

'You mind if I shower?'
     'Mind? I insist.'

★   ★   ★

The Margaret Henley Federal Recuperation Facility in Virginia looks like the home of a software company, but inside the grounds, behind a double-layered security fence, is a hospital and care centre dedicated to serving former members of the law-enforcement agencies. Some have been wounded or maimed in the line of duty, others are counting out their final days, and wish to spend them with some of their former colleagues, men and women who understand what it meant, what it still means, to be a Federal Agent. Margaret Henley was one such, killed by a terrorist bomb in the Federal Plaza two years before 9/11. There are those who want the complex renamed after someone who died in the Twin Towers, but that has so far been resisted. Ms Henley stands for all the people murdered by terrorist bombs everywhere including, Piper supposes, his daughter. It is spooky that his father is to end his days here.

The Wolf is in the small intensive-care wing at the back of the building, all copper-coloured glass and steel, and Vin and his

182

mother are stopped and checked at three separate points on the driveway, before they are allowed to park and enter the hushed confines, the only sound the whirr of air conditioning which, judging by the ambient temperature, is set to minimum. The air feels thick and clammy to Piper, and he finds himself craving a cold beer. After being frisked at the metal detectors, they ask directions at the nurse's station, their ID is examined once more, and they are shown to his father's room.

The Wolf looks far from lupine, an old man surrounded by the usual paraphernalia of such an establishment. Bottles, tubes, several monitors, the low buzz of pumps and the soft click of the heart monitor. Piper crosses to the bed and grips his hand.

'Hello, Dad.'

There is no response.

'He's been sedated,' says his mother.

He feels the thin dry skin between his fingers, follows the ridges of the veins with his thumb, resists the urge to rip the mask from his face and hug him.

'The doctors say the lungs won't expand easily, which puts a terrible strain on the heart. It was a heart attack. When I called you, they said — '

Piper turns, hoping she isn't apologising

for dragging him across the Atlantic. In case she is, he says: 'I'm glad you called me. I'm glad I am here.'

'So am I.'

His mother goes off to find more coffee, and he sits down, staring at The Wolf. His eye catches the thick book on the bedside table, next to the jug of orange juice. He picks it up and flicks it open. The first few pages are signatures and get-well messages from his friends at the Society of Former Special Agents of the FBI, of which The Wolfman is a keen member. The bulk of it, though, consists of newspaper clippings, some of them dating back to the 1950s, the most recent ones in the late 1980s. It is The Wolf's career, encapsulated in a series of journalistic snapshots, from a mere one-line mention to full accounts of Senior Special Agent Piper's role in a particular operation, and even the odd terse, noncommittal quote from his father along the lines of 'I was only doing my job.'

There are pictures too, of the man before him back in his prime, the eyes bright, the hair short, dark suit, white shirt, at the scene of a crime. Other images are of his dad off-duty, dressed in a short-sleeved shirt showing his muscled arms with their faded tattoos, maybe at the barbecue, sometimes with an arm round his son, more often than not sharing a beer with his companions. The contrast between the power of the man in these six by eights and the husk before him makes his tired eyes smart.

He turns the page and there he is. His face is thinner, longer, the cheekbones more prominent. He is smiling. There is no mirth there, just the muscles distorting his features into a shape that looks like a smile. Henry Monroe, the man he last saw moments before he lost his daughter. *'Do yourself a favour. Now. Get her out of here.'*

Piper feels the hairs on the back of his neck rise and a shudder runs through him.

'Coffee, black.'

He reaches up and takes the cup and his mother points at the volume in his hands and says, 'Henry Monroe did that a while back. Had the cuttings all the time. Your father likes to have it around. Go on, read it. I'm OK.'

She sits down on the opposite side of the bed from him, and leans forward and begins to talk to his father, as if they are chatting over dinner. The Wolf shows no reaction, but Piper guesses some small part of his brain might be listening, might be grateful for the comfort of a friendly voice.

Piper flicks the pages until he comes to the section covering the early 1970s, the time when Henry Monroe was his father's partner, and begins to read, trying to turn the various accounts into one coherent picture while, beside him, The Wolf's life ebbs away.

17

The first time his father and Monroe worked together was on the ATM Man case in the 1970s. Automatic Teller Machines were pretty new then, he guesses. The ATM man didn't actually target the machines themselves — those sorts of crimes came later. He simply told his victims to make use of them. In fact, it's possible the *Washington Post* had the best name for the guy — The Time's Up Killer.

The first victim was Janet Fido, who was snatched on her way to school on a bright, clear Tuesday morning. Nobody saw anything. It was eight-thirty, there were a hundred thousand cars on the road in the DC area, school buses, cop patrols. In front of all these people, one little girl was snatched off her bicycle and bundled into a van, the bike left on the grass verge.

The ATM man called the parents fifteen minutes later. This was his schtick: as much money as they could get in eight hours. If they told the cops or the Feds, she'd die. Eight hours. Just to give them an incentive, he put a minimum, a reserve price on their daughter. Ten thousand dollars.

Ten grand was a lot more money back then, of course, but even so not an impossible amount to put your hands on, not for a lawyer and his interior decorator wife. They protested it was too little time and he said: *'Use the ATM.'* It was no good them protesting about cash limits and checking accounts, he put the phone down.

Lots of us, these days, are worth ten thousand dollars on paper. But how many could get it by 5 p.m. that same day? You can't re-mortgage the house in that time, you can't sell stocks and shares and get the cash, you can maybe borrow it if you know someone who keeps notes in their mattress. One thing you can't do is get it from an ATM.

The Fidos did two things wrong. They didn't call the FBI. The Feds would have been all over the case by ten, had a plan by eleven, been out there by twelve. The second mistake was thinking the ATM guy would be happy with part-payment. They proposed seven thousand, with the promise of a similar amount again the next day: fourteen in all. An extra four grand, just for waiting twenty-four hours.

They followed his instructions, made the drop at a truck-stop diner out on the highway, and drove off. Janet was found almost exactly where she'd been taken. She'd been strangled. On her was a note that said: *Time's Up*. He had taken the seven thou anyway. All the parents had to console themselves with was the knowledge that little Janet hadn't been sexually assaulted.

The second child was a boy, Nick Brace, taken on his paper round at 7.30 a.m. Again, the ransom money had to reach the kidnapper by five, which gave the parents an extra hour. Again, '*Use your ATM*,' came the useless suggestion. But this time, he'd doubled the minimum sum to twenty thousand dollars. The parents finally called the Feds at 2 p.m., when they realised they, too, would be short. The Wolf was SAC, the Special Agent in Charge, Monroe his subordinate. They staked out the snatch zone, in case the MO was the same. They ran a sniper and surveillance team into the truck stop. The Wolf pulled funds to make the twenty thou, so if it all went belly up there was no excuse. Except no instructions for a drop ever came. Little Nick was found on a landfill site out in West Virginia. He'd been beaten to death.

However, The Wolf wasn't going to wait for the next kid to go. He tore into the two sets of parents' private lives, to the point where they both complained that he was intruding on their grief. His reason was simple, he told them — he didn't want to face a third set of hollow-eyed parents whose time was up. So he found the link. Both belonged to expensive leisure clubs, albeit at the opposite ends of town, but there was one guy, Albert Windermere, who had worked at, and been fired from, both. He'd had access to family details on the membership log, knew the kids by sight, and maybe vice versa. It had to be him, The Wolf figured.

The Wolf and Monroe got a warrant, searched the home and the house and the car and pulled nothing. Then, when they least expected it, he ran. Vince's dad and Monroe gave chase, and the ATM man was hit by a truck trying to cross the interstate on foot.

Piper reread the notes and the clippings. They eventually found the evidence they needed a couple of blocks away. By then the perp was dead, of course. Nobody seemed too broke up about it.

★ ★ ★

'Vince.' His mother's voice pulls him back from trying to piece together the events of twenty-odd years previously. 'He's waking up.'

His mother has leaned back from her

190

position next to his father's ear. The Wolf's eyes are flickering open, then closing again, then a longer flutter, until the lids finally stay up. His mother reaches across and unclips the oxygen mask, leaving it in place for the moment, and says, 'Vince's here.'

'Damned 'Star Spangled Banner'. Can you hear it? Tell them to turn the goddamn thing down.'

Piper catches his mother's eye and she shakes her head. There is no music. It is being generated in his head, auditory hallucinations caused by blood-supply problems to the brain. She switches on the tape player next to his bedside, and as Sinatra starts singing 'The Summer Wind', he seems to settle down, is less restless. 'Vince?'

Piper stands so he can be seen and smiles down at the thin, troubled face of The Wolf. 'Dad. Hello. I came as soon as I could.'

'What you make of this, eh?' He indicates the neat, pristine room. 'TV, even a DVD player. Now you know where all your tax dollars go.' A laugh, a sound so painful Piper wishes he wouldn't. 'Thirsty.'

A child's feeder bottle is produced and he slurps some of the water back, smacking his lips. 'Never thought it would come to this. If I'd known, I'd probably not have bothered. Should've just let them pull the plug on me.'

'Eddie, now stop that,' The Wolf's wife admonishes.

'Dad, please. Don't speak like that,' Vince adds.

The old man smiles, pleased with having got them so agitated, but all the time Piper is thinking — who could blame him? This is no kind of life, just an extended coda.

'Martha,' says The Wolf to his son.

'Yes?'

'I watched the tape of the funeral. Beautiful. I told Maggie here she should go.'

'I couldn't leave you, Eddie. You know that. We talked about it.' Her tone suggests they've talked about it lots and lots of times.

'Dean Martin.'

'What?' she asks.

'They're playing Dean Martin now. 'Volare'. For cryin' out loud.' She turns up the Sinatra tape and he cocks an ear, listening for the phantom voices plaguing his brain, but clearly there is only room for one Rat Pack member, and Dino has gone. 'You been readin' that?' The Wolf is looking down at the scrapbook in Piper's hand. Vince nods. 'Pretty good, isn't it? Always meant to do it myself. Only thing missing is the stuff on Bruce Hopper's bomb, and I can't take any credit for that.'

'Who's Bruce Hopper?' Vince asks.

'Bruce Hopper? One of the Weather Front. You not reached that yet? They were putting a bomb together in Georgetown. Going to hit something in the capital. Never did find out what. They called it a day, and they all went home, but Hopper decided he'd do a bit more. We dunno what happened. He must have got tired, because somehow two of the wires touched . . . '

The Wolf pauses, the oxygen all used up. Piper only vaguely remembers these people. The Weather Front was an offshoot of the Weather Underground who, like the parent organisation, objected to the Vietnam War and the fascist American state, and somehow had convinced themselves that armed robbery was the ultimate political act.

The Wolf's lungs come back on stream. 'Boom. Up he goes. Now they have a martyr. Now . . . now it is *our* fault. Jesus, Andy Williams. 'Moon River'. Tell them to shut up.'

There is no crooner singing, but the sound of a metal trolley being wheeled along the corridor outside, plates and metal covers clashing as it goes. 'It's mealtime, Eddie. You want to eat?' He nods. 'Maybe you'd like to get some air, Vince?' His mother winks at him. She is conveying to him that he really doesn't want to be here for feeding time.

'That OK, Dad?' He feels his head spin.

193

His body is telling him it is well gone midnight, even though it is barely dusk outside.

'Yeah.' The Wolf reaches out and grabs his wrist. 'You know, he was a bad man, that Hopper. I don't mind one bit he blew himself up. And even now, I don't worry about answering for the others.' It takes a second for Piper to realise who his father is concerned about answering to. In the space between the phantom singers, he has been worrying about his heavenly score card.

'Dad. One thing. The ATM man.'

'Time's Up? Windermere. Bastard. Killing kids for so little. Thing is, it wasn't the money. He didn't want them to get the money. He j-just enjoyed the idea of them trying. He knew damn well you had a limit of a hundred bucks on most ATMs.'

'Why did he run?'

His father eyes flick away. 'I'll tell you after dinner.'

Piper picks up the scrapbook and goes looking for somewhere quiet he can carry on reading, preferably without the looming spectre of Andy Williams to bother him.

*   *   *

They christened it the Circus. It refers to the London social circuit where a man might need a beautiful, well-mannered companion. It could be Wimbledon or Wembley (when it is finished), the theatre, Henley, a day at the races, a corporate dinner or a charity event. For some people it's Springsteen at the Arena, for others it might be a Luc Bondy production at the Royal Opera House.

Wherever it is, over the course of a year or two, the same female faces appear in the crowd and at the exclusive receptions afterwards. Some of these women Celeste would dismiss, the ones who see the other girls as rivals, some of the hard-faced East Europeans who, to be frank, scare her. There are a handful, however, whose company is worth seeking out, who are fun to be left alone with, who understand exactly what game is afoot and how to play it.

The three she feels most at ease with meet her once every few months at Fifth Floor, Harvey Nicols in Knightsbridge, same table, same time. It is one part of the diary that is more or less sacrosanct, unless the offer is so tempting it will make the others jealous. Today, though, there is a full quartet.

To her left is Natalie, the oldest of the group. She is somewhere beyond forty. Her flawless olive skin, and a possible nip and tuck, make it difficult to be more precise. She has a wonderful, sexy French accent, and claims to be from Paris, but Celeste knows she has a son in Beirut, whom she sees three or four times a year. Men choose Natalie when they don't want it to be quite so obvious they have hired that night's help — she is someone closer to their own age, but still a showstopper.

To her right is Timmy, a Croatian who wanted the lifestyle she saw on cable TV shows and came over as an au pair and then went underground. The only way she could support her aspirations and Jimmy Choo fetish was to become a prostitute. Luckily — or possibly because of her long blonde hair and spectacular figure — she managed to slot right in at the top end.

Facing Celeste is Sasha, who claims to work on a glossy magazine and in fact may even go in once or twice a week to advise on some aspect of home design. Sasha talks as if she spent her formative years with Prince Harry on one side of her pram and William on the other, but in fact she is a perfect construct, Mayfair out of Macclesfield, a girl who left home when she was sixteen and ruthlessly stripped down her persona and built a new one from parts lying around the *Tatler* and *Vogue* offices. The accent only slips when she is drunk; hence she never gets drunk, except with very close friends.

'Anyone new?' asks Sasha, cutting into her thin slices of duck.

Celeste shrugs. 'A polo player.' The rule is, no names, just professions. 'You?'

Sasha winks and grins. 'Might be someone.'

'Unfair,' says Timmy. 'You must tell.'

'Can't.'

Celeste eats some more salad and sips a spritzer. These lunches are the only time she drinks during the day. 'Someone we know?'

'Know *of*,' teases Sasha.

Timmy stops eating her chowder and asks breathlessly, 'Have you got a pop star?'

Sasha shakes her head. None of the others have quite the same set-up as Celeste. They all have a roster of clients that expands and contracts, mostly recommended by word of mouth, but each has a core of regulars. 'An actor,' guesses Natalie. 'Some soap star, maybe?'

'Nope.'

'Politician?'

'Not really.'

Natalie, bored with the guessing game, says: 'I've got New York next weekend.'

'Really?' Sasha is mildly miffed they aren't still trying to wheedle it out of her.

'Staying where?' asks Celeste.

'Pierre.'

'Nice.'

'I've been invited to a party at . . . ' Timmy names an Embassy.

'Ugh,' says Natalie.

'Ugh?' queries Timmy.

'Can be ugh,' confirms Celeste.

'Who is taking you?' asks Sasha.

'Billy the Broker.'

'The rugger bugger?' Sasha shoots back.

'Don't go,' says Celeste softly. 'Have a headache.'

'Why?'

Celeste puts down her fork. She made some mistakes early on, and one of them was not realising that 'party' was a very elastic term. Sometimes it was canapés, champagne and chat, and now and then it was a euphemism for a gang bang; fortunately, she had always managed to make her excuses and leave. Things, though, have become more extreme of late. Some of the men like to exchange tapes and discs of the parties.

'Bukkake,' she says, looking at the other girls for confirmation. Natalie and Sasha nod.

'What's bukkake?' asks Timmy.

'The current rage at certain Embassy parties,' says Natalie.

'But what *is* it?'

Celeste looks around, but there are other clients nearby, and a waiter less than a foot

198

away. 'Look it up on the Net.'

'But if you do go,' says Natalie, 'keep your glasses on. It stings your eyes.' She looks at Celeste and smirks. 'So I've heard.'

Timmy looks down at her chowder, her appetite suddenly gone. 'Oh.'

Sasha puts a hand on her arm. 'Just check how many women, how many men, who they are, and where it is to be. Then call me. I'll ask around. OK?'

Timmy nods, and Celeste glimpses the vulnerability that still lurks beneath the surface gloss of this beautiful young woman. She drains her spritzer and says, 'Look, shall we get a proper bottle of wine? Just for once.'

The others nod their agreement and the conversation moves on, the identity of Sasha's new client no longer a topic of interest.

★ ★ ★

The doubts come now and then, usually in the very early morning, as now, when Celeste sits and watches rain crawl like tears down the outside of her bedroom window. Below, the Chelsea streets are winding down to the only three or four hours of quiet they will enjoy.

She is sipping a brandy, unable to sleep, with Beethoven's Late Quartets playing just above subliminal in the background. It is at times like this she wonders whether she took a wrong turn. If, right now, she should be tucked up in bed with a husband, sleeping lightly the way mothers do, always alert for sounds of distress from their children.

The image, however, leaves her cold. She has never craved the normal domestic routine. She knows what people make of her current set-up, she can see it in their eyes. Why is what she does so heinous? It isn't even all about sex, which, as in the normal scheme of things, tended to diminish as the relationship progressed. With some clients, it wasn't even there in the first place.

She knows she isn't like Sasha and the others. They play a different game. One day the cocktail of sex, money and excitement will pall, and they will finally let one man take them away from all that. She knows that isn't likely for her. She runs through the list of possible soulmates for her, ditching each in turn, skipping quickly over Vincent Piper, but returning to him for a different reason. Why had she kissed him like that? Just to illustrate that part of her still functioned normally, she reckoned, to show that she could demonstrate affection, that her choice of career hadn't blunted her capacity for spontaneity. Show him or show herself?

Perhaps there was something in her genetic make-up that precluded the whole love-marriage axis. Roddy was the same. He always had interesting, talented, often beautiful girl-friends, but if they made it to the six-month post they were doing well. Celeste wonders if there is something in their background that explains this, but there is nothing she can identify. There are no dark secrets lurking in the family closet, the sort of abuse or bullying beloved of amateur psychologists. It's just the way they are, for better or for worse. She should accept it. She *has* accepted it, she reminds herself.

So why does she find herself at least once a week looking out onto cold, dark, rain-lashed streets at two in the morning, fighting the feeling that there is a hole in the centre of her life?

18

The Weather Front. Hardly anyone remembered them these days. The organisation had its origins in the non-violent Students for a Democratic Society in the 1960s, whose aim was to attack the status quo on Vietnam, social and political issues. They fought campaigns such as the rights of single welfare mothers, gays — when the term had only just been invented — and civil rights in general.

However, change from using SDS's non-violent methods was too slow for some members, and a radical, more proactive group appeared, with leaders such as Bernardine Dohrn, Kathy Boudin and Billy Ayers. Their name came from the Dylan song 'Subterranean Homesick Blues' — 'You don't need a Weatherman to know which way the wind blows', chosen by member Terry Robbins. The organisation later transformed into the Weather Underground, so as not to appear sexist. Sometime around the mid-1970s there was another split. Sally Borodin and Bruce Hopper, her lover and the father of her child, along with Paul Scanlon and Aaron Masterman, people mostly from wealthy middle-class backgrounds, started a splinter group, the Weather Front.

The Front had a political wing, the Association of Free Minds. Most of those minds were freed by drugs, it seemed, and increasingly the role of the Front was to commit armed robberies to feed the AFM back in their headquarters on 132nd Street in Manhattan. So for two years, the Weather Front hit banks and armoured cars, killing guards and tellers and cops, dismissing them as disposable drones of the establishment who deserved to die. Then came a break-through. After Hopper's death from his bomb — apparently thirty per cent of all home-made detonators are faulty — The Wolf staked out his grave, knowing that Borodin would come back the next time they were due to have a Big Dance, their euphemism for armed robbery. Sure enough, one day Borodin parked the kid and came to say a few words to her old man. Unfortunately, the team that The Wolf placed at the cemetery wasn't up to the job.

★   ★   ★

The call came through to The Wolf five minutes after he had arrived at the new Raleigh Field Office. It had been routed

203

through Washington, because that was where he was normally based, but God or the Devil made sure he was out and in the vicinity of North Carolina that day. He looked across the office and caught Henry Monroe's eye as he took the call, beckoning him over with a finger. Chris Bowden, Raleigh FO's ASAC, Assistant Special Agent in Charge, followed across.

'OK, it was definitely her? And which direction? East. What sort of car? Where is it now? You lost her? How . . . no, no, it doesn't matter. You contact any local police? No, we'll do that. Hold on, willya?' He covered the receiver. 'Sally Borodin. Went to look at her old man's grave.'

Henry smiled. 'You were right.'

'Yesterday you told me we were wasting hundreds of tax dollars on that stake-out. That it wasn't by *MIOG*.' He was referring to the *Manual of Investigative Operations and Guidelines*, which was the FBI's procedural bible.

Henry popped some gum in his mouth. 'Yesterday you were wrong. Today you're right.'

'Yeah, I know, what a difference a day makes.' The Wolf got back onto the field man. 'OK, you can pull off the stakeout. Oh, and good work. Yeah.' He put the phone down. 'Morons.'

'What we got?' asked Henry.

'Ford Fairlane, heading east on 1–49.'

'Heading this way?'

The Wolf nodded.

'Is she Dancin'?'

He nodded. It was at best a guess, but he said with finality: 'She's Dancin'.'

'But we lost her?'

'That's done. Can't put that back in the packet.'

Without being asked, Bowden grabbed a Rand McNally state map from one of the wall pouches. 'Where'd they lose her?' he asked.

The Wolf studied the map, located the cemetery at Rockboro, then traced the route. 'Here. Roadworks. She goes through the Go sign. They didn't. They were three cars back. Trying to jump it would have blown their position.'

Bowden grunted. He could tell from The Wolf's tone that, even if there had been a major earthquake, he wouldn't have lost the woman.

'Henry, I need a list of all banks between here and there.'

Bowden whistled. 'You know how many that is?'

Henry said: 'We'll get onto it. If you are sure.'

'Of course I'm not sure,' said The Wolf.

'But if anyone'd like to put a fifty on it?' There were no takers. 'OK, call Brinks Mat, Wells Fargo, all the other money-movers. Ask where and when there are deliveries today.'

'They won't give us that over the phone,' protested Henry.

The Wolf smiled, and fixed Henry with a hard stare. This was one Dance he wasn't going to sit out. 'Make them,' he said softly.

★   ★   ★

The sound of the scrapbook hitting the floor jolts Piper awake. He looks up at the clock and realises he has just zoned out for a second. He wonders if feeding-time is over yet. Now it is even harder to equate the man struggling for air back there with the sharp operator portrayed on these pages. His father was a better Federal Agent than he would ever be, Vince is sure of that. Partly that is due to The Wolf's generation's tunnel vision. The long and not always benevolent shadow of Director Hoover still fell across them, and this, for all its faults, gave them a certain clarity and certainty of vision. Piper and his peers have never had that luxury; they know they are working in a system that is fundamentally flawed.

He needs to sleep now, his eyes feel

scratchy and dry, but he picks up the scrapbook and carries on reading, wanting to see if the answer to one question is in here. How did The Wolf know to pick Pittsboro?

★ ★ ★

'It's Pittsboro' said The Wolf.

They had left the office, were heading west out of Raleigh, The Wolf driving, hardly touching the brake, swerving through the traffic, making good use of the horn.

'What?' asked Henry.

'Pittsboro.'

'How can you be so sure?'

'It's the third drop-off. Last one. The car will have done Chapel Hill, then the University and then Pittsboro. The crew will be relaxed. Easy.'

Henry grunted. There was no such thing as easy when it came to armed robbery and they both knew it. They had scoured delivery schedules and bank locations, and phoned in warnings to scores of money depots, just asking them to be extra-vigilant, but The Wolf kept coming back to the Pittsboro Brinks Mat run. Monroe settled back in his seat as the traffic thinned and the speedometer crept past the speed limit. He closed his eyes. It was no good arguing with his partner once he

207

had a bone to worry at. The Wolf was well named.

'Can I borrow a pen and some paper?' Piper is at the nurse's station. His head is hurting now, his befuddled brain crammed with names and places. He needs to draw a schematic, showing who was where and when on the day.

'Vincent.' It's his mother. 'He's finished.'

'Right. I'll — '

'He should sleep. I think you should as well. What time is it for you?'

It's four or five in the morning, but he says: 'I don't believe in jet lag.'

'It looks like it believes in you, son.'

He smiles, walks over and puts his arm around her, conscious of her fragile frame. 'OK. Can you give me ten minutes? I want to finish reading that.' He points to the scrapbook open on the chair.

'Don't be long. I'll be with Dad.'

Piper takes the pen and paper and sits down to draw a map of Pittsboro.

It hung heavily in the Carolina sky like a metal fruit, blackened and gnarled from

208

thousands of blows it had made on concrete, brick and steel. They'd been knocking down the Royal Flush Tobacco Company factory at Pittsboro for close on a month. Royal Flush Tobacco had been swallowed by one of the giants five years previously, and had relocated to the far side of Raleigh. Now, the eight-storey redbrick building had to go, having no architectural merit or any windows left after the local kids had finished with it.

The first two weeks were spent stripping out anything of value inside, from copper pipes to the heavy timber floors. Now, a three-man team with a ball and chain were going to take the husk down to ground level. The rubble would be transported in one of the giant hoppers to the landfill site outside Siler City.

As they drove along 1–49 on the edge of town The Wolf could see the team's ball as a black dot in the sky, a mote in the corner of his vision, like one of those floaters, the detached retinal cells that swirl around the jelly of your eye.

Henry checked the map, located the elevated section of the freeway that they were just entering and said: 'Another two miles to the bank.'

'Who's there?'

'Local sheriff. Couple of deputies. I can tell

the sheriff thinks we are over-reacting. Thinks it's a wild-goose chase. That they won't hit the bank.'

The Wolf looked at the wash of brake-lights up ahead and slowed. The mote had caught his attention now, but it took a few precious moments for him to appreciate what he was seeing. A wrecking ball, swinging through the sky, was heading right into the heart of the slow-moving traffic. Even from this distance the sonorous clang reached them as the ball knocked the armoured car off the freeway like a skittle, into a waiting hopper below.

'They won't be doing the bank,' he said, as he swerved the car over onto the narrow emergency lane that was barely wide enough for his car, and floored the accelerator, ripping off his wing mirror within the first ten yards, his hand pressed hard down in the centre of the steering wheel.

'Sonofabitch!' he yelled as a pick-up pulled out in front of him. He braced for the impact as his wheels locked and they smacked into the back of the truck, the front of his car concertina-ing and spewing geysers of steam.

Henry felt as if all his ribs had snapped, and struggled to undo his belt, but The Wolf was out in seconds, his creds — the FBI shield — held up in the air in one hand, gun in the other, sprinting down the lane, towards the gap in the barrier and low wall where the armoured car had disappeared.

★　★　★

It was three miles of agonising bumps over a compacted dirt road into the forest. The Wolf lay in the grit at the bottom of the hopper, next to the deformed shape of the armoured car. He had peered in through the crazed windshield. The driver, a woman, and the guard were both dead, having smashed their skulls together in the impact of the car being knocked off the freeway into the giant container, which was usually used to move rubble. It was both crazy and inspired. As had been The Wolf's leap into the unknown, from the highway, following the armoured car down, his jump hidden by the dust the truck had thrown up.

He'd landed well enough, on top of the side panel of the truck, which bowed under the impact, but as he slid off he'd sprained his ankle on the hopper floor. He could hardly put any weight on it. Now he sat at the rear of the armoured car, gun cocked, waiting for the robbers who would surely come to him as soon as they stopped.

After fifteen minutes the huge Mack rig

pulled to a halt, and the engine was left running, setting up a deep vibration through the hopper that caused The Wolf's teeth to chatter. Soon then, he thought. He scanned the lip of the giant steel container, waiting. He heard voices.

'What if they're still alive?' A woman.

The familiar sound of a pump-action shotgun being primed was just audible above the chugging exhausts.

'They may be alive, but they won't be in no fit state to give us trouble.' This was a man.

'You go first then.' A second man.

'Damn right I will.'

'Can you move it along here? I gotta pick my kid up from the childminders.' The woman again. Sally Borodin?

The sound of two men giggling at the incongruity. ''Sorry, darlin','' one of them simpered, ''just got to leave you here for a few hours while I rob a Brinks Mat shipment'.'

'Move your ass.' The woman sounded annoyed.

The Wolf heard the sound of boots on the external ladder and shuffled to the corner of the rear panel. He held his breath. A head appeared. Then a torso, followed by one leg dangling over the lip. A second joined it. 'I think they're dead,' the man shouted.

212

The next second The Wolf placed four rounds into the guy's chest and he went backwards, arms windmilling, and there was the heavy thunk of a lifeless body hitting the earth. There were screams of disbelief.

'Federal Officers,' he yelled, making sure the plural was stressed. 'Put down your weapons.'

All they needed was to be packing grenades or TNT, and they could blast him to atoms by tossing it in. The Wolf waited for something to come over the side and end his life, but instead he heard another engine cough into life.

There were internal rungs set on one side of the hopper and Wolf pulled himself up as best he could. As he cleared the top, he saw a U-Haul van making a tight turn in the forest clearing, the shadows of a man and woman just visible for a second in the cab. He levelled his weapon and emptied his magazine, but the truck kept on going. Then he slid back down into the bottom of the dusty hopper and lay down, oblivious to the filth, and let himself breathe easy. He'd won.

19

Piper closes the book. He knows the rest. That jump from the freeway into a moving hopper, the shooting of Scanlon as he came over the side, The Wolf's subsequent FBI Medal for Bravery. They had found the U-Haul truck abandoned in a mall parking lot on the outskirts of Raleigh, with blood on the front seat, so he'd hit someone. The Weather Front limped on until the mid-1980s, when all of the members were either in the ground or in jail or, in a few cases, hidden deep in American society, as your friendly next-door neighbours.

The Wolf went on to other cases, but that leap into the unknown, the so-called Wrecking Crew Caper, remained the defining moment of his career. What will his be? Piper wonders, as he stands, stretches and goes to have a last look at The Wolfman before heading home with Maggie to grab some decent sleep.

Piper returns to his father, who looks better, plumper than when he first saw him. Maybe he is just getting used to the changed physique.

'Hey.'

'Hey,' Piper says back. 'Haven't finished it yet. Just done the Wrecking Crew.'

'Yeah. You know, my ankle started to hurt of late. As if it recalled that stupid jump.'

'It wasn't stupid.'

'We should go now,' says his mother.

'Yeah,' agrees Piper. 'But one thing. The ATM guy.'

'Windermere.'

'Yeah.'

His father's eyes widen slightly. 'Why did he run?'

'Yes.' Piper has a bad feeling about this, and The Wolf, for all his feebleness, can see it.

'Have a wild guess.'

Piper licks his lips. 'He was dead before the truck hit him?'

His father nods. 'It's why I never finished the book. Sooner or later, someone would take a look and put it together like you just did. It wasn't me. It was Monroe. You have to remember, it was a different time back then. We still thought we were . . . we still thought the end justified the means. Monroe hit him. You know Monroe did a term in Vietnam? He learned a few tricks there from how they beat up the gooks — the Vietcong. Before I could stop him, he had this guy on the floor, sobbing. Not a mark on him, but sobbing.

215

You go up under the ribs somehow. Can I have some water?' Piper passed him the drinking cup. 'Hurts like hell, but no marks. So he's on the floor, and Monroe has his foot across his throat.'

'That leaves marks,' says Piper.

'Yeah. If you press. He didn't have to press. The guy was pretty subdued. So he's pointing the gun down at Windermere and he explains how he is going to plant a gun on him, after he has blown his face apart, and claim self-defence.'

'What were you doing, Dad?'

The Wolf's eyes slide down. 'Nothing. I know you'll find that hard to believe. Nothing.'

'Nothing?'

'Well, maybe cheering from the sidelines.'

'Vincent.' His mother can see he is agitating his father.

'No, it's OK. I'm not ashamed. So he told us where he had kept the kids. In a lock-up garage a couple of blocks away, in the trunk of a beat-up car. It checked out later.'

'But he could've got the whole conviction overturned. I mean, I dunno where you begin on that . . . '

The Wolf is fading now, the effort having exhausted him. 'He could've. Henry made sure he didn't. Internal injuries, said the

Coroner's report. It was Henry who did it.'

'And the truck?'

'It wasn't hard to call in favours back then. To fake a chase. To substitute a body. Only took about an hour to set up.' He catches the expression on his son's face. 'I saw the photos of the victims. Spoke to the parents. So did Henry. I don't really have a problem with it, Vince. Neither should you. You don't understand, do you? Windermere had killed two innocent kids. We were going to do everything to bring him to justice. Even if it was off the meter. I know it seems wrong . . . '

His dad is getting disturbed, trying to justify behaviour that belongs to another era, a different morality. Piper squeezes his hand. He should be shocked, but his own numbness has dulled any sense of outrage. 'It's OK, Dad. I do understand. More than you know. You did nothing wrong.'

They both know that's a lie, but air wheezes out of The Wolf and he slumps back down, exhausted, and Piper feels his mother tugging at his sleeve. They say their goodbyes, and Piper promises to come again, and as he leaves he tries to understand what he has learned. Not much. His father is only human. And Henry Monroe is capable of extreme violence.

★ ★ ★

That night, when he should be sleeping, he sits in his father's study, at the roll-top desk, spinning the seat round and round, wondering why his brain won't let itself shut down. He can hear snatches of Martha's voice in his head, distant and distorted, heavily sibilant, as if he is trawling through white noise, trying to catch her frequency from the ether through bad atmospherics. There are those who believe you can tape the voices of the dead. He knows, though, this voice is a physical manifestation of longing, of the frustration of a dialogue terminated before it even began properly, as bogus as his father's Andy Williams song.

He scans the prints on the wall, searching for something to focus on. His father had a thing, for a while, about lighter-than-air craft, blimps and dirigibles, triggered by watching the *Goodyear* airship over the Superbowl. So many went down — the *Hindenburg*, the *R101*, the *Roma*, the *ZR-2* and the *Shenandoah*. There is a picture of the latter on the wall, right next to the one of the *Goodyear* platform hovering over New York City near the Empire State.

The *Shenandoah* was one of the Navy's ships, and it was filled with helium, heavier but less flammable than the hydrogen that torched the *Hindenburg*. It was on a tour of the Midwest to test moorings and landing facilities when it hit a thunderstorm on 3 September 1925. The rigid ship was ill-suited to the kind of ferocious weather that builds over the central states, and the seventy-mile-an-hour winds tore loose the airship's main control cabin, which plummeted to earth, killing the captain. It then split into three sections over Calwell, in south-east Ohio. Remarkably, part of it stayed buoyant, and the remaining crew were able to land safely. There had been forty-three men on board; twenty-nine survived.

Despite their appalling safety record, his father loved the idea of these great unwieldy behemoths, obsolete even when they were designed, elegant but potentially lethal. He'd tried to pay for a ride from Goodyear. They'd told him the rides were free, but reserved for corporate customers. Not even a Fed could pull strings to get on board. Piper had bought him a hot-air balloon ride one Christmas, but as far as he knew, The Wolf never took it.

He stares at the *Shenandoah* for a long time, at the image of the broken-backed machine beached on a farm in Ohio, and he feels exactly like the section that survived, something with several parts missing that was

219

miraculously managing to stay afloat. He just has to hang on a little longer. He tries his father's bureau, but it is locked. He spends ten minutes looking for the key and gives up, his depleted body finally conceding it has to rest.

20

It is a meal fit for a hungry polo player, back from the field of combat. Around the corner from Tim Brogan's flat in Holland Park is Lidgate's, one of the best butchers in the world, with a window display that Celeste swears would make a lifelong PETA (People for the Ethical Treatment of Animals) member drool. The choice of cuts and pre-cooked dishes is just too much. And the pies . . .

She asked her old friend Gennaro what to cook and he has suggested *porcetta* — stuffed pork belly. She prepares it according to his detailed instructions, and it has been roasting for two and a half of its three hours. There is chocolate cake for dessert, a crab linguine for starters and she has just opened a Viognier, which she sips while she waits for Tim to come home.

Brogan is a good addition to her portfolio. He is young, with a family base — and a fiancée — in Hong Kong. His likes are simple — good food and wine, sport and athletic sex. Indeed, the latter is the best she has had for some time. The fact that he usually winds down from a session by watching the European sculling championships — or whatever other arcane activity requiring testosterone and brawn is on offer on cable — is only a minor disappointment. Cinema is an interest, as long as it is a blockbuster, the theatre not at all, and some way below that is classical music. He is the sort of man who likes Simply Red and doesn't mind admitting it.

Such is the state of his CD collection, Celeste has taken to bringing her own over. She is in the midst of an Arthur Honegger obsession — not the likes of the brutally modern *Pacific 231*, but the later neo-Romantic works. She puts on the Fourth Symphony and lets the sound wash over her, thinking of the man composing such beautiful phrases in the Swiss mountains, while the dying embers of war still smoulder across the rest of Europe.

There are other parts of the Honegger canon — which is vast — which she doesn't care for. The man spent some time in New Orleans, and the syncopations he picked up there, to her ears, sit badly with his Bach-influenced wellspring. Perhaps Vincent Piper, with his love of jazz, might feel differently.

Yet again, the American has popped into

222

her thoughts. It happens several times a day. Why that should be eludes her. He is totally out of her frame of reference. Glorified policemen are not her cup of tea, even ones with a cute accent who come trailing a cloud of melancholy. It could be a legacy from that shared time in the car and the hospital, from being there when his daughter died, but even when she has seen him subsequently, even when he has behaved like a prick, she has been left with a feeling that somehow Vincent Piper is her business, her concern. She is incapable of walking away entirely.

She laughs when she realises what it is. Somehow the usual white knight syndrome has reversed itself. It isn't uncommon for men, once they discover what she is, to start strutting around like Lancelot, the Hollywood version at least, wanting to save her from herself and a life of degradation. Somehow the wires have got crossed, and she feels she wants to rescue Vincent Piper from the pit he appears to have fallen into, to heal what is clearly a very fragile soul. It is a ridiculous position for a woman who has taken her particular career option.

Is it a career option? Or is it just a twenty-first-century variation of the oldest game in town? In her heart she knows she feels different from the other Circus girls, she hopes not superior, but certainly more in control. Perhaps she should have become a vet like her father wanted. Good job for a woman, he always said.

As the music finishes she hears the door slam and stands to welcome Tim. It is when she hears his gear and mallets hit the wall of the hallway with some considerable force, followed by a string of foul oaths, that Celeste realises all is not well. There is the noise of a man punching a wall, oblivious to the damage he is doing to his hand. Celeste feels her throat go dry, acknowledging, as she hears him storming through the flat towards her, that stuffed belly of pork is unlikely to be able to repair whatever has gone amiss.

★ ★ ★

As he drives through the rolling hillsides, pushing ever deeper into rural Virginia, Piper remembers learning about the things that went on here a century and a half ago, and the grudging admiration he felt for Colonel John Singleton Mosby. His sympathies were meant to be with the Union armies, of course, but during the latter stages of the Civil War Mosby controlled approximately 1,600 square miles in five Northern Virginia counties west of Washington DC. So complete was his grip that the area became known as 'Mosby's Confederacy'. Mosby used irregular troopers and tactics in a way that would now be called guerilla war or Special Ops. He tried to kidnap the Governor of Maryland, for instance, perfected lightning hit and run raids and would ride behind enemy lines with a select band of infiltrators to capture key personnel.

Incredibly, Mosby lived until 1916, and there is a myth that one of the people he inspired along the way with his tales of the glory days was a young boy called George S. Patton, whose own son seemed to pick up some of the irascible Mosby's traits and talents.

Piper turns his car off Route 50 and onto 15, carrying on south-east until he passes the Mount Zion Church and its grounds, which served as both hospital and battlefield during the war. It was here that John S. Mosby defeated his Federal pursuers on 4 July 1864. He remembers who had told him all this as the low stone-clad building on the ridge in front of him comes into view. Henry Monroe. It was Monroe who was a Mosby fanatic.

★   ★   ★

'Thanks.' He takes the coffee from Kate Monroe's shaking hand. They are in the living

225

room with its large plate-glass window that gives onto the very fields where Mosby fought the cavalry skirmishes that are now known as the prelude to Gettysburg, although at the time, of course, neither Mosby nor his opponents knew about the carnage to come. 'Nice view.'

'Yes. Henry loves it.'

Henry might not be seeing it again, Piper thinks, but says nothing. He sinks into the huge floral-motifed couch. Kate Monroe sits in the matching armchair next to the fireplace.

'I'm sorry about your father.' She has already expressed her sympathies about Martha. 'How is he?'

'Better. I mean, better than he was, thanks.' It is true. His heart, it seems, is stronger than his doctors give it credit for. There is even talk of him going home. 'Have you heard from Henry? My father was asking about him.'

He thinks Kate Monroe is going to cry. She is a more substantial woman than his mother, but it is only the shell that is robust. Behind the fleshy face, he gets an impression of decay and fragility. 'I got a postcard. From Paris.'

Paris? His heart blips down for a fraction of a second before he remembers that arranging for cards to be sent from other cities is one of

226

the simplest methods of throwing off the scent. 'What is he doing, Kate?'

'I don't know. I think he's running away.'

'From what?'

'From me. From . . . Eric. From what Eric has become. I know it must be tough seeing The Wolf sick, but your father's not a young man, and Eric is.'

She looks over at the side-table, where a healthy Eric stares back at them, lounging on the beach, sailing, riding on his dad's shoulders. There is even one of Piper and Eric together, even though he and the Monroes' son were never really great friends. There were a couple of years when the age gap between them seemed like nothing, but he had hit puberty first and a chasm opened up. By the time it might have closed, Eric was in England with his parents, and upon his return the space between them was larger than ever. When Vince was ready to enter the Academy and had a wife with a child, Eric was ready to get stoned and stay that way. Last he heard, the guy was working in a video rental store in Fairfax.

'Where is he now? Eric?'

'In a clinic in Arlington.'

'Can I see him?'

Kate smiles and shakes her head. 'No. You've seen enough illness on this trip.'

'I'd like to.'

'You should remember him the way he was.' Her eyes glisten now as she looks over at the array of frames containing images of her healthy son. 'Maybe that is what Henry wants.'

'How did you . . . how did you discover about his cancer?'

'Cancer?' She shakes her head, as if she still cannot believe that word applies to her only child. 'I knew he was ill this one time when I heard him laugh. That sounds strange, doesn't it? That someone's laugh can tell you something is wrong.'

'Not if you know them well.'

'I was speaking on the telephone to him and he made a joke about something and he laughed. And it wasn't him. It was someone else's laugh. An animal cry. Vincent, he sounded like . . . like a monkey.' She starts to sob. He holds out his handkerchief and she dries her eyes. 'I never told anyone else that.'

'I apologise for prying. Really.'

'How is London? Oh. Now that's me being insensitive.' She appreciates that any gloss the city had for him had been well and truly tarnished by Martha's death there.

'No, it's OK. It's fine.' He remembers what Sandler had said. 'I can't blame the city. You liked it, didn't you? London?'

She nods enthusiastically. 'Happy times.'

'Highgate, wasn't it, where you lived?' A guess.

'No, we were further up north. A place called Whetstone.'

'Nice part of town.' He's never heard of it.

'You know it? Yes, very pleasant. Long way from the Embassy, though. That was why Henry got the apartment.'

He sits forward. 'What apartment?'

'Oh, if he had to work late, he would stay at our apartment in Bayswater. Well, my apartment. We put it in my name. It wasn't smart, but it did the job. We kept it on, and that was good, because with London property prices as they are now, it'll be a great pension. Although with the cost of Eric's care, I don't think we can wait that long to sell it.'

Piper tries to keep his voice steady. 'You have an apartment in Bayswater?'

'Yes. Queen's Terrace.'

Got you, Henry Monroe. Got you. Now let's find out what you meant. '*Do yourself a favour. Now. Get her out of here.*'

Explain that, Henry. And it better be good.

21

As has happened for the past decade, a Renault truck with an electric tailgate drops off the majority of the hotdog stands that operate between Notting Hill and Oxford Circus at or near their trading spots. It carries eight carts at a time, always pulling up at the kerbside, regardless of traffic or parking restrictions, and the two drivers laboriously unchain the nearest cart and slide it onto the tailgate and lower it to the ground, where the vendor — well wrapped against the night air these days — takes it and heads for his chosen pitch.

There have been changes these past few weeks. There are three delivery men now, one of them designated to ride shotgun. Plus there are more no-shows — times when the truck pulls up, but there is no vendor to take his cart. The hidden watcher can see the anger on the men's faces when that happens, hear their cursing of the spineless hotdog sellers.

Better spineless than headless, he thinks. The *Evening Standard* had made the biggest splash with the story, highlighting this 'gruesome new escalation in the Dog Wars' which it 'believed to be about the control and supply of ecstasy and amphetamines on the London streets'. Legitimate purveyors of street snacks were 'terrified and concerned, fearing it was only a matter of time before an innocent vendor was killed'. That makes him laugh. None of them were innocent.

Still, it is almost time to move the war on, to spread it beyond these pond scum. He has ideas of how to make more people pay. He has been doing his research at Colindale, scouring the newspapers in the library there. He's read all the journals — the exposés in the *Fourth Way*, the *Lobster*, the *Green Arrow*. The harrowing articles in the *Guardian* and the *New Scientist*.

A cover-up, that's what it has been. Many of the people responsible for the scandal are retired now, to their cosy little jobs in business. Usually the food business. The *Fourth Way* people preached a return to old, sustainable ways. Very worthy, but he has come up with something else. The Fifth Way. Kill the bastards.

Standing in the doorway of Selfridges, watching the rain dance through the yellow streetlight, he sees the Renault truck approach and slow, the three men in the front scanning the crowd for their customer. No passers-by stop walking, nobody even looks up from beneath their umbrellas. There is no vendor. Another one scared off the streets. He smiles to himself. He's done his job for the moment. A month or more and they'll be back, but by then he reckons his campaign will be over and everyone will know his story.

From his inside pocket he takes the photocopy of a page from the *Sunday Times Home* section, which tells him that former MP and Cabinet Minster Charles Greenslade has bought a nice family house in a place called Amersham, out in Berkshire, where he doubtless gets to see his healthy, beaming son Ben go off to Eton or Harrow or some other famous school. No, probably Oxford or Cambridge by now, the kid must be old enough now. The chances are, he won't be getting much older.

★   ★   ★

Piper is still tired from the transatlantic flight back to the UK. Hiring a car and driving up north to see Judy was probably not the brightest decision, but his time in the US has left him with an urge to build bridges. At least, before he goes to Queen's Terrace.

His father is at home now, and out of immediate danger. The Wolf's heart has rallied for him, although the oxygen mask is on almost permanently. The auditory hallucinations have been diagnosed as vascular dementia, which has been treated with low doses of anti-psychotic drugs and a bedside radio, which has given the brain something to focus on. The chances are it was caused by a small stroke, or a narrowing of the capillaries in the brain.

Miles is on the hired Alfa's CD player, *Live at The Plugged Nickel*. It's not his favourite album — the trumpeter's playing seems harsh and jagged in places — but there is lots of it, enough to keep him company on the drive from London to Cheshire.

As he turns off the M6 he spends thirty minutes negotiating roundabout after roundabout, increasingly irritated by British road planners' inability to come up with any other solution to traffic flow than a big circle of concrete. Eventually he is into the suburbs, and at his final destination, he pulls up in the drive. He rubs his weary eyes, hoping this will go OK.

Her mother opens the door and her face folds immediately into an expression of hate that is so powerful, it alone is almost enough to drive him away, but instead he tries his best smile.

'Judy,' the mother shouts, but Piper puts a

finger to her lips. She almost bites it off, but thinks better of it.

The hallway is large and square, quite grand, with lots of stained glass and ornate woodwork, but also plenty of hideous vases on fussy stands, and the air smells of furniture polish. Judy doesn't have to be called. She is at the top of the stairs, dressed in faded jeans and a thick cable-knit jumper.

She can't quite believe what she is seeing. 'Vince?'

'Shall I call the police?' her mother asks.

I am the police, he almost says. 'I just want a couple of minutes. I drove up, straight from the airport.'

'Judy.' Her mother's voice is hard and unyielding.

'Can we go in here?' He points to the front room. The woman moves to block his way.

Judy comes down the stairs and beckons him to follow her into the floral nightmare that is the house's 'best' room. 'I'll be OK,' she says to her mother, who reluctantly steps aside.

She sits on the sofa, straight-backed, legs together. 'You look tired.'

'I know. I flew coach.' He lowers himself into an armchair. His back is sore; he needs a good run or swim, and some sleep.

'You should treat yourself to Club.'

'Yeah. My dad always told me it was a waste of money. I shouldn't have listened.'

'How is he?'

'My father? Not good.' He updates her on The Wolf's condition.

'I'm sorry to hear that. He was always good to me. Would you like some coffee?'

'In a while, maybe.'

She waits for him to say something, but he just stares at her. 'Why have you come, Vince?'

'I wanted to see you.'

Judy gives a little laugh, unsure of how to answer that.

'I was looking at all my mom's photographs, of us, of Martha.'

'And you remembered how it was.'

'Yes.'

'That's all there is now, Vince. Memories. It can never be that way again.'

'I know. I also wanted to say, I think I know a way to find out what happened to Martha. Why she died. Who did it.'

Now he has her attention. She shuffles forward. 'Who was it? Have you told the police?'

'I have to check I'm right first. I have to find someone.'

She shakes her head. 'Don't go playing The Wolf Cub, Vince, always trying to be like your dad. Let the police handle it. Who do you think did it?'

'I'll tell you that when I'm certain. I just wanted to let you know, in case anything happens to me. I'm doing this for you and Martha.'

Judy shakes her head vigorously. 'No, Vince. Go to the authorities, don't go vigilante. Otherwise, you're doing this for yourself, not us.'

'Possibly.'

'Look, I know you'll find this hard to believe, Vince, but part of me still cares for you, despite everything, and I don't want you to get yourself killed in my name. Or Martha's. She wouldn't have wanted it. I don't want it.'

Vince stands up. He'll get coffee at a services. There is nothing else to say, except, 'Don't worry. It's not me who is going to get killed.'

22

Ben Greenslade emerges from the kitchen with the bottles of Grolsch and looks down at his coffee-table in horror. There are six fat white slugs arranged in rows along the centre, and a rolled-up tenner next to them. At least, there had been six. Josh is now sniffing wildly and dabbing at the ghostly remains of one with a damp finger, which he rubs along his gums.

'Burns,' he says at last, turning to Harry. 'What's it cut with?'

'What the fuck are you doing?' asks Ben.

The five faces turn to him. 'Drugs,' says Ali, with a giggle and a flick of her blonde hair. They have just got back from the pub. The idea is to have some more drinks in the flat, listen to music and maybe watch some television. Ben's flat has been nominated because he is the only student they know with a thirty-two-inch plasma TV. 'You must have seen them before, Ben,' she adds.

'Oh no, I can't have this. Christ, the trouble it could cause.'

'Ben.' There is disappointment etched into Fiona's voice, as if her nearly-boyfriend is

237

letting the side down. 'Lighten up.'

'You can't do that here.'

'Watch.' Harry leans forward and does his line, coming up grinning, and Ben loses it. He drops the cans of beer, walks over and blows as hard as he can on the table, swirling the drugs up into a cloud of particles. There is a howl of outrage from his new friends, and a look of disbelief on Harry's face.

'You stupid cunt,' he says. 'That was almost half a gram. Do you know how much that cost me?'

Ben pulls out two twenties from his pocket and throws them down. 'That should cover it. Now fuck off.'

The five of them rise, most of them not catching his eye as they gather up their gear. Ben can feel his face glowing with a mixture of embarrassment and anger. His heart sinks a little when Fiona also fetches her coat, but he knows it's no good protesting.

As they go, Harry says quietly, 'You know, Ben, it's not as if your father is the fucking Prime Minister.'

'He's not even famous,' adds Ali, as if this is the worst insult she can think of.

'I'll see you Monday,' says Fiona softly.

'Not if we see him first.'

The door slams and Ben stands alone in the small flat, only the whining of Thom York to keep him company. He fetches the vacuum cleaner from the cupboard in the kitchen and sucks up as much of the drugs as he can find, but he is in no doubt that if a forensic team came they would be able to pinpoint Class A drugs.

Had he behaved like a prim prig? He supposes so. But ever since he was a boy the importance of supporting his father had been impressed on him. Public figures don't need scandal of any kind was the in-house motto, and for the past ten years, whenever there was a new craze — from shoplifting sweets to smoking dope — his friends knew to count him out. This new group would get to know him soon enough. Or had he blown it with them once and for all, and with Fiona? He laughs when he thinks of the outrage on their faces when he puffed the shit up into the air. It was like a scene from one of the old Woody Allen films his father liked.

It might have been easier if he had gone to Cambridge, but his grades had been off, and he had chosen Reading rather than a re-sit. Maybe that had been a mistake. Still, his father has bought him this flat in the modern block, ten minutes from campus, and he has a new Porsche Boxster promised for Christmas, which will certainly ratchet up his standing. If not Fiona, there will be someone else who won't mind being squired around town in a thirty-odd-grand slab of sexy automobile.

There is a knock at the door. It must be Fiona. She has slipped away and come back, doubtless feeling sorry for him. He'll happily take pity for the moment, if it means she stays the night.

He runs and opens the door, and the lead-filled cosh simultaneously breaks his nose and stuns him, making it easy for the man to push him down onto the couch, while he brings in the two bulging supermarket bags from the hallway.

'Hello, Ben,' he says as the boy comes to, his face aflame, his clothes splattered with blood, to find a stranger has bound his hands with flexicuffs and is doing the same with his feet.

The man finishes the bonds and disappears into the kitchen. He hears the sound of a knife being sharpened. There is the clack of the cupboards being opened and shut.

The man has fetched salt, pepper and a plate, which he lays out on the coffee-table. There is the chink of glass on glass, and he returns with ketchup and mayonnaise bottles. He shakes them both and unscrews lids gummed shut by unwiped drips. Now he leans across him, smiling. He licks his lips, an obscene and repugnant gesture.

'Well, Ben,' he says. 'I don't know about you, but I'm starving. Shall we begin?'

★   ★   ★

A bright morning in Hyde Park. Roth is walking behind Beckett, the Federal Bureau of Investigation's Senior Legal Attaché, effectively the man in charge of the whole operation in London. Beckett is almost fifty, and looks tired. Ten years ago, this job was a sinecure. Now it is a testing ground. The man has another year before he can take retirement, and he has earned it. This is an informal briefing before the Ambassador's big 'pow wow' as he calls it, when Beckett and Atkins, his opposite number at the State Department, and other senior staff meet for coffee and doughnuts.

'Anything back from Quantico on the Charing Cross Road?' Beckett asks.

'Bits and pieces. Some restored CCTV footage I haven't seen yet. The bulk is still being processed.'

'He'll ask for details.' Beckett means Sandler.

'I'll get something on your desk within the hour. I'll make a call to SO13, get a status update.'

'It's still blank, isn't it?'

'Yes, sir.'

'The Ambassador doesn't want to hear that,' Beckett sighs.

'Neither do I, Bob.'

'You have to understand how it looks. He launches a programme to promote travel to the US, then we have a few bombs here and bookings from the States to the UK drop by thirty per cent. One orchestra cancels, so do a couple of jazz outfits, a heavy metal tour is postponed, two Hollywood stars pull out of premieres . . .'

'I know. I read the 'cowardly Americans' headlines too,' Roth says dryly.

Beckett nods, knowing he is preaching to the converted. There had been so many explosions in major cities in the past four years, he had thought bombs had become part of the fabric of life — joining the Acts of God such as car accidents, train wrecks and plane crashes as just one of the prices for modern living. He is wrong, of course. They still scared people out of all proportion to their actual danger.

'What about Piper?' Beckett persists.

'On light duties.'

'Not what I meant.'

Roth stops walking and watches an airliner pencil a thin line of vapour across the baby-blue sky. He, too, is beginning to wish he was on one. Some sun on his face would be nice.

Beckett looks at him. 'I know he's your friend, and I know he's had it rough, what with his daughter dying and his father being sick and all, and I know he used to be a good agent but now, of all times, we don't need passengers.'

'What do you want me to do, Bob?'

'I don't think he should be in London.'

'I have no argument there,' Roth agrees quietly.

'Good.'

'But he's staying,' says Roth.

'Why?'

'The memorial dedication.'

Beckett shakes his head. 'Shit. I forgot about that. What the hell is that all about? I mean, she wasn't Princess Diana, was she?' He sees the look on Roth's face. 'Sorry. Uncalled for. But do we normally honour dead daughters of FBI Agents? And the guest list? Have you seen it?'

'Marion put a copy on my desk.'

'Ken Livingstone?'

'He's the Mayor of — '

'I *know* who Ken Livingstone is, Stan. I have sat next to him at enough rubber-chicken lunches. But why him? Did he ever meet Martha Piper?'

Roth doesn't correct him, but it will not say Piper on the dedication. Judy Saxton has seen to that. 'You know what this is as well as I do, Bob.'

'Does Piper?'

'I guess, although he'll take the gesture, forget the politics.'

They are both aware that Sandler is using the whole concept, and especially the actual day, as a means to show that bonds between the two countries, strained during the recriminations over the flawed intelligence that launched the Iraq invasion, are being reforged in adversity. That this is all their war now. It will also help elevate the profile of Jack Sandler back home, because it is fairly certain that a relatively young man like him, still in his forties, and an ambitious one at that, isn't going to see the UK Ambassadorship as the pinnacle of his career.

'OK, listen. About Piper. We have to handle this gently. It musn't appear insensitive or arbitrary.' Beckett is referring to the increasingly alarming habit of Federal employees suing the government when they think the proper procedures have not been adhered to, or when they think there is the chance of a couple of mil of spare change from the government's coffers. Or both. 'Once the ceremony is over I want a full PPE on him.' A psychological performance evaluation, something they all had to submit to each year. 'Then I want it compared with his last one.'

'And?'

Beckett waves a hand to indicate that what follows is a foregone conclusion. 'And it'll show that there has been a deterioration in his capability due to high levels of personal stress. Perfectly understandable, nobody is being judgmental, but we will recommend reassignment. Understood?'

Roth nods. Nobody will be judgmental, but Beckett knows damn well that will be the end of Piper's career in the FBI. He kicks at a pile of leaves, watching the larger ones lift and swing lazily back to earth.

'Do you understand?' repeats Beckett.

'Consider it done,' says Roth wearily.

23

There are so many messages on his answerphone that the machine has run out of memory. Piper sits down with a notepad and goes through the stack. There is a request from the Ambassador's aide asking him to call to confirm the arrangements for the dedication, three from Sarah, one asking to see him, another inviting him to witness the casting of Martha's work, and a slightly more frantic one repeating both those sentiments. There are several from Roth, a terse one from DCI Fletcher, recorded the day before his return, and two from Celeste, one hoping his father was OK, another, the last on the machine, saying she would be out of town for a few days and not to call her.

He plays this one back, listening to her voice, feeling increasingly unsettled. She sounds odd, like she'd had major root-canal work. Maybe she had. Her chosen career demanded she be as unblemished as possible and, for an English girl, she had good teeth, so she needed to look after them.

He dials the first four digits of Sarah's number, then presses the cradle. He gets to five next time before he puts the phone back and rings Celeste.

'Hello?' she asks in a muffled voice.

'Celeste?'

'Who ith thith, pleathee?'

'It's Vince. I was hoping to catch you.'

'Mmff.'

'You OK? You sound funny.'

'Yeth. Howth's your father?'

He explains The Wolf's situation.

'That'th thad, Vin. I mutht go.'

'Celeste?'

'Mm?'

'Can I see you?'

'No. I'm going away for a few dayth. Thoon. It'th not a put-off. Nobody elthe involved. No fwends.'

'I'd still like to see you.'

A sigh. 'Me too. Thoon.'

'Take it easy.'

'Yeth.'

He sits in the gathering darkness, listening to *Clifford Brown With Strings*, knowing he should call Sarah, but put off by a growing sense of unease. The conversation with Celeste worries him. *Fwends? Yeth?* There was something about her pronunciation that really worried him. *Fwends?* Did that sound like dentalwork? Does dentalwork take a couple of days to heal? In the midst of

Brown's take on 'What's New', Piper gets up and goes downstairs to take a taxi to Soho.

* * *

'Vincent.'

Roddy is just locking up the office. He looks haggard and drawn from too many late nights, far too many cashflow worries. It looks like his salvation may not lie in greyhound gambling on the Net either. 'Just leaving. Dinner at Zagora. Celeste isn't here.'

'I know. I just got off the phone with her.'

'Ah. She told you?'

'Yes.'

'I'm surprised. Mind you, she seems to quite like . . . ' Roddy stops, seeing the concerned look on Piper's face. 'She didn't tell you, did she?'

He shakes his head. 'Tell me what, Roddy?'

Roddy shrugs. 'It's none of your business, old chum. Sorry.'

Piper grabs him by the lapel of his Richard James suit. 'Listen, *old chum*, Celeste was there for me when she could have just walked away. If something has happened, I want to know about it. No, she didn't tell me. But you're going to.'

Roddy pushes the American's hand away and steps back, straightening his jacket and shirt. He looks into Piper's flint eyes and decides there and then that, regardless of how furious Celeste will be, he is going to have to do as he asked. He is going to tell Piper everything.

★ ★ ★

'What did you do to your hand?'

Sarah Nielsen reaches across and touches his swollen knuckles, and he winces slightly. 'I punched a door.'

'Do you do that a lot?'

'More and more these days.'

The waiter slaps menus down in front of them and swirls off.

'Do I have to order pizza?'

He sips his beer. 'It's a Pizza Express.'

'You said it was a jazz club.'

'It's the Pizza Express Jazz Club.'

'You missed that bit out. I thought it was a swanky supper club. Now you are offering me American Hot with extra pepperoni.'

She is teasing him. It is two days after he has seen Roddy, a day after seeing Celeste, and when Sarah called and he told her he was going to cheer himself up with some jazz, she had said she would join him. On the stage in the low dark basement room, a polyglot band is warming up. A French saxophone player with a Mohican haircut, a short but explosive Italian alto, a Dutch drummer and an English trumpeter, the sextet completed by Hammond organ, trombone and bass players of indeterminate origin. She'd like this music, he was sure. It wasn't just a blowing band, there were tunes and complex arrangements as well as fiery solos.

'So will you come?' she wants to know.

'To the foundry?'

'Yes.'

'I think so. I'd like to. I am just feeling strange about it all.'

'What's the worst that can happen?' she asks.

'Ladies and gentlemen, welcome to the Pizza Express on Dean Street. Before we start, if I can just remind you of the Club's silence policy. If you would please keep the conversation to a minimum during the set . . . '

'So we can't talk?'

'In between numbers you can.'

'How long does a number last?'

'Twenty minutes or so.'

'You'll come?' She smiles at him, and he feels his worries draining away.

'Yes, I'll come.'

'Good.'

As the first trumpet notes pierce through

the smoke, she squeezes his hand again, and he remembers how it got to be so swollen and sore.

★ ★ ★

You have to take a big man by surprise. Tim Brogan was a big, fit polo player, not yet thirty, with a stomach that looked like something off the cover of *Men's Health*. In his office Roddy had a file on him that told Piper everything he needed to know, including the twice-weekly squash sessions at the Lab West Fitness Centre. It was Roddy's partner Lennie who got him the membership card.

Lennie had picked it up in the steam room at the Porchester Hall Baths where he was having his usual sauna. 'The geezer won't miss it for a day or two. You just swipe it. They never look at the screens to see if the name and face match. Just go in behind a couple of others, it'll be fine. When you're done, give it back and I'll hand it into Lost Property here. How's that?'

It was perfect. On the day he used the card, Piper had cycled and swum for half an hour while Tim Brogan played his game with Max Galbraith, his usual partner. He had gone to the changing room and used the sauna while

251

he waited for them to finish. Two of them. Was he up to two? One day, not so long ago perhaps, but the toll on his body of the past couple of months had been fearsome. He would have to use the advantage his fury gave him.

He stepped from the sauna, showered and then dressed, seemingly oblivious to the two loud-mouthed men as they stripped and padded next door. He wondered which one would emerge from the white-tiled enclave first. There was nobody else in the changing room, but it wouldn't stay that way for long. Time was of the essence.

In the event, it was Brogan who appeared, knotting one towel around his waist, drying his hair with another. Piper had a foot on the slatted bench, apparently doing his shoes up, and he waited until Brogan was level with him before making his move.

No matter how strong and fit the man, the abdomen is always a weak spot. Legend has it that Harry Houdini was killed by an unexpected punch to the stomach by an overeager young fan; it ruptured his appendix before he had time to tense his abdominal muscles. Piper wasn't out to do that, but it would be a bonus.

Piper jabbed his fingers hard into the solar plexus, aware from the resistance of well-toned muscle bands that he had been right to use maximum force. He grabbed a tuft of Brogan's curly black hair and brought his knee up sharply into the face. The first blood flicked onto the tiles. The elbow to the throat sent him into the metal lockers with a crash, and he could see Brogan's mind fighting to find ways to regain the upper hand, as his body finally realised what was happening. But a naked man is a vulnerable man. Piper yanked the towel away, stepped back, and buried his steel-capped shoe deep into his groin. Tim Brogan sank to his knees and vomited messily across the floor.

Piper knelt down to be on his level, careful not to mess his shoes. He made sure Brogan saw the gun in its holster under his jacket. 'Your contract with Celeste is now terminated. You contact her again, in any way, and you are a dead man. Understand?'

The merest nod, but Brogan's eyes told him he had got through. The sound of the shower stopped next door, and Piper stood and walked calmly out of the room and away from the health club.

★　★　★

Roddy had drawn the line at giving Piper Celeste's address, but it took the FBI assistants less than fifteen minutes to match it

253

to her landline number. He hadn't called ahead, but she didn't seem too surprised to see him.

'I suppose you'd better come in.'

The sitting room in the house just off the King's Road was a light, airy room, cream except for the deep brown leather sofas, two bold pieces of modern art on the walls, a few books on the glass coffee-table and an expensive Bang & Olufsen hi-fi.

'Roddy warned me you might be over.' She handed him a glass of Scotch. 'You've cut yourself.'

He looked down at his hand and wiped away the blood. The knuckles were enlarged, but the skin was unbroken. 'It's not mine.'

'Oh.'

'It's Tim Brogan's.'

'Oh.'

He rubbed his sore fist, trying to remember when he had punched him. Before or after the kick to the groin?

'Am I meant to be grateful?'

'No. I owed you one.'

She shook her head disapprovingly. 'Just what I always wanted. My own pet Rottweiler.'

He walked across and put a finger under her chin. Most of the bruising on her face had gone, although he suspected there was more he couldn't see underneath the atypically heavy foundation. 'How are the ribs?'

'Roddy told you that, did he?'

'Everything.'

She waved a hand dismissively. 'It's an occupational hazard.'

'Why are you mad at me?'

'Because this time the bastard deserved it. But I'd already ended the relationship. Refunded him his money. Vince, I can't have you running around as my own personal avenger. I'd have got over it. Is he badly hurt?'

'About the same as you were.'

'He has a match next weekend.'

'Not for a month or two, he hasn't.'

'Oh God, Vince. You really are the end. It's sweet of you to care, but next time, ask me first.'

'You wouldn't tell me. You didn't tell me this time.'

'If there is a next time, I will. Promise.'

'Deal,' he had said and fished out one of his cards. 'All my numbers. Mobile, office, home. If you have any problem, contact a man called Stanley Roth on that main number. He'll know where I am, anytime, if I am on duty.'

Celeste took the card. 'Thanks.' She seemed to relax, and sat. He did the same.

'Why did you come back to London, with your father so ill?'

'I had business to finish.'

'What business?'

Something made him tell her that, too. And, like Roddy, he told all of it, from Monroe in Soho, to his wife in Virginia, the whole shooting match.

★   ★   ★

A few hours after his confession to Celeste, Piper is watching the little Italian guy on stage at the Pizza Express in the middle of his solo, standing on tiptoes, tearing up the joint. He looks over at Sarah and she smiles at him.

'Noodling,' she whispers.

'You want to go?'

She nods apologetically.

'After this number,' he says, hiding his disappointment. One day he'll find a woman who can sit through a sax solo. They must be out there. Or perhaps, he thinks, as the applause breaks out around him and the band plays the final chorus, he is just getting greedy now.

24

Roddy makes to kiss her on the cheek, but Celeste pulls away. He puts an arm around her waist and guides her inside the doorway and up the stairs to the private dining rooms on Greek Street for lunch. They are shown through to their table, and Celeste busies herself with reading the menu. Roddy reaches over and gently takes it from her. He wants her attention, but he gets a frown.

'Are you angry at me?' he asks.

'A little.'

'Why?'

'Because — '

'Because I told the American what Tim had done to you? Or because I didn't find out about his temper when I checked him out?'

Without looking at the wine-list, Celeste orders a bottle of Springfield Estate for Roddy, water for herself, and says: 'A bit of both.'

'I said I was sorry.'

The wine arrives and they make small talk until the waiter has gone. 'You look fine now,' Roddy said.

'Fine isn't good enough. And the bruises

257

here,' she points to her torso, 'are taking an age to fade. Oh, I don't know, Roddy.' She feels the once-unfamiliar tug of despair and doubt. 'I just think . . . '

'You've had enough?'

Celeste reaches over and touches his arm. 'I'm not really angry with you. This was all my choice. A grown-up option in an adult world. And it was all going tickety-boo, but now it's blown up in my face.'

'I blame your friend Vince.'

'Do you? Good God — why?' Roddy has always been adept at shifting responsibility, ever since they were children. The phrase 'Celeste did it!' comes back to her across the years. But she wants to hear his justification this time.

'No reason. He's a bit of jinx, though, isn't he?'

Disappointed, she snaps: 'Not really. Can we order? I'm famished.' She thinks over what Roddy has said while she pretends to examine the menu. Bad things certainly happen around Vince, that's for sure. Does he attract them? She shakes off the idea as silly and superstitious, then puts him out of her mind for the time being. Vincent Piper is occupying too much of her time as it is. She has spent a sleepless night thinking about his crackpot ideas, worrying for him. Enough.

She must worry about herself.

'What are you doing later?' asks Roddy. 'After lunch?'

She smiles. 'Letting LuLu put me back together.'

★ ★ ★

Piper is in DCI Fletcher's office in New Scotland Yard, with rain hammering against the windows, and steaming cups of good coffee in front of them. Piper takes a sip. It is a deep, strong black and almost hot enough to crisp the skin, just the way he likes it.

'I'm sorry I was late,' she says. 'One of the kids is unwell.'

She has two young children, both under ten, whom she feels she doesn't see enough of, while the childminder sees far too much of them. Her husband is some kind of financial consultant in the City, who lost his job when Arthur Andersen went belly-up. These days, he has to work long and hard to make sure he is never in that position again.

'That's OK. The coffee was worth the wait.'

'Are you fully functioning at the office?'

'More or less. They are keeping me away from anything to do with Martha.'

'Understandable. They get anywhere tying

anti-globals to the bombs?'

'No.' Roth has given him a heads-up on that. Every organisation they had raided and picked over had been clean. They'd even found DAGGER. As he'd originally thought, the outfit consisted of one guy and a dog-eared copy of *No Logo*. Now, though, he has another avenue to explore. The road to Queen's Terrace. 'Got anything for me?'

'Yes and no. No US victims,' Fletcher tells him.

'Good.'

'But two perpetrators who are.'

'Go on.'

'The first one is an assault at a health club. In the changing room.'

'A misunderstanding in the showers?'

'I don't think so. Our man was worked over pretty thoroughly. By an American.' Piper takes the folder and looks through the stark images of a battered and bruised body. He had been harder on Brogan than he remembered. 'Ouch,' is all he says.

'We think it was a pro job. Someone hired to warn this chap off.'

Piper makes sure his scabbed knuckles stay out of sight. 'Why do you think that?'

'Look at the build of him. It needed someone good to take him down, to do that much damage.'

Thank you, he almost says.

'And the man had a gun.'

'Any ID on the type?'

'He didn't get a good look. An automatic pistol is the best we've got.'

'Any leads?'

'No. Nothing on the CCTV. Apparently they don't run it twenty-four-seven. Typical. Victim insists he has no idea why it was done. Don't believe that for a minute. Must think we were born yesterday. We are checking the membership records, who was signed in and out of the club.' You'll not get me like that, he thinks, but concedes he was lucky with the surveillance tapes.

'The thing is,' she continues, 'I get the impression from the interviewing officer that this man won't be pressing charges, even if we can find the attacker. His squash partner was the one who called the police, who insisted on the photos, not the victim.'

'What do you want me to do?'

'Nothing, for the moment. Just file it away — that there might be American muscle for hire in Town.'

No, the American muscle works for free. 'Consider it filed.'

'This one is from Thames Valley Police.' She passes a second file across the desk and he opens it, the shock of another bruised face taking him aback. 'It's just a kid,' he says.

'Nineteen, Ben Greenslade. Student at Reading University. Badly beaten by an intruder.'

'Robbery?'

'No.'

He flicks the pages. 'Is he dead?'

'No.'

'I give up. What?'

'He was force-fed about ten pounds of sausages.'

Piper suppresses the urge to laugh. He can't even visualise what ten pounds of sausages look like. A lot, he guesses. 'Jesus. What kind of — '

'Sausages?' she interrupts.

'Sicko,' he concludes, 'would do that?'

'One who forces him to eat at gunpoint. Sausage after sausage.' She leans forward. 'It gets worse.'

He thinks for a second. 'They were raw?'

'They were raw,' she repeats.

'How is he? The boy?'

'More poorly than you'd think. They had to suck most of it out of him. But he'll be all right. Physically at least. I doubt he'll be able to look a banger in the eye again, mind.'

'So why is this of interest to me?'

'He had an American accent.'

'The sausage king?'

'Yes.'

'Another one? Is he sure? The kid?'

'Seems to be.'

'Could it be the same American as at the gym?'

'Why should it be?'

'Yeah. Just thinking out loud.' And blowing smoke. He takes another sip of the coffee, stands and looks out of the window, watching the rivulets of water run down the glass. He turns. 'I don't get it. The sausages.'

'You don't know about Ben Greenslade's father, do you? The stunt he pulled.'

'No. Tell me.'

'You aren't going to believe this.'

★ ★ ★

Celeste Young is lying face down on a table at the BodyBliss Day Spa, just off Kensington High Street, keeping her weekly appointment with the serene LuLu, her favourite masseuse in town. She is in the green treatment room, where the walls are covered in swathes of muslin dyed the appropriate hue, which rustle and shift in the artificial breeze. Soft, jungle sounds leak from the Bose ceiling speakers, with the occasional trickle of water. The ambient touches are corny, but they work. Celeste

263

can feel the tension leaching out of her.

She had booked in for a Beauté Neuve facial, but LuLu took one look at her and rescheduled her for the works — a salt and oil scrub, followed by the BodyBooster massage. Celeste has no secrets from LuLu who, at £120 an hour, knows that total discretion is part of the package. She has never seen Celeste like this before, but then she has never been used as a punchbag before. Despite what she told Vincent, it shouldn't be an occupational hazard, not at her end of the game.

'Ow,' she says as LuLu touches one of the yellow splodges on her side.

'Bastard,' says the masseuse, and Celeste rolls slightly on her side to look at her. She is Balinese, has trained at The Four Seasons on the island and was brought over by the owner of the spa, who discovered she gave the best Lulur on the planet (hence her adopted name, when she quickly realised that English people could grasp and spell it much easier than her original one).

LuLu is a great advert for massage and relaxation. She has a flawless honeyed face, rarely without a smile, and a healthy glow that seems to extend several feet around her. Celeste suspects that such would be the case even if she were working in some rice paddy back home. So it is a surprise when Celeste rolls onto her side and sees those features darken with disgust at the man who hurt her.

'LuLu,' says Celeste with mock admonishment.

'Sorry, ma'am.' She slips back into her normal cloak of serenity.

'You are right, though. He is a bastard.'

'You press charges with police?'

Celeste finds herself laughing, even though it hurts because of the pressure on her ribs. 'Well, in a manner of speaking.'

'So he's sorry?'

'Oh, he's very sorry.' She feels guilty about taking pleasure in his considerable misfortune, but then she remembers that look on his face, the detached, stone-cold expression as he worked on her, as if it were a clinical exercise in removing his frustrations on an inanimate object. The food and wine smashed onto the floor, the twenty-five minutes of hell before the first, ridiculous, feeble apology came.

'Shall I start with your neck? Very hard, very tense.'

'Yes, LuLu, whatever you think. I need this body back as soon as possible. I have had to empty my diary until I manage not to look like I have come from a refuge for battered wives.'

As LuLu's long, sensuous fingers start to dig deep, generating another, almost delicious type of pain, Celeste reluctantly reverts to thinking about Vincent Piper.

Twice now he has come to her aid with violence. DeVaughan in the restaurant, a man who was lucky, she now believes, not to be more seriously hurt, and Tim Brogan in the health club. Both times in public, taking a terrible risk of discovery. Did the man have a death wish? Was she dealing with a dangerous psychotic?

She supposes her main worry is that his unpredictable force could end up being directed at her if she displeased him in some way. Yet there was no sign of that. It was as though she had gained another brother, brawn to Roddy's brains. Roddy, of course, made it clear over lunch that he didn't agree. He felt she'd gained a nutcase.

'Oww,' she says again.

'Just some knots to work out.'

Yes, the story of her life. *Just some knots to work out.* What she can't quite grasp is the knowledge that Vincent is going to take his solitary vendetta one step further. He is going to find this Monroe and kill him. The thought should horrify her, but the concept of turning the other cheek has lost its appeal recently, and if Piper is right, and this man *is* blowing up buildings . . . But what if he is wrong? What has he got to go on but a hunch? And if he isn't way off the mark, will he even bother to ask why Monroe is doing this before he kills him?

As the endorphins — or whatever it is LuLu can conjure into her bloodstream — are released, she drifts to thinking about Monroe. What Piper can't see, says the Voice of Reason within, is that there are similarities: here is another father in pain. He has a son, dying of cancer.

She thinks of Kate Monroe and the discovery of their boy's illness. No. No, that isn't right. It doesn't play. She rewinds and tries again. There is still the clang of a false note. From the recess of her mind something is calling to her, a long-neglected memory, one scary and traumatic enough to have been filed away.

Now she has it: *the laugh*. Like a monkey. She jerks as if the table is electrified, squirming to throw off the towels, and LuLu protests.

'Sorry.'

Piper had described what the mother, Monroe's wife, had said, and now she is certain there is another explanation for the laugh. The Voice of Reason tries to dismiss it, but reason and logic have no role here. She is dealing with two sick men, who have ended up in the same desolate place for two very different reasons. She sits up and says to LuLu: 'Look, I'm sorry. We'll start again in a second. Can you get my mobile out of my bag? I need to make a call.'

'Is it urgent?' says LuLu with an undertone that suggests it had better be.

'Yes. It's to Professor Winslott. My doctor.'

25

Number 14 Queen's Terrace is part of a row of late-Regency houses on the eastern edge of Bayswater. Several of them are now Bed & Breakfast hotels, catering for long-stay families and the odd bewildered tourist. The rest are subdivided into flats, none of them remaining as the single-occupancy homes for which they were once intended.

Like the others, number 14 is painted cream, although it is flaking badly in places. The window-frames and sills are marbled with shrinkage lines, and large sections of putty have fallen away from the glass, leaving some of the panes held in by nothing more than old paint and a couple of rusty nails. They rattle fitfully as the wind swirls down the streets.

The internal hallway is also in need of attention. The dark green paint is depressing in the extreme, and the carpet only extends two flights. Above that are cold, cracked marble steps, flanked by gap-toothed bannister rails, some of the more elaborate sugar-twist uprights replaced by plain, square wood.

The Monroes' apartment is on the third floor — the one the Brits call the second — and the unit above it is vacant and for sale, so it is on this landing that Piper sits in the dark, taking the occasional hit from a half-bottle of Scotch to help keep him warm on the cold surface. Maybe to help him keep his nerve, he isn't certain.

He has checked the ammunition in the Sig Sauer. As he expected, it is a soft-nose 9mm. Maximum knock-down power, minimum penetration. One shot is all it will take, if he gets a clear target. It will make a hell of noise, though, but he has no idea how to go about finding a suppressor in London. The FBI has them in the armoury, but he wants no chance of a trace back to him after this hit. If that is what it becomes.

'Do yourself a favour. Now. Get her out of here.'

Sometimes he wonders whether he even heard those words. The scene has run so often in his head, it feels worn and scratchy. Perhaps grief, not the truth, has driven him to this peculiar situation, where he waits on a dank stairwell to kill a man.

Take him down first, Piper. Before you kill him. You have questions that need answering. Such as: why?

OK, OK. I know.

He hears a noise downstairs, the timer light flicks on, the bulb above his head starts buzzing, he closes his eyes to keep his night vision intact. There is the echo of footsteps going down, then the heavy front door slams, rattling those windows. The light snaps off, and he opens his eyes again.

He wonders what his father, Eddie the Wolfman, would say if he could see him now, a bitter man, cradling a stolen gun, whisky at his side, a sickness in his stomach. Would he approve? Somehow, he thinks not.

Perhaps this is what they mean when they say it is 'too personal'. That your higher processes stop working in the accepted manner, you obsess, working a few isolated strands into a full-blown theory, which you are determined is the only correct one. Now he is on the final straight, he can feel the drip-drip of uncertainty at the back of his mind.

Have you read this right. Vince?

He feels the cold metal press just behind his right ear. A perfect spot. A slight breeze ruffles his hair and he shivers. The door is open behind him. His prey has come out of the top-floor flat, not his own. This man worked with The Wolf. He learned from the best, then added one or two touches of his own. Like killing suspects and covering it up.

271

'They have fire escapes out the back,' says the voice, close to his ear. 'You didn't case it properly.'

'No.'

'I guess you just buzzed an apartment and came on up.'

'Yes.'

'How did you find out about this place?'

'From Kate. By accident. I saw her when I went over to see Dad.'

'How is The Wolf?'

'Dying.'

'Yeah. That's a damn shame. You have a gun?'

'Yes.'

'Radio?'

'No.'

'Back-up?'

'No.'

'No?' Monroe giggles, an unsettling sound from a grown man. 'You wanted all the glory for yourself? Maybe you are The Wolf's son after all. Stand up, very slowly.'

'What do you mean, me being like The Wolf?'

'Grandstanding. Look at that jump he made that time.'

'The Wrecking Crew?'

'I was right behind him. He should have waited. We could have formulated a plan. But no, he jumps, he gets the headlines and the Medal for Bravery.'

Monroe's left hand frisks him expertly, and removes the Sig Sauer. He carries on checking. He finds the phone. It is off. He switches it on, examines the screen suspiciously, listens for the tone.

'It's just a cellphone,' Piper tells him honestly.

'You're not wired?'

'No.'

'So nobody else knows you are here?'

'Is this all about The Wolf?' Piper asks. 'Is he the key to this?'

A shake of the head. 'Just making conversation, Vince. Nothing to do with your dad. I'm real sorry about what has happened to him. Downstairs.'

He prods him forward and keeps well back as Piper descends the stairs to the next landing.

'He told me about the ATM man. What you did to him.'

'Someone had to pay.' His voice is hard and flat. 'You remember the phrase 'by all means necessary'? We appropriated the slogan of the other side, that's all.'

'The other side? You mean civil rights?' Since when was that the 'other side' he wanted to add, but thought it best to keep out of that minefield.

'Yeah, some of it was about civil rights. Some of it was about other things.'

Monroe elbows the hall light switch, finds his key and opens the apartment door, the suppressed gun unwavering all the time. He ushers Piper in.

'Why did you blow up that bookstore, Monroe? Why did you kill Martha?'

There is a hiss of anger, and Piper waits for the bullets in the back of his head, the flash of bright pain. Monroe simply says: 'Through there. Lie on the bed, face down. Arms outstretched.'

Monroe throws the phone and the Sig Sauer onto the armchair in the bedroom, but hangs onto his .22, leaving one hand free to do the work.

Piper's arms are bound to the heavy brass bedhead, his ankles taped together, then roped down to the bed. Piper can smell rank body odour coming off the pillows and sheets. It is some time since they have been changed.

'Can you at least answer my question?'

'It wasn't me.'

'Monroe, I saw you there. You warned me — '

'It wasn't me. For fuck's sake, what do you think I am?'

'I think you've turned into a monster, Henry.'

Monroe hits him, with his fist, not the gun, thank the Lord, but a short, sharp punch to the side of his head that leaves Piper blinking away starbursts. Then he jabs Piper under the ribs and a blinding pain makes him swoon. That's a taster of what he did to the ATM man.

He can hear Monroe panting hard, as if fighting to regain control. He has touched a nerve.

'Are you going to kill me?' he asks. He turns his head so he can see him. 'Like you did the ATM man?'

There is silence, just the hum of traffic from outside, the shudder of the window-frames as a bus changes gear.

Eventually, Monroe says, 'You are just in my way, Vincent. I don't want to have to kill you. You're The Wolf's son. He's got enough to deal with.'

'So what now?' Piper asks.

'I'm not sure. I'm going to have to leave you here until I get back. I'll have to tape your mouth. It is no good struggling. They are Quantico knots. You know all about them.'

He hears Monroe walk from the bedroom, and as he returns, the sound of him ripping off a fresh length of duct tape. He approaches and Piper can smell the adhesive as the strip is presented to his mouth. Then the man hesitates.

'You thought I did that bomb?'

'Yes.'

'Why? Why would you think that?'

'Because of what you said to me in the street. About getting Martha out of town. About it not being safe.'

'Oh, Jesus. You idiot. You want to know the truth?'

'Yes.'

'You first.'

'What?'

'Show and tell, Vince. Tell me what you think you know, I'll tell you how it really is.'

'And then?'

'Then we go back to me gagging you. I need time to think what happens afterwards, something that suits both our purposes. But at least, whatever happens, you'll know the truth. Or at least my part of it. Deal?'

Piper's mouth suddenly feels furry with the taste of stale alcohol. 'I need some water before you tape me.'

'Agreed. Is it a deal?'

Piper nods as best he can. 'It's a deal.' Then a thought strikes him. 'You leave me trussed here in Quantico knots. What happens if you don't come back?'

Monroe laughs quietly, and Piper senses the madness beneath it. 'Well, I think you'd better pray I do.'

26

Andy Williams has retuned. The Wolf can hear him crooning. 'Can't Take My Eyes Off You' came first, then the 'Hawaiian Wedding Song', followed by 'Born Free'. He was beginning to think this was some kind of revenge for watching the goddamn *Andy Williams Show* whenever he was at home. Wasn't there something about a bear and cookies? Oh jeez, he thinks, there is always the Osmonds to torture him with.

He is in the corner of the living room, on the bed, his permanent home. This is where he eats, sleeps, shits and, he has discovered, pisses himself. He remembers feeling as though he ought to go, then . . . bam. It's out.

The Wolf pushes himself up in bed. He wheezes with the exertion, listening to the tick-tick of the gas regulator as it makes sure he doesn't get too much of the oxygen.

Maggie, his wife, is out, he can sense that. Apart from that pump, there is no other sound. When she is here the house seems to breathe, to have rhythm and soul, but without her it sinks back to a cold, functional shell.

Maggie takes about an hour and a half to

do the grocery run, sometimes more. If she has only just gone, he probably has just enough time for what he has in mind. But does he have the strength, the energy? There is only one way to find out. His study is at the back of the house. Two seconds away for a healthy person, as distant as Siberia to him.

As he slips onto the floor, his feet find his slippers and he slides each foot in turn into them, wriggling his toes in pleasure. *Ready for extra-vehicular activity*, he jokes to himself. As he straightens up, he feels the thin plastic tube of the oxygen supply tighten and stretch. Time to cut the umbilical cord, it seems.

The Wolf unhooks the elastic side from the mask. He forces his lungs to work for themselves. He wobbles like a tightrope walker for the first few steps, arms out-stretched, muscles and balance sensors trying to recall how this thing works. It takes ten minutes for him to reach the door.

The hallway now, the longest section, but in some ways the easiest, because he will be able to rest his back against the wall and slide along. Even so, the pressure through his depleted flesh onto his bones builds up quickly, so by the time he is halfway along, he is sweating with the exertion. He hears a car outside, slowing with a squeal of brakes, and thinks he is doomed, caught red-handed, but the driver guns the engine and moves on.

He gathers his strength to reach the entrance to his study, and uses the last of his energy for the shuffle across to the far side. He almost falls the last few feet, landing heavily at the rolltop bureau and slumping down into his swivel chair, folding in half with exhaustion.

He locates the key taped to the underside of the chair and unlocks the desk, sliding up the top, releasing a cloud of dust. Yes, it's been quite a time since he needed to sit down here and write a report or a letter or an assessment of some kind. Quite a time.

The metal box is at the rear, behind the old diaries and journals he has kept. Andy chimes in with 'Love Letters', but he ignores him.

The pistol is old-fashioned, almost an antique, and it dates to a previous era in the Bureau, when you had some choice of weapons. His back-up had always been a Colt Detective Special, because it was simple and foolproof. It was in continuous production from 1927 to 1986, so it must have been doing something right.

These days, of course, it is all Glocks and Berettas, which have their place, but as he grips the lightly knurled wooden handle — his being one of the 1967 anniversary models — he feels he is holding a real cop's gun. He pulls back the thumb catch on the left side of the frame and allows the cylinder to swing out. Empty. He presses the ejector rod to make sure all the moving parts are well oiled, and with shaking hands he slots in six of the .38 special rounds. Half-forgotten reflexes help him flip the chamber back into place with a single twist of the wrist. He looks for somewhere to hide the gun in his pyjamas. As there is no safety, he has to be careful in his clumsy state and, in the end, he decides to carry it.

More relaxed now that his mission is accomplished, he retraces his steps to the living room. He just has time to slip the Colt under the stack of pillows, strap the mask on and pile his aching bones into bed, when he hears the crunch of Maggie's tyres on the gravel outside. He sucks on the oxygen, gives a sigh of relief and falls into a satisfied sleep.

★ ★ ★

'Vin. It's Celeste. Pick up, please. Are you there? Look, I have important information about your man. I can't put my finger on why, exactly, but it makes me uneasy. I . . . think you might be wrong about him. If you get this, call me.'

★ ★ ★

'Vin. Celeste. Where the hell are you? Call me. I am going out of my mind here. This is not a drill or whatever it is you say. Vincent. *Please.*'

★ ★ ★

In a musty room in Queensway, illuminated only by streetlights and the headlamps of passing cars, Vincent Piper listens to his mobile phone play its refrain four times and click over to the message service. It is feet away from his hand, sitting on the armchair, but he can't reach it. Quantico restraint knots are keeping his arms stretched rigid. If he struggles, the blood supply to his hands will slowly be squeezed off. He is facing up to the fact that he will be like this until someone comes to get him. Or not.

27

He nibbles on the over-sweet cereal bar as he looks in the estate agent's window. Most of the houses staring out at him are lavishly appointed — three-car garages, a bathroom for every bedroom, heated pools, that kind of thing — but, irritatingly, there are no prices. POA. Price on application. What does that mean? Hey, we don't want to give you a heart attack right out here in the street, we'd rather tell you how many millions of dollars we are talking about inside, while you are sitting down and we can get water and do CPR on you while you recover from the shock.

Monroe finishes the bar, climbs back in the scruffy Ford Mondeo he bought earlier that day in Streatham for cash and throws the wrapper on the floor. He knows where he is going, the estate agent stop was just out of curiosity. He wanted to get an idea of how much the man was worth. POA my ass, he thinks. The guy is loaded.

He steers the car, which is running rough, down the leafy avenues of the commuter town, the roads illuminated by yellow sodium lamps, and lots of them, the houses all snugly tucked behind high box hedges and tall ornamental trees.

Monroe hasn't quite decided what to do about Piper. The fact that he is The Wolf's son has saved his life. It was true, that man loved his share of the limelight and most other people's as well, revelled in being The Wolfman, but hell, he had been his partner. He had suffered the loss of his grand-daughter, the loss of lungs, soon his mind would go. His son being shot, that would probably strip out the last of his reason, tumbling him over into complete senescence.

But he didn't have to kill Piper. He had in his pocket a whole new identity, painstakingly put together in Paris, that would get him out of the country and into the safety of Europe. Who was going to find him in Budapest or the backwoods of Slovakia? Interpol? Unlikely. So what he'll do is, make a call in a day or two to the cops, telling them where to find Piper, and his conscience on that one will be clear.

He pulls the car to a halt, opposite the man's house, and turns off the ignition. The car judders as the engine kicks and spits, as if reluctant to stop. Piece of shit, thinks Monroe. He opens his case and takes out both guns. The Sig Sauer isn't threaded for the silencer so if he uses that, there is going to be noise. It's a neat one-shot weapon, though, as he is sure Piper considered when he was going to use it to take him out. The Secret Service like them, because there is little chance of the soft-nosed rounds going through the target and damaging civilians or fellow agents. In the end he puts both weapons into his overcoat pockets.

He checks inside his jacket, finding the letter he will leave on the body. It is no good just killing Greenslade — people have to know why. The letter takes the chain of events back to a windy day in May 1990 at a country show photo-call. It then leads the reader through the politician's less than illustrious career to Greenslade's current position as a director of ZanCo, pioneers of something called PCR-negative techniques, according to the Colindale newspaper library.

Monroe rereads the letter, wondering if it will sound deranged to the people who find it. Probably. However, he tries to make the point he has banged on about ever since he discovered his son's condition. Along the line it has to be *someone's* fault. Which means somebody has to pay. OK, Greenslade might not be point zero, but he helped propagate the circumstances that led to his son's illness and, more importantly, he continues to do so to this day.

Monroe folds the letter away and returns to the matter in hand. He already has his MOE, his method of entry, having captured the electronic garage door code in the black box in his left hand when Greenslade's wife and kids left earlier in the evening to visit the hospital, where the boy is being treated for a ruptured stomach. On most cars the frequencies of the electronic door signals are changed after each use, cycling through hundreds of variations, so that thieves can't do what he has done. It has taken garage door manufacturers a little longer to come up with a similar system. They are hardly ever retro-fitted. All he has to do is make sure he is not seen approaching the side of the house, and he can get the doors up and be inside within a few seconds. Well, the British passion for gardening certainly helps with that. There is more cover here than there was in Da Nang, when he was posted out there to assist the MPs.

Monroe steps out of the car, checking his gloves are pulled tight, feeling the weighty swing of the pistols in his coat, and crosses the road to kill Mr Greenslade.

★ ★ ★

Maggie Piper looks down at her sleeping husband. It isn't fair. He should have had ten, fifteen more years of active life. Not this interminable twilight.

She knows fairness has got nothing to do with it. If there were some kind of equality or checks and balances in this life, then Martha would still be alive and her son wouldn't have that haunted look in his eyes. It chilled her when she saw it. Like the empty, thousand-yard stare you saw in shell-shocked vets. She knew then that it was going to be a long struggle for Vincent before he found any kind of peace.

The Wolf snuffles in his sleep and she presses the boost button, letting a pocket of oxygen-enriched air settle over his mouth. His eyes are moving under their lids.

She bends over to kiss him and her hand connects with something hard under the pillows. She reaches between them and pulls out the revolver. She remembers this gun. The last time she saw it, the weapon had been in his desk, safely locked away. But if it is here . . . ?

She walks out into the hall and looks down at the study, trying to spot evidence of the journey. The old fool. No wonder he was sleeping. How many days' energy did he expend on making it down there and back? Now she does begin to cry, quietly, stifling the sobs, knowing how his desperate mind must be working.

She considers putting the weapon back from whence it came, in the desk, but something stops her. She considers for a moment, sniffs, retraces her steps and, after a few moments, slides the gun back where she found it between the pillows.

★ ★ ★

Even in the most security-conscious houses, the door between garage and living areas is often the weak spot. The Greenslades' is no different. It takes him fifteen minutes to work away the wooden lip around the catch and, praying there is no bolt or deadlock, he pushes the thin steel plate, the size of a credit card, into the catch. It rolls back smoothly, and Monroe is inside.

He waits, listening, taking the pulse of the house. There is classical music coming from down here somewhere, but otherwise, all is quiet.

He slides inside, the silenced pistol in his hand, held close to his chest. This is a side hallway of some kind, running alongside the staircase, off the main, more extravagantly appointed, entrance space. He steps forward and peers up through the stair railings. Lights are on upstairs, but there's no sound or movement. Just the music, which is leaking from behind the door on the opposite side of the hall on this level.

Monroe pads across the hardwood floor and stops outside the glossy, white-panelled door with its polished brass fittings. Yes, he must be in there, listening to his Mozart.

He eases off the safety on his pistol and makes his move, measured and fluid. Handle down, shoulder against the door, weapon already being extended, checking the room, spotting his man sitting at the desk, even as Symphony Number 38, the *Prague*, swells in his ears. Greenslade looks up.

'Armed police! Drop your weapon!' A yell from behind.

'AFOs!' Authorised Firearm Officers. 'Put the gun down or we open fire.'

A radio crackles.

'Clear sighting!' roars a voice from his left.

'Armed police! Drop the fuckin' gun or we drop you.'

A dragon light flares up from across the room, blinding him, and the shouts become more heated. He can see figures emerging from behind curtains and chairs, hear the thump of thick rubber-soled boots on the stairs.

Monroe manages two shots into Greenslade's chest before the chatter of Heckler & Kochs snuffs out his life.

28

The letter that Roth hands across to Beckett, the FBI's Senior Legal Attaché, is sealed in plastic, a separate transparent sheath for each of the four sheets. There is a dark stain in one corner — blood — and a hole through one edge, made by the police marksmen of SO13. The document had been over Monroe's heart.

In ten minutes Beckett will take a walk from his office, catch the lift to the next floor, and brief the Ambassador on the previous evening's events and the aftermath. He needs to get it straight in his head. He wants to take in solutions, not problems. Hence the presence in the room of Diana Napper, the Senior Press Secretary, a good, no-nonsense operative, six-two of Armani trouser suit and bottle blonde hair. You didn't argue with Ms Napper. This woman could make even hardened news-hounds cower with one of her steely expressions.

'Should I read this?' Beckett asks her. 'Or do you want to precis it for me?'

'I think you'd better see it for yourself,' says Roth. Napper nods her agreement.

Beckett reads quickly, his lips moving as he does so.

' 'To the British authorities. The man I have just executed is, as you are probably aware, Charles Greenslade. He is a former Member of Parliament, and in 1990-91 was a Junior Minister in the Department of Agriculture. In the spring of that year he, and several other members of the Conservative Government, undertook a series of stunts designed to put the public's mind at rest regarding the issue of food safety. In May 1990 Greenslade was at the Hampshire County Show and Fair. As he was entering, when asked questions about the industry by reporters, he purchased two hotdogs from a roadside van. He ate one of them, and he fed the other to his young son. He stated that he would hardly put his own child's life at risk, would he? Yet, that is exactly what he did. Not only that, he put everybody else's children's lives at risk by refusing to acknowledge that there was a serious situation in the British food chain'.'

The phone rings and Beckett picks up. He listens and replaces it before saying to Roth and Napper: 'I have two minutes.'

'Carry on,' suggests Roth. 'It's worth it.'

' 'Furthermore',' he reads, ' 'this cavalier attitude, to not just the UK's health but to

290

the world's wellbeing, continued when Greenslade lost his seat in Parliament and within two weeks became a director of ZanCo. This company has, through its Dutch subsidiary, pioneered the use of PCR-negative techniques to inject chickens. This amounts to a crime against humanity'.'

He stops. 'PCRs?'

'It explains later,' says Napper. 'Polymerase Chain Reactions are used to detect a particular species' DNA. As far as I can gather, and I am no expert, this Dutch company can disguise the origin of meat products.'

'Why would you do that?'

'It means you can pump hydrolysed beef or pork into chicken, which makes it hold more water, and makes your chicken fingers, or whatever, fatter and nobody'll be any the wiser. Then you sell 'em to schools, hospitals . . . '

'I still don't get what is going on here,' says Beckett, irritated. 'Monroe killed this guy because of some contaminated chicken?'

'Monroe was saying that beef waste-product continues to get in the food chain,' offers Roth. 'Look at page three.'

Beckett does so, mouthing the words this time as he speedreads. It more than explains Monroe's madness. 'Ah.'

'You disguise the DNA,' says Roth. 'Nobody knows what is going where any more. You buy chicken pâté, it could be goat for all you know. No way to prove otherwise.'

'Shit. What is our line here?'

Napper clears her throat and says: 'That Monroe, a former Federal employee — the term FBI will not be used — who had spent time in London, was hired by a business rival to intimidate Mr Greenslade, firstly by attacking his son, and when that failed, by going to his house with a gun. However, after the incident with his son, Mr Greenslade had police protection.'

Roth grunts but doesn't say anything. He knows that wasn't how the cops came to be there. But they all need to keep Piper's name out of this.

Napper continues, 'The police were waiting, and despite repeated warnings, Monroe used his weapon. He was shot dead at the scene by Authorised Firearms Officers of the Thames Valley and Metropolitan Police Forces.'

Napper hands a transcript of the statement across.

'Impressive,' says Beckett after he has scanned it.

'It took two hours to agree on the wording.'

'Is it cleared?'

'Yes.'

'At what level?' asks Beckett.

Roth interjects. This had been his department. 'Home Office. Metropolitan Police Commissioner's Office. You think even this government wants the alternative version to appear? Nobody comes out covered in glory when you start looking at how this country feeds itself.'

Beckett stands and gathers his papers for the meeting. 'Thank you both.'

'It'll play for two days then go away,' Napper reassures him.

'Good. How is Greenslade?' asks Beckett.

'In shock,' says Roth.

'The cop who stood in for him?'

'Took two to the chest. The Armitron stopped them both. Good old made-in-the-US technology.'

'Well, that's something. One more thing.' He is looking at Napper.

'Yes?'

'Check the provenance of the meat in the catering facilities here, will you? The canteen. And the trolley service.'

She smiles, ahead of the game. 'I already have. It used to be guaranteed from the US of A.' They were all aware that the last year had seen outbreaks of various bovine diseases in the US herds.

'And now?'

'Organic from never-contaminated sources.'

'Good. Now bury the rest of the story. Quickly.'

★ ★ ★

'You're mad at me?'

'No.'

'Little bit?' teases Celeste.

'No.'

'Honest?'

'Why should I be mad at you?' asks Piper.

'You could lose your job,' replies Celeste.

'I could have lost my life.' He reaches across the restaurant table and touches her hand, hoping she is not going to misconstrue the gesture.

'One fettucine, one chef's salad,' says the waitress, and Piper removes his hand and sits back as she puts the dishes down. They are in Nicole's, in Bond Street, her idea for lunch; the chattering ladies with their piles of branded purchases that surround them are not really his scene. She'd earned the right to select this, though. He owed her yet again. That made it twice. He must make sure there isn't a third time.

They are both on water, the mood too subdued for wine, he feels, even though part of him just wants to go and get steaming drunk. Maybe later. 'Pepper?' asks the waitress. They both refuse.

As he picks up the first strands of his pasta, he says, 'I was about to say thank you.'

'You are very welcome. Perhaps that makes us quits?'

The bruises on her face have faded and she has no need of sunglasses. 'You mean I should stay out of your business from now on?' he asks.

'I'm glad I stayed in yours.'

'Me too. What I don't understand is, how did you know?'

She delicately inserts a leaf in her mouth and chews for a second before explaining. 'It was when you were telling me about the son and the laugh. You see, my father died of a brain tumour, so I knew all the symptoms. And the thing about the laugh, the monkey laugh — that rang another bell. I knew I'd read about it somewhere, maybe in *The Times* or the *Telegraph*. It's not the kind of thing you forget. So I contacted my doctor and he confirmed that such a laugh is an early symptom, sometimes, of CJD. So I knew there was something else going on here, something you hadn't considered.'

'Go on, make me feel stupid.'

'Well, why should you know?'

'It's my job,' he says, adding ruefully, 'or maybe, it *was* my job.'

'Look, it was just guesswork. I knew it gave the case a whole new dimension, if only as a motive for behaving in such a crazy way. So I rang the number you gave me and said I needed to speak to you urgently. Your friend Roth told me he could locate you. And I said — '

'He told me.'

'Oh.' She'd said that he should find Piper before someone got killed. So Roth had used the PPT, the Bureau's Pin Point Technology, to locate his mobile phone, which they could do within a couple of hundred yards. Only, however, if it was switched on — which Monroe had done for him when he was checking it wasn't a fake. PPT, of course, hadn't been around in his day.

A team from the Embassy and the British police had eventually found him by standing in the hallway of number 14 Queen's Terrace, listening for the ringtone, just as he had done to locate Martha all those weeks ago.

Monroe, of course, had nothing to do with Martha. As he'd begun to suspect, Piper's fevered imagination, stoked by his heartache, had concocted that. Monroe, his father's old friend, had his own, equally crazy agenda. Lying there in the dark, Piper had concluded that the balance of both their minds was disturbed. Hoping his father would forgive him for putting the life of his old partner on the line, Piper told them about Monroe's plan to go after Greenslade. They had put an SO13 team in that night.

'It's hard to believe that all this was because his son contracted that,' he struggled for a moment, trying to remember the correct term, 'Variant CJD.'

'Is it? You were going to kill him when you thought he had been responsible for your daughter's death.'

'That's different.'

'Is it?'

'Of course it's diff — ' Piper pauses and rethinks. 'Maybe not. Maybe I'd gone a little way along that path, too.'

She forks some more salad into her mouth. 'Only a little?'

Piper feels himself redden. It has been hard to admit it to himself, or Celeste, but for the last few weeks it feels as though he has been in the grip of a virulent fever. Everything had been twisted to fit the deranged theory that Monroe was responsible for Martha's death, the nagging suggestions that he might be wrong dismissed time and time again.

It was as if something had to fill the void in his life, to give it meaning. And into the vacuum came a form of madness. Doc Turner had told Piper that Monroe might have been suffering from mood-incongruent psychosis, a grand delusion triggered by depression. Possibly, he wasn't the only one. 'At least my agenda wasn't as big as Henry Monroe's.'

According to Kate Monroe, who had been interviewed by Washington Federal Agents, her husband had insisted the public was told that his boy had cancer, and the 'shame' of being the second case of Mad Cow Disease in the US was kept from the public and press.

'You know you can't tell if it is this vCJD until you perform a post mortem,' explains Piper. 'And the son isn't dead yet.' It would have been much kinder if he had been taken quickly, and it might have prevented the hate festering inside Monroe.

'But Monroe would have been sure.'

'Absolutely.' The discovery of Mad Cow Disease in Washington State only spurred Monroe on. He had convinced himself that the ultimate source of the US infection was back in the UK, which allowed its animal husbandry industry to experiment with cannibalism.

Of course he needed a link to back up his suspicions. Before Eric's mind went completely, he had made his son describe his time in London, trying to pick up a clue, to establish a crude form of epidemiology. It wasn't easy for either of them, but he impressed on the boy how he had to tell him everything, no matter how much he might think his old man would disapprove.

He sifted through hours of tapes and notes. The clincher was the weekends, when all the kids from the various Embassies bought their pills and went clubbing. Ecstasy, coke, amphetamines, all were readily available from certain hotdog stands scattered across London.

To cover the deal, of course, you had to buy something and Eric, like some of the others in the group, developed a taste for hotdogs, would have six, seven over the course of a couple of days. Monroe became convinced it was this poorly regulated trade that had infected his son with the prions, the rogue proteins that had punched large holes in his brain, reducing him to the level of an animal. He has been howling, day and night, for over a year now, locked in a padded cell, violent and filthy, wracked with those strange spasms called myoclonus jerks and, mercifully, unaware of who he once was.

'But the chances of it being the hotdogs . . . ' muttered Celeste.

'Are slim,' he agreed.

'Could it have been the drugs rather than the food?'

Piper shook his head. 'Even more unlikely. There is a long history of drug-taking in this world. We know what they do. At Monroe's home they found evidence that he had traced other kids in the Embassy clubbing clique. From France, Brazil, Sweden . . . he eventually tracked down four similar cases. One had died, three others were still in Eric's state. You see, when they're young and strong, it takes a cruel time to finish them. But now he had a cluster. Just like in Cherry Hill.'

'Cherry Hill?' Celeste repeated.

Piper nodded. He'd got up to speed on this subject very quickly. 'At least eleven people who worked or ate at the Garden State racetrack in Cherry Hill, New Jersey, died of some form of CJD. That's all that links them. They all worked at or visited the track. In fact, there are those who are convinced they can all be linked to the track's upscale restaurant. The Phoenix.'

'And Monroe would know about this cluster?'

'For certain.'

'And would be sure that the hotdogs were a similar case?'

The same way Piper was once sure that the man was the instrument of Martha's death. It takes so little to topple the bereaved over the edge. 'Yes. He would also realise he had little chance of standing it up. The people who uncovered the race-track cluster have been denounced by everyone from beef farmers to the Centers for Disease Control. He had to act alone if he was to get what he felt was justice.'

Once Monroe was in the UK and had access to more detailed history at the Colindale Newspaper Library, he discovered that various people in the UK had known about the risks and had blithely ignored them. And were still ignoring them. So he had targeted Greenslade, whom he was convinced had been paid by the food industry all along.

'*Do yourself a favour. Now. Get her out of here.*'

Monroe hadn't been referring to the bomb, he hadn't even known about it prior to its detonation. He had meant London in general. Get out of London, it isn't safe. He was more right than he knew.

'Vince?'

'Yes? Sorry. Miles away.'

'What will happen to you now?'

'Stan Roth has claimed I was on surveillance for him, following up what we thought was a tentative lead, and got overpowered by Monroe, who panicked when I questioned him. The fact that the cops got

Monroe, before he got to Greenslade, that kind of fixes everything. For now.'

'Won't Greenslade have to make a statement?'

'Only to say that his company has plenty of secrets worth stealing, and that he would never succumb to threats or blackmail, and the share price will probably go up, because if the opposition want something from them that bad, then ZanCo must have technology worth having.'

'Cynic.'

'You buy a thousand shares and watch.'

'I don't think I want anything to do with them.'

'No. Me neither.'

'You know, it leaves one big question, Vin.'

He smiles bleakly. This is hardly news to him, he has thought of little else all night. 'I know. If Monroe didn't plant that bomb . . . '

They continue eating in silence. He looks at his watch. The time has gone quickly, and he realises he has overrun. 'Christ, I forgot — they are casting the statue today. I said I'd be over for the great reveal.'

'Where?'

'Whitechapel. You know where that is?'

'I know the Whitechapel Gallery, it can't be far from there. Eat up, I'll give you a lift over.'

29

Celeste has replaced the M Class with a Volvo XC90 SUV, and the inside still smells of new hides and ripe synthetics. The leather makes him think of cows, and cows lead him to beef. Piper has never given too much consideration to the provenance of food before, but he can see it will preoccupy him now. How much more it must have festered in Monroe's mind, as he thought about the iniquity that had blighted his son's young life, turning him into that poor creature whose brain was dying inside his skull?

It must have infuriated Monroe that a few industrial food-processing companies, keen to maximise profits, started feeding beef waste to cattle, which allowed BSE to thrive. And it is still spreading. Piper vaguely remembers reports of Mad Cow reaching Canada last year, and of outbreaks within the US. Roth tells him there are more than one hundred and thirty cases of this new form in humans now, mostly in young people, mostly Brits, clustered in low-income families. Eric Monroe and his friends had simply been unlucky. How many more people had been similarly infected,

Piper wondered, but hadn't yet found themselves with an unsteady walk, or a laugh like monkey's?

'Nearly there,' says Celeste.

It is a scabby part of London, all cheap wholesale shops and uninviting pubs offering big-screen sports. A streetmarket sprawls along one side of the road, the fruit and vegetables and flowers a welcome burst of colour. Opposite is a mosque, and it doesn't take Piper long to spot the plain-clothes officers on the fringes of the crowd. Since they downgraded the global activists in the search, Muslim extremists are still the main suspects for the Barnes & Noble and Banana Republic bombs. There have been no more since, no more communications received, but the alert remains high.

There is a clattering overhead, and Piper strains to look up. A red and white shape flashes through the sky.

'Air ambulance,' explains Celeste. 'Lands on the roof of the London Hospital down the road.'

The foundry is in a side street that runs alongside a pathetic patch of green, hardly big enough to qualify as a park. It consists of a series of grimy brick buildings, the date, 1850, etched into one keystone above a doorway large enough to drive a truck through. Celeste pulls up outside.

'There you are.'

'You want to come in?' he asks.

'No. I shouldn't.'

'Why not? You are part of this now. What I mean to say is, you are part of this, if you want to be.'

She hesitates for a moment. 'I'd like to be. But . . . '

'You can't stay long.'

She smiles. He is beginning to learn. She has five o'clock drinks with Denis. 'I can't stay long.'

★   ★   ★

The foundry is surprisingly clean inside. He is expecting something Dickensian, with piles of iron filings on the floor, and misshapen workers wheeling hideous lumps of metal while furnaces roar and spit. All, however, is calm. The foundrymen, none of them disfigured as far as he can see, wear brown coats and busy themselves at benches, polishing and filing various pieces of metal. A huge gas furnace occupies one wall, with smaller systems scattered around the perimeter; two large fans on either side of the room suck the air out, and push fresh in. There is, however, still a taste of steel that sits on the tongue, and Piper finds himself swallowing, wishing for a drink.

Martha's work is in one of the rooms at the rear, sitting in the centre of the concrete floor beneath steel girders and chains and pulleys. It is a grubby grey colour, nine feet high, a massive rectangular slab. It reminds him of the monolith from the movie *2001, A Space Odyssey*.

Sarah is there with a small cluster of her pupils, mostly dressed in jeans and sweat tops, all looking solemn. A small flicker of surprise registers on her face when she sees Piper has company.

'Sarah Nielsen, Celeste Young,' he says. 'Celeste — '

'I know. I know what you did for Martha that day. How do you do? I am very pleased to meet you.'

They shake hands rather stiffly, and Celeste indicates the slab and asks: 'Is this it?'

Sarah nods. 'We have to break the mould. The outer casing is fibreglass. Within it is heatproof plaster and inside there — '

'It's the lost wax method?' Celeste interrupts.

'Yes,' says Sarah, without missing a beat. 'I know it's considered old fashioned — '

'But it works.'

Piper zones out while they discuss the

306

relative merits of various casting procedures, only surprised yet again that Celeste can call upon an inexhaustible supply of arcane knowledge. She claims most of it is bluff, the use of a few key words, but it fools him every time. *She probably had a 'friend' who was a sculptor*, he tells himself.

'This is Geoffrey,' says Sarah as one of the brown-coated men approaches, this one with oiled-back hair that went out of fashion forty years earlier. 'The best foundryman in London.'

'Well, that's because there's not many of us left,' he says with a wink, and shows a set of yellow, uneven teeth. 'How do you want to do this, miss?'

'The students would all like a chance to contribute to the chipping away of the investment,' she turns to Piper, 'that's what the casing is called. And at least some of the finishing, although I will do most of that, if that is OK?'

'We can move you to one of the workshops out the back for that,' says Geoffrey, pointing through a grimy window that hasn't seen a cloth in a century. 'You can have some peace and quiet. It'll take you a few days, mind, size of it.'

'The ceremony is in a week,' Sarah says. 'That's enough time.'

'You'll all have to mask up, I am afraid. Health and Safety. Even if you aren't going to grab a chisel.'

White masks are issued and slipped over heads, although Celeste opts to hold hers in place with her crimson-tipped fingers. The girls begin to chop away, tentatively at first, and Geoffrey directs them, making suggestions on how to strike the chasing tools for maximum effect. The room fills with the staccato rhythm of metal on metal.

'When you see it, don't be shocked,' comes Sarah's muffled voice from behind the mask. 'It will be rough, crusty with plaster, warty with air vents and sprues. You might think it looks more like scrap. It will need finishing and polishing. Trust me, it will be beautiful.'

'I do trust you,' he says, and Celeste notices the eye-contact between them. She has to stop herself giggling, not because she is embarrassed by a couple of lovebirds, but because she has just identified the sudden hollowness in the pit of her stomach. Jealousy. Oh, grow up, she tells herself.

'OK, hold on. Stop.' It is Geoffrey. 'Can I give it a go?'

Geoffrey has a power tool, and sets it running, the blade hammering back and forth in a blur. It looks brutal, but he applies it delicately. After a few minutes, he stops, examines his handiwork, fetches a ladder, and works on the top of the casing. He lets the students have another session, then spends a further fifteen minutes of chiselling, before he finally steps off the ladder and beckons Sarah over.

'Shall we?' he invites.

'Together?'

'Yeah.' He fetches two pairs of gloves, hands one pair to Sarah and slips the others on. He digs his fingers into one of the fissures and pulls, and a large chunk of plaster breaks free. Sarah tries the same, and she, too, is left holding a large section of the investment. They tear at the rest of the casing, until dull metal shows through.

'Leave the base,' he says. 'We can clear that later.'

Piper finds himself stepping closer to Celeste as the form gradually emerges from its plaster cocoon, the figure he saw on paper, the woman reaching for the skies, and even from this distance, he can feel the residual heat in the metal reddening his face. It is, as Sarah suggested, rude and unfinished, the metal flat and tarnished, but somehow the elegance of the vision still shines through, giving it more power, perhaps, than the final worked version will have.

'It's beautiful,' whispers Celeste. 'Beautiful,' she repeats in a louder voice, and for the first time Sarah and Geoffrey step back and admire their handiwork, both panting from their efforts.

Sarah takes off her mask and there is no hiding the pleasure in her face. 'Yes. Yes, she is, isn't she?'

The students break into a smattering of applause.

'What is she called?' Celeste asks Piper.

'*Stripped*,' he says.

Celeste raises her eyebrows. Such a short, nasty word for something so exquisite and graceful. But maybe it does fit. Perhaps it is just how Vincent feels.

'What about the . . . whatever it is?' asks Piper as Sarah walks over to them.

'What?'

'In the drawing she is holding something.'

'Ah. That. We are making that at the college, so the students are actually involved in the process for one small part of it. It will be put into place a few days before we transport it to the Residence.' That reminds her. 'Have you seen the guest-list?'

'No. I think there is one waiting for me at the office. I'm just the father, after all.'

Sarah pulls a tongue at the sarcasm and from her bag on the floor she produces

310

several folded sheets of paper, each with closely typed names on them. 'Look.'

Piper takes it and begins to read, waiting for a familiar name to jump out. He finds one fifty down. Sarah Nielsen, then a 'plus one' and the name Mrs Anita Nielsen. 'Well, I'm glad to see you are on there. Who is Anita?'

'My mom. I hope you don't mind. I asked if I could have one guest apart from the students. She's coming to see me, from the West Country, and I thought as she is here . . . If it's a problem . . . '

'No, no, that's fine. God, there are a lot of unfamiliar names here.' As he reaches the end he can sense Celeste at his shoulder looking for her name under Y. It isn't on there.

'Oh,' escapes from her lips.

He flips back and checks it isn't under C by mistake. It isn't.

'Not to worry,' she says, in a voice heavy with disappointment.

'Must be a mistake. An oversight.'

'What is it?' asks Sarah.

'Celeste isn't on the list.'

'Well, that's ridiculous,' she says with genuine indignation.

He hands the list back and turns to Celeste. 'I'll fix it.' When she makes to protest he repeats firmly, 'I'll fix it.'

She nods and walks over to chat to the

311

group of students, leaving Piper and Sarah together. Celeste congratulates them on their efforts. 'Well, it's Sarah who is behind it really,' says one. 'We have her to thank.'

Let him put me on the list, thinks Celeste, as the students chatter on about their tutor and Martha, and eventually, she tunes out. Maybe I'll just stay away from the ceremony. Perhaps I've done my bit. Time to leave Vincent Piper and move on.

★   ★   ★

'We ran a security check on everyone on the guest-list six days ago. Special Branch did the Brits, we did the US citizens and foreigners. Your friend wasn't the only one who got struck off, Vince.'

'No, but she is the only one who stopped and helped me get Martha to the hospital. Under normal circumstances, she would have saved her life. She deserves to be there, more than almost anyone else, Stan.'

Roth shuffles the papers on his desk, embarrassed. 'Look, Vince, I hate to be the one to break it to you, but your friend Celeste — '

'Is a whore.'

Roth looks up. 'I wasn't going to put it quite like that.'

'No?'

'I was thinking more of courtesan. A kept lady. I know she isn't a streetwalker.'

'And this makes her a security risk how?'

'You know how,' says Roth pointedly. 'Or you would have once.'

'Remind me.'

'All right, I'll tell you straight. It was the Brits. They have gate responsibility for the Residence. And if you know your history, you'll be aware that they've been kinda sensitive about paid escorts ever since a certain Christine Keeler slept with a Defence Minister called Profumo.'

'That was forty years ago. And I'm not sleeping with Celeste, Stan, nor is anyone in the government. You're being unfair.'

'No, I think you are, giving me such a hard time.'

He is, and he knows it. Roth has saved his ass in the Monroe debacle, even managed to make him look something of a hero, which took some doing. He should be thanking him.

'Sorry.'

'Yeah.'

'Look, her morality or lack of it does not make her a security risk. I mean, slap an agent next to her for the whole ceremony if you want, but she has to come, Stan.'

'Or?'

Piper shrugs. 'I'm not going to threaten you.'

'Good. Because if you had, she would have definitely been out. No matter what you said. As it is,' he picks up the guestlist once more, 'I'll talk to Beckett. See if he'll lean on the Brits a little.'

'Thanks, Stan.'

'I said I'll see what I can do. Jeez, Vin.'

'I know. But we don't always pick the people who become our friends.'

'Well, maybe you should at least try and stick to ones with regular jobs, huh?'

★ ★ ★

'Roddy, please.'

Celeste is on the phone in Denis's Mayfair apartment, trying to persuade her brother to do her a favour while she towels her hair dry. Denis is her oldest client, in both senses of the word. They have had sex, and he is dozing fitfully in the other room. She has showered and is about to get ready for dinner at the Connaught which, given his wine preferences, will cost Denis the best part of £400 for two. It's good food, but sometimes she wishes he would settle for something a little less formal, somewhere she can kick off her shoes and slump and laugh. That, though, isn't Denis's style.

'What am I, a dating agency?'

'Roddy.'

'Hold on.' She hears muffled voices. Roddy talking to Lennie, his partner. 'Look, Cel, I don't have time for this.'

'Two grand,' she says.

'What?'

'You get me some results within four, five days, I'll pay two thousand.'

'Cel,' he says, sounding hurt, 'it isn't the money — '

'How about five?' It is always the money with Roddy these days, she knows that.

'Five?'

'Five, cash.'

'Bloody hell, Cel. OK, for that money I can farm it out.'

'No. For that money you can bloody well do it yourself. Please.'

Denis appears in the doorway, in boxer shorts and socks. She grimaces at him. She has told him many times about how unappetising men in socks are.

'OK. How much do you want?' Roddy asks.

'Everything. I want everything, Roddy. Like with Tim.'

'Yeah, that worked out well, didn't it?'

315

'This is different. I don't want to fuck this one.'

There is a sigh at the other end. He knows when he is beaten. 'Leave it with me.'

She puts the phone down, knowing he will be very thorough this time. 'My brother,' she explains to Denis.

'Roddy? How is he?'

'He's fine,' she says distractedly, and not entirely truthfully, while her insides tell her she's just wasted five thousand pounds on a petty whim. A phrase has stayed with her though, running around her mind, refusing to be ignored. *'Funny, we always thought she hated her.'*

30

'Tell me about Monroe.'

Piper is sitting in the APPLE office, opposite an uncharacteristically frosty DCI Fletcher.

He recounts the approved version of the story, right up to his rescue.

'How did you get suspicious about Monroe?'

'I met him, casually, and it was something he said. A hunch.'

'When was this?'

'Why are you so interested, Fletch? The story is dead.'

'When was this?' she repeats forcefully.

'Three weeks ago.'

Fletch gets up and walks over to the slim LCD screen. She presses the video player and an image flickers into view. It is grainy and distorted, but he recognises it as Soho. 'When the CCTV coverage on Charing Cross Road was so poor, they widened out the scope to the streets around. You were unlucky. It's just a meeting in the crowd. One of dozens. But on what must have been the fiftieth viewing, one of the Branch's officers recognised you.'

317

She presses the pause button on her remote.

There he is, turned to face the camera, just calling to Monroe minutes before the bomb detonated, minutes before Martha died, the rolled-up magazine in his hand.

'Look at the time. And the date.'

'I know the time and date,' he says flatly.

'What the fuck have you been doing?' she asks. 'Why didn't you mention this meeting to anyone?'

'It wasn't relevant.'

'Everything is relevant.'

A knock and a WPC's head appears around the door. 'Just doing lunch orders. Usual chicken salad, Ma'am?'

'Yes. No. Cheese. Make it cheese.'

'And DI Reed is here.'

'Fine. Tell him we'll be a few minutes.'

'Reed?'

'X-Team.'

He stifles an urge to laugh. X-Team? It sounds like something from the Golden Age of Marvel Comics. He asks: 'And the X-Team are?'

Fletcher turns off the television, pats her hair back into place and sits. 'Yesterday morning, AFOs performed a digout in N5.' He translates as she goes along: armed police on an early-morning raid in North London. 'Some outfit called the Burning Joy of Allah. The entry team had an expo with them.' An

318

explosives officer. 'He recovered material that he has sent to PERME.' The Propellant, Explosive and Rocket Material Establishment. 'They confirm a match for the Barnes & Noble bomb. Now, one thing we don't want is a fuck-up on evidence. So it is practice for a team to hand all their notes and investigations over to what used to be called a B-Team. New set of eyes, making sure nothing has been overlooked. Some bright spark thought B sounded derogatory, so they switched it to X. Makes them feel like Mulder and Scully. One of the things they do is re-interview witnesses. See if anything has struck them in the interim.' She looks at him. 'My point is this. What are the X-Team going to make of you and Monroe speaking just before a bomb goes off? Then of you finding Monroe a few weeks later and him trying to kill Greenslade?'

'How do you think it looks?'

She scowls. 'I think it looks like the FBI has been playing silly buggers with us and are about to get their arse kicked, Special Agent Piper.'

★ ★ ★

DI Tom Reed looks as if he still has teenage acne. He is tall, lanky with close-cropped hair and, young though he might be, he makes it clear he isn't intimidated by Piper. Piper has given Fletcher a fast outline of the genuine Monroe story and, despite her anger at his maverick behaviour, she has agreed not to enter it into the current conversation.

'Special Agent Piper,' the Detective Inspector begins.

'Vince.'

'Can I just check what time you had arranged to meet your daughter?'

'Seven p.m.'

'And you were late?'

'Not much.'

'How much?'

'Fifteen minutes. Maybe twenty.'

'Is that usual?'

He looks at Fletcher who shrugs. 'Special Agent Piper is usually very punctual.'

'I'm very punctual,' he confirms.

'So your daughter might be concerned?'

'It's possible.'

'You had arranged to meet her in the coffee-bar?'

'Yes. She needed to buy some books. I said we'd hook up at seven. I bought a new shirt, which took me maybe ten minutes.' There is something here Piper isn't getting, something he doesn't like. The discovery of the tape has unsettled him. Is everything about to unravel?

Are they going to charge him with withholding evidence, obstructing the course of justice, that kind of thing? 'Can you tell me where this is going?'

'It isn't going anywhere, Special Agent. Just confirming a few things.'

'Have you got the in-store tape yet?'

'No.'

'Why not?'

'Because the FBI seem to have put us at the bottom of their in-tray over at Quantico.'

He has no real answer to that, but the jibe rankles. Every fucker sent stuff to the FBI, millions of items a year from hundreds of police forces and sheriffs' offices all over the US, let alone the stuff the Brits couldn't hack. What were they meant to say? 'Hold on, guys, we got some Brit stuff here, drop everything?' 'I'll chase it up.'

'OK, so we have established that your daughter — '

'Martha.'

'You've seen the outside camera footage of her?' asks Fletcher.

'No.'

'Why not?' asks Reed.

'I couldn't . . . no.' He taps his head. 'I don't have to see it. It plays in my head every day. Every hour. Heavy rotation. She stands, looking around, probably for me. She reaches into her bag for her mobile phone, puts it to her ear. I guess she's calling me, wondering where I am. Then, it's gone. *She's* gone.'

The other two don't say anything for a few seconds, then Reed speaks quietly. 'Yeah, that's about it. You know, if you'd kept that appointment, you'd be dead as well. It went off on the first floor.'

'I know. Somehow, that doesn't make me feel better. In fact, there are days when I wish that's how it had gone down.'

'Can you re-check this statement,' says Reed, handing over a copy of the one he'd made to Cardew and Simons, 'and see if you wish to change anything.'

Piper is aware of Fletcher's eyes on him as he scans the document. 'No. That's correct.' He hands it back over. 'We done here?' he asks.

'For now,' says Fletcher. Reed nods his agreement.

They shake hands and Piper leaves, checking his messages as he strides down the corridor towards the lifts. The first text is from Sarah. It is succinct and to the point: 'I need a fuck.'

★ ★ ★

Once Piper has left, Fletcher looks at Reed. 'After talking to his dad in the States, Piper became convinced that Monroe planted the bomb,' she says. 'That's why he went after him. The Feds had no idea about Greenslade or the dog wars. That's crap. They retro-fitted Piper into the frame.'

Reed nods, hardly shocked by the revelation that an organisation like the FBI protects its own. 'He couldn't have been more wrong, could he? The PERME boys swabbed Monroe's body. That man had not handled explosives.'

'No. Piper knows that now.'

'But he didn't share his suspicions with us?'

'Or his superiors. He tracked him down alone.'

Reed whistles. 'Shit. Withholding that kind of lead? They should can him.'

'I know.' She also knows the FBI have a department called the Office of Professional Responsibilities, the OPR, that ought to be informed of what they call 'lack of candour'. She wasn't going to be the one to tell them. Would Roth?

'Will they can him?' asks Reed, reading her mind.

'I don't know. Your daughter gets blown up in front of you, you get cut a lot of slack.'

'Enough to hang yourself with?'

'Maybe. He could be RIP'd.'

Reed is not as familiar with Federal jargon as Fletcher and his eyes widen.

'It means Retired In Place, Tom, not whacked. So, you boys think it was the Burning Joy of Allah that did Barnes & Noble?'

'Burning Light of Allah. We got the 'Joy' last month.' He considers for a moment. 'Look, we've been here before, and jumped to the wrong conclusions. Even if it is the same explosive, Ma'am, you know these people are often supplied from the same batch. It's like we all shop at Tesco or Sainsbury's. You find a packet of Red Label tea in my flat and one in yours, it doesn't mean we have ever met.'

'True, but there are fewer explosives wholesalers than supermarkets.'

'Doesn't seem like it sometimes.' Reed begins to bite at his nails. His fingertips are a mess. She looks down at her own. Not too elegant, either.

'Something bothering you, Sergeant?'

'Yes.'

'Me, too. Look, this is none of my business.'

'But?'

'I'd put a couple of men up behind him,' she suggests.

'Close surveillance on Piper?' He can't keep the surprise from his voice.

'If you can you spare the manpower. Just in case.'

'Just in case of what?' He winces as he tears a piece of cuticle off.

'Just in case the Yanks are really bullshitting us.'

Reed watches something form on her face, tentatively at first, as she runs through the possibilities. It takes a minute or so to harden into a certainty of sorts.

'Or maybe *they* are being bullshitted too.' She picks up the phone. 'There is something here I don't like. Amy, get me the Home Office.' She covers the receiver. 'I'm going to need your Super's backing on this.'

'What are you doing?'

'Putting my job on the line.' And a couple of friendships, too, she thinks.

'To do what?'

'Swab someone else for explosive residues.'

★　★　★

'It never ends, does it?'

Piper turns over to Sarah and kisses her, running his hands over her body, feeling the sweat in the small of her back, inhaling her perfume, reminding himself there is something to be said for live humans, when you spend all your time thinking about dead ones.

In fact, the closer your proximity to mortality, the more you need this antidote. 'I think I might have reached the end.'

'Nonsense,' she says, tickling him.

He strokes her upper arm, then down to the crook of her elbow, where his fingers snag on a patch of dry skin. She pulls away, embarrassed. 'I get it when I am stressed. Guess I am nervous about Martha's statue.'

They are in bed in her flat, curtains pulled, Verdi playing on the CD and he has just done his best to fulfil her text request. Then he explained about the whole circus with Monroe and how he feels he has even lost the trust of DCI Fletcher now.

He pulls her close, enjoying the feel of her breasts against his chest. 'You shouldn't worry about her statue. You should be proud of it. Of her.'

'So should you. Maybe tomorrow will be some kind of closure. Maybe the misery will end then,' she suggests. 'The end of a long, long road.'

'God, I hope so.' The following day the ceremony in the Residence garden will finally take place.

'Do you have your speech ready?' she asks.

'Me?'

'You have to say something.'

'I can't,' he protests.

'Jack Sandler will.'

'He is a politician. It's a glorified photo-call for him.'

'That's unfair.'

He nods. 'Maybe. But he was going to invite CNN till the security people vetoed it.'

'He's just trying to get coverage.'

'For himself. He's doing an interview with them the next day.'

'I thought you liked him.' she says.

Piper sighs. 'I do. I'm just not comfortable with all the crap that spins around something like this, I guess. He's just doing his job. Look, why don't you say something instead of me?'

'Don't be ridiculous,' she says.

'You got to know her as well as anyone this last year or so. It's your monument, it was your idea. Please.'

She squirms. 'I hate speaking in public.'

'You'll be perfect. Judy or I would go to pieces. I think you're stronger.'

She considers this. 'OK.'

'Thanks.'

'I guess I will have to write something.' She looks across at the clock. 'And I have to pick Mom up in a couple of hours from Paddington station.'

'What time is her train due in?'

'Seven.'

'Have to leave here at six because of traffic,' he calculates, rolling on top of her. 'Which gives us about ninety minutes.'

'Ah. A quickie, then.'

31

The Wolf's eyes snap open as he accelerates out of the deep sleep and into the light, the speed of his emergence causing his head to spin and stomach to drop. He gulps air frantically, and tries to still his poor heart. Something has happened, his body is telling him. You stopped breathing, maybe, just for a second. He lies and waits for his internal storm to quieten down, for his stricken body to find its painful equilibrium.

The house is quiet, but for the groans of the sidings as an east wind knifes through the suburb. Maggie must be out, perhaps changing the oxygen cylinders or getting drugs. He shifts position, feeling the tapes of the special pants he has to wear pinch into his skin. This is it, he tells himself. If not now, when? He chuckles at the thought of that famous phrase. Indeed. If not now, when?

He has heard about Monroe. Maggie has told him, and he finds it hard to believe. He was such a straight arrow. Well, apart from roughing up the ATM guy, but that was different. But what does losing a kid do to you? What has it done to his Vincent? And losing a child in such a terrible way, to a disease nobody really understands, one that cannot be detected and sits inside you for maybe decades before it bursts forth.

He worries about Vincent. He is in a mess, too. All because he let his cock do the thinking. At his son's age, he had already taken down the Wrecking Crew and had a name for himself in the Bureau, had his Medal for Bravery. Vince was a long way shy of that. Not that Vincent was a coward, just that the modern generation of Agents seemed more confused, less focused than his.

Mind you, maybe he was the one out of step. He stayed true to the Bureau's ethics right the way through the late 1960s and early 1970s, when even some of his colleagues got tempted by what they called the permissive society. He'd stuck by Maggie, never even put a joint in his mouth, let alone inhaled, couldn't imagine that sniffing drugs up a dollar bill was more fun than a six-pack and a piece of steak on the barbecue.

Monroe, he thought he'd been a by-the-book guy too, even if it wasn't the same volume the kids used now. He knew his partner never much cared for all the media fuss after he made that jump into the hopper with the armoured car. That wasn't his doing, though. The Bureau had taken some bad publicity hits, the legacy of Hoover was being eroded by increasingly fanciful claims. Here they had a straightforward case of the good guys winning. Hardly anyone supported the various Weather Undergrounds once they decided that armed robbery was a political act and shooting cops just a day at the hustings.

Those who had been captured were up for parole about now, looking forward to the rest of their lives outside, while his was rapidly shrinking to nothing. And what about those who really went underground, who hid as nurses and teachers and librarians and handymen? He wondered if they still started at every ring of the doorbell, an early-morning knock. He hoped so. Innocent guards killed, a policeman shot, and for what? Nothing.

He rolls onto his side, moving his shoulder back and forth until he is comfortable, and reaches under the mattress for the gun, its new hiding-place.

The Wolf looks at the revolver, at his shaking hands, and knows that in a few more days he won't have the strength to pull back the hammer. As it is, it takes both thumbs to make it snick back into position. He turns and places the short barrel against his head, manoeuvring it until he is absolutely sure it is in the right place, at the right angle, and he mentally kisses Maggie goodbye.

★ ★ ★

The traffic out west is the usual crawl, and there are road-works around Paddington. Sarah parks her little Mazda in the parking lot and they sprint for the station, skidding through the crowd milling around in the main hall, groaning at the signs and the Tannoy announcing that the Heathrow Express is suspended due to a security alert.

The train is up on the board as having arrived at Platform 6 about two minutes earlier.

When they reach the gate, the first passengers have alighted and are streaming out.

'That was close,' she says.

'I blame you,' he says.

'Why?'

He mimics her voice: ''Slow down, don't go so fast'.'

She slaps him playfully on the arm.

'Have you told your mother about me?' he asks.

'Uh-huh. Of course. I have no secrets from her. She is looking forward to meeting you.'

Something makes Piper's neck prickle and

he looks around. There are armed police in conspicuous evidence, but that is par for the course at stations these days. At one point he would guess Kevlar-armoured cops with H&K subs were a shock for the British public, but they are as much a fixture as WH Smiths these days.

'Tell me about her.'

'She's a very special lady. Very brave. I'm proud of her. You'll see.'

He does see, he sees the man by the news-stand, perusing the magazine. He'd noticed him in the car park. He doesn't appear to be waiting for anyone or in a hurry to catch a train. He's been tagged. By whom? Roth? Well, Roth was concerned about him, but he knew the Monroe business was over. Fletch. It had to be Fletcher. The Brits don't trust him any longer.

He looks around. Normally an 'up behind' surveillance would take many men, but he suspects they wouldn't get approval for a full-scale number. Too expensive. They can't even cover all the genuine terrorists they know are in London properly, let alone one rogue Fed. Piper thinks about going over, telling the guy he has been made, but thinks better of it. If he's any good, he knows already.

'Here she is! Mom!'

It takes a second for Piper to realise Sarah is waving at the old, bent woman being pushed out in a wheelchair by a porter. He fixes a smile on his face and goes forward to help.

★ ★ ★

'I take it all back.'

'Take what all back?'

'What I said about the Yanks, Ma'am.'

DI Reed is on the speakerphone to DCI Fletcher who is trying to get on top of her correspondence, much of it from an irate US businessman who wants to sue the Met for the way they treated his son, just because he bit two officers while resisting arrest outside a nightclub. 'What did you say about the Yanks?'

'Oh. Maybe I just thought it.'

'DI Reed, can you get on with it? I have to deal with a Texan gentleman who thinks the Metropolitan Police has a spare thirty million dollars to give him.'

'How'd you get on with the Home Office?'

'It'll take three days to get permission to exhume the body. As long as the family don't object,' she said brusquely. Of course they'll object. 'Tom? What about the Yanks?'

'The boffins at Quantico salvaged the shop's melted security tapes, rebuilt them

334

using computers to fill in all the gaps. They are enhanced and absolutely playable apparently. They're being Fedexed over. They'll be here tomorrow morning.'

'Can't they email the lot?'

'Worried about security, I suppose. But it looks good. The Feds did email a short clip over just to show the quality. They've got the coffee-shop cameras, Ma'am. We'll be able to see who the bomber is.'

*   *   *

'Eddie?'

Her voice hangs in the air, and his limpid eyes look at her. The gun is still pressed to his forehead, has been for ten minutes now, while he waits for whatever reserve of character it needs to reach the critical mass to enable him to pull the trigger.

The Wolf's wife walks over and gently takes the gun from his hand. He glares at her reproachfully, and she removes the mask and kisses the blue-tinged lips.

'You took the bullets.'

'Yes.' Before she placed it back under the pillows she'd slid out the shells. At one time, he'd have known by the weight that the gun was empty. In his diminished state, he couldn't tell.

'It's so hard.'

'I know.'

'For you too.'

'Don't worry about me.' She checks her watch and dials her son's number in England. When he comes on there is a cacophony in the background. She says it is about Dad, and before she can say anything else, he tells her he'll find somewhere quiet and ring back.

She crosses the room and refits the oxygen mask. Within a minute Vincent calls back and she explains.

'Put him on,' Vince says.

She hands the phone over.

'Dad.'

'Vince.' He tries to make his voice big and strong. He knows it is but a feeble echo of The Wolfman's growl.

'What are you doing, Dad?'

'You don't know what it's like, son. Nobody does. Knowing you will never, ever be well again. What's the point?'

'You wanted Mom to find you like that?'

'Those old soft noses don't make much mess.'

'And if it wasn't a clean shot?'

'You think I don't know how to shoot? At this range?'

They both laugh at this, one transforming into a sob that catches in the throat, the other a tight wheeze.

'Dad, I know it is difficult. I need you to promise me something.'

'I can't.'

'You don't know what it is yet.'

'I can guess,' croaks the old man.

'All I want you to do is wait until I get back. We've got Martha's dedication tomorrow at the Ambassador's Residence. Then I'll fly over. You want to finish it, we'll find a way to do it together. With us all there. I want to be holding your hand when it happens, not five thousand miles away. I won't try and talk you out of it, Wolf. Not if you don't want me to. That's my promise.'

'Couple of days?'

'At the most. What do you say?'

There is a long sigh. 'Hurry home, son.'

★   ★   ★

Lennie Ryder spends forty minutes in the flat. This is just like the old days, before he got into the sports and computer business with Roddy, before he went legit. Truth is, he has rather missed this excitement, the ball of fear in the stomach, the danger of discovery.

He spends ten minutes on the living room. Nothing. He boots up the laptop and examines the desktop, opening a few files at random. He isn't good enough to do much else, and if things are hidden, Lennie isn't the man to find them. He copies the hard disk onto the black box Roddy gave him and shuts the machine down. Roddy can trawl through the shit on there later.

The bathroom cabinet yields a large quantity of hydrocortisone and the usual make-up and shampoos and tampons, but again, nothing to raise so much as an eyebrow.

He finds them in the bedroom, bottom drawer, underneath the fancy underwear. There are fifteen in all. He flips through them, memorising what they depict, finds two that are almost identical, and pockets one. He'll just have to hope it won't be missed.

32

It is almost 11 a.m., and Winfield House, the Official Residence of the US Ambassador to the Court of St James, is set for a day of mourning, celebration and remembrance. The marquee where drinks will be served to the hundred or so guests has been erected just to the north of the dell where the statue has been placed. At the moment the bronze monument is wrapped in a billowing calico shroud. Rain has been forecast, but although the London skies remain leaden, it has stayed dry. As usual there are British AFOs deployed around the house grounds, plus a decent number of US Secret Service Agents within.

The driveway of Winfield House is a one-way system. Guests are checked at the barrier, their invitations scrutinised, names ticked off the list, and directed round to the right, where the cars are examined by the Metropolitan Police's C7 Explosives Officers — expos — with long-handled mirrors, electronic detectors and old-fashioned sniffer dogs. They are then directed to park up on the grass verge, well away from the house itself. Nobody will be allowed back to their vehicle unless they are leaving the party.

A string quartet is setting up and, at the climax of the ceremony, it will play two pieces by Alan Hovhaness that Judy and Sarah have chosen. One of them, *A Prayer of St Gregory*, with a featured trumpeter, Piper has heard in rehearsal, and he knows it will rip his heart out, and do the same to anyone in the audience who possesses one.

Judy has already arrived, having travelled down the previous day, and is inside the house with Mrs Sandler. She looks stunning in a black two-piece, hair drawn back, and she exudes a glacial beauty that hurts him inside. She is cooler towards him than he expected, as if making the point that only Martha was left to join them at the end, and that umbilical cord will finally be cut today.

'You OK, buddy?'

He turns to see Jack Sandler. They shake hands.

'Yes, Mr Ambassador. This is . . . well, thank you.'

'I've been talking to your wife. I think I've heard enough thank yous for one day. But you're welcome. My idea is that this isn't just for Martha, but for all fallen Americans, and their families who have suffered in this war. And it is a beautiful thing. I saw it being set in the ground before they covered it.'

Piper nods, but he hasn't seen the finished sculpture. Sarah had only fixed the pod onto the upstretched hands the previous day. She has now gone to fetch her mother from her flat. He feels bad about the meet at the station and its aftermath. He should have stayed with them, helped entertain, or at least push around, her mother, but he felt drained after speaking to his father. He had explained what had happened, sparing them the worst of the details, then gone home and drained a bottle of Riesling. At least he hadn't gone for his normal heavy red — his head would be paying that price right now.

'Look, Vincent, there are drinks afterwards at the house for a few people. I asked your wife. If you'd like to stay on . . . '

He thinks about Sarah, and then about Celeste, and he wonders what exactly each would do post-ceremony. He hadn't thought beyond the unveiling. Then there was Judy to consider. How did he end up with three women in his life? He has never managed one properly.

He should stay with Sarah, but he wants to speak to Celeste, and he shouldn't leave his estranged wife alone in the Ambassador's Residence. No, he couldn't be seen to go off early with any of them.

'Yes, that would be good,' is what he says. 'Thank — '

'Ah. No more thank yous.'

'Yes, sir. I'll be there.'

'Good.' Jack Sandler slaps Piper on the shoulder. He nods to an anxious woman whom Piper recognises as the head of the Embassy Protocol Office, who is acutely aware of the pecking order at such events. 'I have to go and greet and smile and be the Ambassador.'

Piper looks around the gardens. Most guests have gravitated straight to the champagne in the marquee. Groundsmen are putting the finishing touches to the thick rope barrier around the statue which will keep the crowd well away from the people gathered at the base. There is a small wooden podium, with a microphone, from where the speeches will be made. A police helicopter occasionally thrums overhead, drowning out the harsh, amplified sound of the muezzin from the nearby mosque. Here and there dark-suited men speak into their cuffs, confirming their positions and status.

Piper doesn't have a radio, but he does have a Glock 9mm under his jacket, which he managed to persuade Roth to authorise, today being an 'exceptional circumstance' involving Orange Level protection. It is the highest they can go to outdoors — a Red Level would mean the whole ceremony would be conducted in the house, with an armed man at every entrance, which is hardly practical. The gun won't be needed, of course, but it makes him feel better, as if he is a real law-enforcement officer once more.

'You know that Monroe had two weapons on him when he was killed?' Roth asked when Piper applied for permission to carry.

'Really?'

'One of them was the Sig someone took off the Secret Service guy at the Fairmont.'

'Son of a bitch.'

'Yeah.' Roth had held his gaze, but Piper hadn't flinched. There was no way to trace it back to him, unless they fingerprinted it, and even then the chances of a clean lift after Henry had handled it would be slight.

'So it must have been Monroe at the Fairmont,' Piper had suggested.

'It must have been,' came an unconvinced reply. Roth had moved on, the subject closed.

He sees Sarah wheeling her mother from the car park and raises his hand in greeting. Just get through this day, he tells himself, and then go and see The Wolf. Maybe then, when that bridge is crossed, along with this one, he can pick up his life once more.

★ ★ ★

Celeste's day has started badly. She returned
from Denis's an hour late, having overslept
because he had wanted to stay up until three
in the morning with some of his old London
pals and she'd had to play the happy hostess.
Her resolve not to attend this ceremony has
melted away over the previous few days. She
doesn't want to hurt Vincent, doesn't want
him to think she is snubbing him. So she will
go along, say the right things, and then
distance herself. He has a love affair to get on
with.

In her bathroom, still dressed in her
underwear, with ten minutes to go before she
must leave, she leans forward to apply the
touch-up pen to disguise the dark circles that
have colonised the thin skin under her eyes.
Not perfect, but not bad. She expertly applies
the rest of her make-up, keeping it as delicate
as possible, as befits the occasion, and in the
bedroom takes her dark blue Marc Jacobs
suit from the wardrobe, just as the phone
rings.

'Hi.'

'Roddy? Can't talk now, have to dash. I'm
late for the ceremony. I was going to call you
from the car. What have you found out?' she
asks, jamming the phone under her chin as

344

she struggles into her skirt.

'She's clean. She's who she says she is.'

Celeste suspected it had been a silly idea. 'So I did waste my money.'

'No, not entirely.'

'What do you mean?' Impatience creeps into her voice. 'Tell me now, Roddy.'

So he does, and she feels her heart race as she pulls on her jacket, trying to understand what he is saying to fit it into a bigger picture. It's as if someone has mixed up two jigsaws, and she is trying to sort one from the other. 'Roddy, thanks. I've got to go. And thank Lennie.'

'Cel.'

'Yes?'

'Be careful.'

'Of what?'

'I don't know. Just be careful. I told you I have a feeling your American friend attracts very bad things.'

She picks up her handbag and the invitation, checks herself in the mirror, and decides she will call Vincent Piper from the car on her mobile, see if what Lennie has found makes any kind of sense at all. As she opens the door, she is aware that the frame is blocked by a large presence. The unexpected blow hits her hard and she feels the man's rings slash into her skin. She staggers back,

345

the coffee-table scything into her calves, and she goes down in a shower of breaking glass and water as the vase and its flowers hit the wooden floor.

She hears the door slam and looks up, blinking to focus, wondering if her jaw has been broken by the backhand slap. As the man steps further into the room, she realises who it is.

Tim Brogan.

★   ★   ★

Piper looks at his watch. Five minutes to go and no sign of Celeste. Was she still annoyed that she hadn't been on the original list? Roth had smoothed things over and had her security rating reversed. He'd even called to apologise, so that was unlikely. As surreptitiously as he can, he dials her number, but it switches straight through to voice message. He hopes she isn't having problems at the gate.

At the entrance to the marquee he asks one of the Secret Service men to check if she has been ticked off the list. The guy whispers into his wrist and waits for the reply through his earpiece. 'That's a negative, Agent,' he says. Nor is there anybody waiting in line at the entrance.

The Embassy ushers begin to move people

from the interior of the tent to the designated spot outside. The majority of those present have formed a semi-circle behind the velvet rope, although a few chairs had been laid out on level ground for those who might not be able to manage on their feet for twenty minutes or so.

He helps Sarah wheel her mother to the lip of the dell, where she can see over the heads of the assembled crowd. Anita Nielsen looks up and smiles at him, her face crinkling into lines. He tries to guess her age. She looks sixty or more but if, as she has said, she had Sarah in her early twenties she can't be. It looks as if the constant back pain Anita admits to suffering from has aged her considerably.

He kneels down next to her, his elbow resting on the padded armrest. She is fiddling with her camera. 'You OK, ma'am?'

She bristles in mock anger. 'I told you. Drop the ma'am.'

'Sorry, I'm on duty,' he explains. 'Hard to shake it, Anita.'

She wraps a bony hand around his forearm. 'This is a great day for you. At least, as great as any can be after what happened.'

'It is, I know. Thanks to Sarah. She has to take some credit. And I appreciate you coming.'

'I would do anything for my daughter. And vice versa. I hope she does us proud up there.'

'She has already.' He glances over at Sarah, and allows himself to think of some of the times that lie ahead. That's as far as he dare project the relationship just now. It will go on, there will be good times, and if it leads to something else, more permanent, so be it. He indicates the thickening crowd of guests. 'It's quite a turn-out.'

She squeezes his hand. 'You all deserve it.'

As he looks over the guests towards the sculpture, Piper catches Judy's eye, winks at her and gets a smile in return. Maybe the day will be OK after all.

Sarah steps over and points down the slope to the statue and checks her watch. 'I think I'm on.'

Piper gives her a kiss on the cheek, wondering at the same time if Judy will notice. 'Good luck.'

A wind swishes across the gardens, rustling the trees, generating a low, mournful moan. Hands flash up to hats and down to skirts. He can feel the moisture heavy in the air. The atmosphere has become oppressive, just right for a wake. He tries Celeste again on the mobile phone. Nothing. She is going to miss it. He tries to rationalise that, but fails.

Maybe one of her clients is in town. After all, they pay the rent.

'My daughter looks beautiful,' says Anita.

'Yes, she does. And I can see where she gets it.'

Anita giggles. 'I'm afraid that's from Bruce, her dad. How is your father?'

He looks down at her and thinks back to his promise to go back to the States. 'Not good.'

'You should take care of him.'

'I will.'

'Ladies and gentlemen, thank you very much for coming, and welcome to the garden at Winfield House. You may be interested to know . . . ' On the podium Jack Sandler goes through his well-rehearsed history of the Residence — the hunting lodge, Barbara Hutton, the German bomb, the sale to the US for a dollar. How he had thought Winfield referred to some Lord who had hunted on this land, but discovered it was named after the Woolworth's in-house brand. So he was living in a nickel'n'dime palace.

He says some words about the war on terror and its civilian casualties, and dwells on the solidarity the British people had shown after 9/11 and the Afghanistan and Gulf Wars. He promises to return to read a citation before the unveiling, then hands over

349

to Sarah, who takes her place at the lectern.

'Thank you, Mr Ambassador.' Her voice is strong and determined, and carries well, despite the wind. 'I am here to say a few words about Martha Saxton and also to explain what this work we are about to unveil represented to her. Firstly, though, I think there should be someone down here for that unveiling. By the nature of their role, Federal Agents shun the limelight. But this is one moment he will have to endure it. If Vincent Piper, Martha's father, could join me?'

There is a smattering of applause, and when he remains rooted to the spot, she repeats, 'Vincent Piper,' and the applause grows louder, urging him forward.

He looks down at Anita, who nods her encouragement, and he moves down the grass slope. As he skirts the assembled guests, he swerves into the melee and, before she can object, pulls Judy to his side.

'Vin, no,' she hisses.

'She was your daughter, too.'

They step over the rope and walk the fifteen yards to the statue, its shroud now snapping loudly in the wind. 'Thank you,' says Sarah. 'I first met Martha Saxton . . .' she begins, and he closes his ears. He is going to have to fight not to cry. Perhaps it is just as well Celeste isn't here to see him.

The second blow has wedged her firmly between sofa and coffee-table, and there she lies, panting, looking up at Brogan's face as he sucks air through his bared teeth. Her mobile rings and he rips it from her bag, throws it down and stomps on it till it stops. Then his anger seems to drain away.

He reaches down and pulls her up effortlessly, and she knows that she should squash any faint hope she has of overpowering him. He sits her down on the sofa and stands before her, a kind of serenity on him now. 'Where is he?'

'Tim — '

'Where is he?'

'Where is who?'

'Your hired muscle.'

'I don't have any hired muscle.'

He grabs a handful of hair and twists and she squeals.

'Maybe he does it for free. Or for blowjobs. But he's muscle.'

'I don't know where he is.'

He twists harder and forces her to rise as he raises his arm. He lets go and she flops back into the cushions, her scalp aflame.

'I'm going back to Hong Kong,' he explains. 'My territory. He can't touch me

351

there. So I can settle up with him before I go. I need to know who he is and where he lives.'

'Tim. He is just a friend, I didn't ask him to do anything. He found out what you did to me and just flew off the handle.'

'I don't care whether you asked him or not, you fucking whore. He did what he did. I can't let that lie. *Who is he?*'

The arm is back, ready to strike, and she knows she can't take many more cuts from those rings.

'His name is Vincent Piper.'

The arm lowers slightly. 'Good. Now where is he?'

She glances at the clock on the wall behind him and says in a low murmur, 'I can take you to him.'

'Yeah, right.'

'I can't phone him, can I — warn him? This way, you'll have the element of surprise, just like he did with you.'

'Get up.' Brogan yanks her to her feet, his fingers digging deep into her biceps. From his pocket he takes a Swiss Army knife and unfolds the largest blade. He doesn't really need it, Celeste already knows she is powerless against his strength and fury. He rummages in her bag and tosses her the Volvo's keys.

'OK, let's go and see your Mr Vincent Piper.'

33

'Martha called this piece *Stripped*. She wrote that it symbolised the way governments and the industrial-military complex conspire to strip everything of value from ordinary people around the world. Their money, their food, their livelihood, their dignity, their children.'

Piper detects a ripple of unease in the crowd as Sarah speaks. He has to remind himself that Martha was a young girl, with the views and slewed rhetoric of youth, when everything is black and white. As she hits her stride, Sarah seems to grow at the lectern, raising herself up to her full height.

'She also believed in taking sides. One of her favourite quotes was: 'There is no excuse for not struggling to make things better. To not act, to not do anything is criminal, and is complicity'.'

He looks at Judy. She shrugs her ignorance of the source. It rings a distant bell, but Piper has never heard Martha use it. When he last spoke to her, her favourite quote had seemed to be 'whatever'.

'In a few seconds, I will ask Mr Jack Sandler and Martha's father to pull the cords that will unveil this remarkable tribute to a remarkable young lady. First, however, the Crossley Quartet with Martin Hyams on trumpet will play Alan Hovhaness's 'Prayer of St Gregory'. As you may know, St Gregory was the man who took Christianity to Armenia in the year 301.' This is news to Piper. 'He was rewarded by being cast into a pit without light for fifteen years. After which he cured the King of his madness as forgiveness for what he had done. This music is a prayer from that darkness.'

The low drone of the opening bars begins and Piper bites his lip. He joins in the clapping as Sarah steps down and strides up the slope to rejoin her mother. As the strings soar, picking out what seem to be parts of every hymn he remembers from childhood, the trumpet comes in over them with its plaintive melody, and Piper steals a glance at Judy. He takes out a handkerchief and slips it to her and she dabs at her eyes. The smile she gives him this time is rich with the old warmth.

It is as the volume of the music lowers towards the end, the strings soft and lush, the smallest hint of daylight breaking through into St Gregory's all-consuming blackness, moments before the soaring trumpet returns to restate the main motif, that Piper hears the squeal of tyres. At the same time, he recalls exactly where Martha's 'no excuse' quote comes from.

★ ★ ★

Celeste enters the Outer Circle of Regent's Park, just north of Baker Street, and travels clockwise, heading for the landmark of the London Central Mosque. Next to her, Brogan shifts in his seat. 'Where are we going? The Zoo?'

'He's at a function up here. I'll point him out to you, I swear.'

He flicks the Swiss Army knife from his sleeve and stabs the point into her leg, causing her to wince. 'You'd better be doing this straight, m'lady.'

She passes a parked police car, the yellow dots on the rear windows indicating it is an ARV, Armed Response Vehicle. However, it is empty. She glances across at Brogan. The face is still set in a mask of hate. She needs to get away from him.

'Just ahead,' she says.

She waits until she is level with another ARV that marks the entrance to the Residence and spins the wheel on the SUV hard. The electronics that are meant to prevent a rollover are sorely tested as the big vehicle lumbers into a ninety-degree turn, but the Volvo remains mostly upright. Brogan is thrown against the window and the knife slides out of his hand onto the floor.

She can see the various figures ahead at the security barrier suddenly taking notice. *Look at me*, she wills them. *Look at me*. Her only idea is to leap out and tell them to arrest Brogan, hoping she can make them understand.

She brakes, hard. Guns are raised towards her.

'What the fuck are you playing at?' Brogan is still struggling to sit upright. Beyond him she sees the ceremony, the tight crowd, the cluster of VIPs at the base, and Sarah at the top of the dell.

Someone is yelling at her, but she can't hear what they are saying.

'*Turn off the engine and exit the vehicle. Now.*'

Sarah is talking to the woman in the wheelchair who is holding a fat-lensed camera, and the pieces that have been spinning through her mind lock into place, producing a blinding insight.

The camera. Sarah. It fits in with what Lennie told her he had found in the flat, hidden in a drawer. Photographs. Obscene photographs.

She knows what is going to happen, where it will end, how it will end. With lots of bodies.

Brogan bends down, scrabbling for the knife.

'Exit the vehicle — '

She spins the wheel again, squealing the back end of the Volvo round so it is parallel with the barrier across the road, the tyres disappearing in a cloud of acrid smoke. All the security at Winfield is designed to protect the house, not the gardens, and she finds her way blocked only by a low concrete beam, sloping away from her at forty-five degrees.

The Volvo's bonnet crumples, but the four-wheel drive system pulls and pushes it up the ramp, and the big car launches itself over the barrier. The chassis crashes down on the top, cracking it, but still it drags itself over with a teeth-clenching squeal.

There is panic and pandemonium. A hundred pairs of eyes have turned towards her. Brogan sinks his fingers into her arm as she floors the accelerator. The damaged Volvo shudders and creaks but lurches forward.

The first rounds from the security detail hit the back and sides of the vehicle, a soft *pink-pink* sound as the metal punctures. The car bucks and skids onto the grass as a rear tyre explodes, its run-flat technology unable to cope with a shredding by nine-millimetre slugs. It is crabbing down the slope and she is barely in control. A spider's web appears in the windscreen, then a second — each with a small neat hole at the centre.

She is thrown back against the seat by an impact, and her shoulder turns white-hot. One side of her body goes numb. She can't feel her hand on the wheel.

Then Brogan, his eyes wide with terror, makes the mistake of reaching across and grabbing the steering-wheel.

★ ★ ★

DCI Fletcher walks into the C7 ops room and stops. The blinds have been drawn, and it takes a second for her to adjust to the gloom.

'Hello, Ma'am,' says DI Reed. There are six officers from what used to be called the Bomb Squad, all facing the LCD screen of a computer, but he doesn't make the introductions. 'Are you ready for this?'

'You've seen the tapes already?'

'We have, just now. Very clever. Fire damage, then water damage — but the Feds used a computer to link up whole passages with fragments of images. It looks a bit odd, but you can see exactly what happened.'

'Go ahead, then.'

Reed points the remote and the screen is instantly filled with a grainy complex image. It is a view of a coffee-shop, the Barnes & Noble coffee-shop, taken from high-vantage points. A few people sit around, chatting. For two minutes nothing much happens. Jacqueline Fletcher keeps quiet, simply eyeing the time frame in the corner, counting it down to when she knows this place went straight to hell.

She watches a figure come into frame, wearing combat trousers, a brown cord jeans jacket, and holding a selection of carrier bags. Recognition hits her.

Carrier bags. Heavy ones.

'Christ. Did we know this? Did we know she went inside first?'

'No,' says Reed.

'There's nothing on the outside CCTV to confirm it,' says one of the nameless ones.

On screen, in jerky unco-ordinated movements, and in silence, Martha Saxton/Piper sits, orders a coffee and examines her watch. She takes out her mobile phone but the waitress says something to her. She points to the sign on the wall.

'Barnes & Noble make a big play of not allowing mobiles in the London shops,' explains Reed.

Martha speaks to the waitress and points at

her bags. She moves off, out of frame. Why? Where is she going? After a second, the waitress takes the bags and places them behind the counter.

'Shit,' says Fletcher. 'She told the waitress to mind her bags while she went to make the call to her dad and she put them out of the way for safekeeping.'

'Which signed the poor girl's death warrant.'

There is a white flash on the monitor; the screen goes blank.

Fletcher struggles to come to terms with what she is seeing. But the implication is clear. The images don't lie. Martha, Vince's daughter, had planted the bomb that killed her and the others and maimed dozens.

Several PRs and telephones squawk into life at once, bringing sudden cacophony to the room, scrambling Fletcher's thoughts. Reed answers his personal radio and slams it down. 'IR room, quick.'

Together they race along the corridor as fast as they dare. They burst into the Information Room, where six monitors show the same scene, shot from a helicopter hovering above Winfield House.

Fletcher speaks for them all: 'Oh, fuck.'

★ ★ ★

As the guests panic, and either run or dive to the ground, Piper feels the world around him slowing. Only he is moving at normal speed. He grabs Jack Sandler and throws him over the low rope cordon, before doing the same with Judy, yelling at them both to get clear. The Volvo is heading down the hill towards him, trailing steam, smoke and rubber; the wind-shield is peppered with shots, the driver probably dead. But still it comes on.

At the top of the dell he can see Sarah, silhouetted against the gunmetal sky, the only one still standing up there, frozen to the spot next to her mother. Anita is holding her camera, Sarah is pointing with her right hand. Her movements look as if she is underwater, and he realises she is still going to be standing when the Volvo gets near them.

Piper runs, hurdling the rope and, with a turn of speed that The Wolf in his heyday would envy, is up there in seconds.

Her face is contorted, she is still pointing something at him, right at his chest, but he is on top of her, pushing her down and using his body to shield her. 'It's OK. It's OK,' he says. 'Sarah.'

He doesn't recognise the woman snarling up at him.

The burning pain in his back makes him arch and he rolls off her, a scream on his lips.

As he spins round he sees Anita, raising the knife once more, the four-inch blade she has slid from her chair wet with his blood. He kicks as hard as he can, catching the old woman below the knees, and she goes back with a scream, crashing into the abandoned wheelchair.

Sarah is on her knees now, swearing, pointing her device at the still-shrouded statue. Piper watches in horror as the carcass of the Volvo ploughs into his daughter's sculpture, sheering the figure at ankle level from its the plinth, tearing what is left of the muffler from the underside of the SUV as it mounts the stumps, careering through the stands and seats where the string players had been sitting seconds before.

What is Sarah doing? What is that in her hand?

'Oh shit!' she yells. 'Shit, you bastards!'

'Sarah, drop it.'

She looks at him as if he is beneath contempt.

Piper raises himself up on one elbow, pulls out the Glock, sights Sarah for a shot. It feels like madness.

'Sarah, stop!'

The Academy had drilled into him, time and again, that going for anything other than a complete knockdown is stupid. But he can't. What if he is wrong once more?

She is on her feet, arm outstretched.

'Sarah.' He is pleading now.

That look, only even darker this time. 'Fuck you.'

The Glock kicks as he fires, and he blows out a large section of her upper thigh. She should have gone down — the arc of bright blood spraying over the grass means a hefty hit. It causes her to stagger, but she recovers. She touches the wound and examines the bright red smear on her hand.

Go down, damn you. End it now.

He raises the Glock for a second shot when the door of the Volvo swings open and he freezes. Celeste. She falls out from beneath what looks to be a lifeless body, the head and chest of the man a bloody pulp where several rounds have hit it. It is hard to tell whether she is injured. There are certainly plenty of sickeningly dark patches on her face and clothes. On legs of rubber she half-totters, half-runs away from the car, away from the mangled statue which is now resting across the windshield and roof.

She is almost clear when Sarah staggers several steps down the slope. She presses the detonation device and the radio beam gets a clear signal through to its target at last. For the second time in a few cruel weeks, Vincent

Piper sees a woman he loves disappear into the debris as an explosion rips through the air, the sound of his own gun lost in the reverberations.

34

Roth and Beckett are in a hotel bar near Marylebone. It is late, and they are the only customers. They have spent the last twelve hours piecing together what happened at Winfield House. They are trying not to be judgmental about Piper's role in the whole mess. It is difficult.

'The daughter planted the bomb at Barnes & Noble.'

'The daughter *carried* the bomb at Barnes & Noble,' corrects Roth.

'Did she know what she had in the bag — what she was carrying?'

'We don't know. It was apparently inside a plaster model. Only the Nielsen woman knows whether the Saxton girl was just a mule or not.'

'And is the Nielsen woman talking?' asked Beckett.

'If she makes it she might. Piper got her ass with the second shot, but nicked the femoral artery with the first. She lost a bucketload of blood. The grass where she fell'll grow greener than the rest for years to come.'

'He should have killed her.'

'You didn't hear that,' says Roth to the barman, who shrugs in a heard-what? attitude. 'And if he had, we'd have no chance of getting to the bottom of this. Same again?'

'Sure. We got the mother, though.'

'The mother ain't saying jack, so far.'

'Well, either way, whether Martha Piper — '

'Saxton.'

'Whether she knew what she was doing or not, she didn't deserve a statue to the fallen,' says Beckett, and laughs. 'So it's just as well it got trashed. Did you tell Piper what was on the tape?'

'Worse. I showed him.' Roth shudders at the recollection of the man's hollow eyes as he watched his daughter walk into the coffee-shop carrying a lethal gift. 'He, of course, is convinced Martha was suckered by the Nielsen woman. Tricked into taking a bomb to the meeting. He thinks he was meant to take it home, some kind of present from his kid, and it went off prematurely. He says thirty per cent of all detonators malfunction.'

'You don't buy it.'

'For a start the tech boys say it is ten per cent.' Roth picks an olive off the tray of bar snacks and pops it in his mouth. 'You know what happened at the ceremony? They'd rigged it to detonate with a remote car key system, instead of the usual mobile phone.'

'But?'

'But some of those systems are glitched by nearby radio sources. I used to have a Ford Explorer here. Wouldn't start if you were near the BT tower. There is a good chance the phone tower just outside the grounds saved a lot of lives.'

Beckett thinks on that for a second and asks: 'What about this idea that the daughter was a stooge?'

'OK.' Roth takes another olive. 'What if Sarah Nielsen had managed to convince Martha that her father was a legitimate target?' He spits the stone out into his hand. 'Hell, he'd left the mother for some bit of tail, so he was certainly no angel. And, of course, as a member of the FBI he was The Man, as they used to say. The Government's blunt instrument of oppression.'

'Aren't we all?' Beckett swirled the ice in his fresh drink. 'You believe that outline?'

Roth shrugs, refusing to be drawn. He doesn't like it any more than Piper would. Which is why he isn't going to spell it out to him, not until he can stand it up. Or knock it down. 'I'm going to run it as a possible scenario. One of several,' he adds.

'There is one way to be sure.'

'Yup,' says Roth. 'Exhume the body and

swab the girl for residues. Prove she handled the explosives rather than just carried them. The Brits are way ahead of us on that one. Fletcher already had an exhumation request into the Home Office. She was going to pull the girl up anyway.'

'And?'

'Deferred for the moment. They are waiting for some of the dust to die down. Piper leaves the country in a few days. They'll pull her up as quietly as they can, get us an answer.'

'Are we sure Piper *isn't* an Agent of Satan?'

Roth shakes his head. He knows Beckett does not share his opinion of — or latent affection for — Vincent Piper. 'He's the son of The Wolfman. In the end, I think, that's why those people wanted him dead.' Roth raises his glass and they chink. 'The rest can wait for tomorrow. Right now, I think I need a couple more of these.'

★ ★ ★

The day has dawned miserable and smudged, matching Piper's mood as he pulls up to the private hospital at the north end of Harley Street. Traffic is snarled along the Marylebone Road, and the air is sharp with fumes. He can feel the grime sticking to his skin. He hates this town.

Piper feeds the meter with an hour's worth of coins — a Queen's ransom — and takes his flowers from the back seat.

Celeste is on the first floor in her own room, propped up by pillows, her face glowing, just a hint of pain in her eyes. The bullet wound in her shoulder is heavily bandaged. She smiles when she sees him and takes the flowers. 'Lovely. Jane Packer.'

'If you say so. Selfridges.' Then: 'I don't know where to begin,' he says. 'I read the debrief. What you did . . . '

'God, I thought those Agents were going to spend the night with me,' she says. 'The nurses had to throw them out.'

It is three days since the explosion, the first time he has been allowed to see her since the incident. 'How are your car premiums?'

'Sky-high, I would imagine. I might have to start taking cabs.' She laughs then grimaces. 'Careful about making me laugh. I've got some stitches.' She touches the back of her head with her free arm, the site where most of the metal from the bomb has been extracted. 'How about you?'

'Yeah, Anita stuck me pretty good.' The blade, though, had slid around his ribs rather than penetrating his organs. The woman hadn't had time to shiv him properly before he got her down. He touches the tight tapings under his shirt. 'I was lucky.'

'So was I. They told me the expos — see, I'm getting the jargon — the expos say the charge was primed to blow from the oval shape the statue was carrying, down into the crowd. Into you. Most of it went into my poor Volvo. And Tim Brogan.' There is just a undercurrent of regret when she says his name, as if he didn't deserve what happened.

'I think the FBI owes you a new one.'

'What, a lover?'

'An SUV. And don't feel sorry for Brogan. Best thing he ever did was take the hits for you.' Tim Brogan had leaned across at just the wrong moment to grab the wheel, and had been the recipient of several H&K bursts from the security team.

'I don't think they owe me anything. There was just something that one of the students said to me at the foundry — that at first, Sarah had seemed to hate Martha. Then, a few months before she died . . . '

'When I came to the UK,' he says flatly.

'She became teacher's pet. The girls were just chatting, saying how surprised they were that Sarah was doing all this, because at one time they were convinced she hated her. Then . . . ' Her mouth tightens a fraction. 'I think I had better get some more pain relief.' She presses the button to summon a nurse.

'You know, I didn't really put it together until I got to the ceremony. It's weird, isn't it, the way things sometimes just click into place.'

Or get jammed, he thinks, as they did with Monroe. 'What tipped Roddy off about Sarah?'

'It wasn't Sarah, it was the mother, Anita. Nothing about her was right. The name, the social security numbers. Oh, they were all right for a couple of years back, but the name on her passport wasn't Anita Nielsen when she flew in from Canada. Roddy accessed her medical records from the hospital in Plymouth where she had an op eighteen months back, and found that she'd had an old bullet wound in the back. That was what crippled her. She claimed it was from a mugging that happened in the US. There was no way Roddy could verify that, but he said he suddenly had a very bad feeling about the Nielsens.'

'The bullet was from The Wolf,' Vincent tells her. 'Anita was in the U-Haul after the armoured-car robbery. My dad had emptied a magazine into it. Looks like he hit her.'

'Why didn't the security vetting at the Embassy pick up on this?'

'Mother was a late addition, remember?' he says. 'The daughter came up clean — who is going to look too closely at the old crippled mother?'

371

'Roddy,' she said.

'Yes. Thank the Lord for Roddy.'

And the five grand, Celeste thinks. 'You have to remember he felt bad about giving Tim the OK, when he really turned out to have this little problem with losing. So he went the extra mile. He sent Lennie to burgle her flat.'

'What? Sarah's apartment? That's not in your debrief.'

'No. I think we keep that one quiet, don't we?'

'I guess'. Piper was shaken. 'What did he find?'

'Photographs of Martha taken with a long lens. Going into the bookshop. Coming out. The aftermath. The dead. The injured. Pictures of you . . . ' She shakes her head at the callousness. 'Photographs of you holding Martha, running with her.' It was the sight of the mother sitting in the wheelchair, aiming a camera, that had somehow made everything click for Celeste, made her sure that Sarah and that bitch were the danger.

'Shit. She was watching the explosion?'

'Sarah was watching that day, from a distance. A first-floor window, by the look of it.'

Vince is going to have a hell of a time explaining this to The Wolf. That Anita

372

Nielsen is really Sally Borodin, one of the last fugitives of the Weather Front, who had survived the Wrecking Crew incident.

Sarah is her daughter, Buttercup, whom she had picked up after the fiasco of the Big Dance, having managed to avoid capture. The father was Bruce Hopper, the man who'd blown himself up making a bomb to detonate somewhere in Washington.

After the failed heist, Anita had scooped up her daughter and fled over the border north to Canada, where they lived a blameless existence. Then came CANAL, the programme that involved sharing of fugitive information with Canada, which made their unmasking likely. So they'd moved to England on Canadian passports.

She hadn't come away from the ill-conceived escapade unscathed, though. The Wolf's bullet saw to that. The hatred that grew inside her also seems to have infected her daughter and it's just possible it was passed on to . . .

No, no, he reassures himself, Martha was an innocent player. And what about the other bomb, at Banana Republic, and the note at Starbucks? They must have been to throw them off the scent, send them scrabbling after the anti-global camp, until this neo-Weather Front was ready to try again properly. Piper figured that, although they couldn't get back to the US to get at his dad, they could exact revenge of sorts by killing him and gloating about it to The Wolf, making the old man's last months even worse than they were going to be.

The quote at the abortive unveiling wasn't Martha's, of course. It was by Bernardine Dohrn, one of the original movement's heroes, the pin-up of the Weather Underground, both sister organisation and arch-rival to Borodin's group. They all shared a vision of themselves as Robin Hoods, albeit ones that shot cops and security guards with impunity while claiming to stand up for the oppressed. The words Sarah had used had been slightly doctored — since Dohrn had made it clear that violence was the prime instrument of 'fighting behind enemy lines' as she put it back then. Where was more behind enemy lines than the grounds of the US Ambassador's Residence in London?

Of course, he could blame Sarah and Anita — or whatever their names really were — all he liked, but the fact remained that there was something he would have to live with: one night, in the aftermath of a raid in which people died, Piper had slept with a woman who wasn't his wife. The butterfly flapped its wings, and a couple of years later a storm raged through London. His storm.

Without that infidelity with Rachel, Judy would never have moved back to England, and Martha would never have ended up at the American College of Art where a twisted mind was already at work, doubtless unable to believe her luck that a chance for revenge for her mother had been tossed to her. In one sense, killing The Wolf's son and granddaughter, he guessed, would have been almost as satisfying as getting the old man himself.

'Vince?'

'Yeah?'

'One thing has been puzzling me.'

'Oh, I wish I only had one.' There were enough questions to keep Special Branch and the newly announced Serious Organised Crime Agency, SOCA, busy for months. Such as how a crippled woman and her daughter managed to obtain explosive material and make and plant bombs without detection. Did they act alone, or were there other cells/sympathisers in the UK? 'What's yours?'

'Why didn't Sarah just kill you? She had plenty of opportunities.'

There were dozens. She could have slit his throat while he was sleeping. Drugged him. She could have done what she liked on those days and nights when they were in bed together. Had that all been an act? It must have been. Phony passion, fake enjoyment. Not on his part, though. Only in retrospect does it seem sick and contrived, leaving a nasty taste in his mouth and a cloud over his heart. How could he have been so stupid? Because, once again, as with Rachel, he wasn't thinking with anything above his spinal column.

He shakes his head at her question. 'I think she wanted a public execution. A Big Dance, as they used to call it. A show of strength.' And no doubt the way they had planned it, once the statue exploded, mother and daughter would have been long gone before an investigation had even started to focus in the confused aftermath. No, they wanted the world and The Wolf to see his demise.

'What'll happen to them now?'

'Well, Sarah's prints were on the Barnes & Noble bomb, which is a British concern. However, the Winfield House grounds are US Government property. They committed crimes on American soil, and my feeling is your people won't put up much of an objection to them being extradited and put on trial back home. Plus Anita — Sally Borodin — has to pay for the Pittsboro heist.'

'What about you?'

He takes her hand and strokes the long fingers. In a world where everybody — including

376

himself — has a confused and often duplicitous agenda, it seems ironic that only Celeste, a woman society would condemn as amoral, is good and true. 'I have to go to the US and fulfill a promise I made to my father.'

The nurse enters, Celeste explains that her shoulder is throbbing and uncomfortable, and she leaves to fetch some medication.

'I'd better go. I have a plane to catch.'

'Will you be back?'

'I don't know.' He rubs his tired eyes, dreading the flight already, anxious about what he will find at the other end. 'Do you want me to come back?'

'I'd like you to, yes.'

'Then I'll come back,' he says, kissing her hand, unsure himself whether he is leaving her with a lie.

Acknowledgments

I would like to thank Marie from Paris, who inspired Celeste, and Dan (NYC) who did the same for Vin. Both have jobs roughly equivalent to their fictional counterparts, and they'd make a lovely couple if they ever met. When I wrote *Steel Rain*, there was no Fairmont in London, although now it looks likely it will take over management of the Savoy. I am sure security there will be better than depicted here. Similarly, Barnes & Noble and Banana Republic have yet to make it over. And apologies to Jesus Adorno at Le Caprice. He'd never allow such goings-on.

Jack Sandler's speech on the history of Winfield House is based on one given by Raymond Seitz when he was Ambassador. His book *Over Here* is highly recommended as an insight into the minutiae of the job. The crash of Sandler's dad's Lockheed Lightning is based on a real event. The details are in *Final Flights*, a book about aviation archaeology by Ian McLachlan (Patrick Stephens Limited).

The Weather Underground (formerly the Weathermen) was active in the 1960s and

1970s. From liberal student beginnings, the organisation quickly moved to bombings (including the Pentagon) and violent demonstrations to try and bring down the US Government. Bernardine Dohrn was the group's glamorous spokesperson (there is a famous portrait of her taken by Richard Avedon, at the height of 'radical chic'), who explained that the aim was to 'build a white revolutionary movement' to support the Black Panthers. (Dohrn now teaches law at a US university.)

By the late 1970s the WU was in disarray, but elements of it had linked up with the Black Liberation Army, part of whom believed armed robbery was a political act, with the side benefit of funding a drug-dealing cartel. At least one of their heists, on a Brinks Mat armoured car in October 1981, was codenamed Big Dance. For more details on the robbery and its aftermath, see *The Prisoner* by Elizabeth Kolber in the *New Yorker*, the 16 July 2001 issue.

Back in the 1980s and early 1990s the hotdog stands of London were a source of various recreational drugs. The idea of a CJD cluster traceable to them, though, is fictional. So far.

However, Caroline Smith DeWaal, Director of Food Safety for the Center for Science in the Public Interest, told the *New York Times* in December 2003 that US consumers should avoid 'hotdogs, salami, bologna and other products that contain not only ground beef but beef from machinery that squeezes out bits of meat that cling to the spinal column.'

There is an on-going controversy about the CJD cluster centred on people connected with the now-defunct Garden State racetrack in Cherry Hill, New Jersey. It was established by Janet Skarbek, who noticed in an obituary that the person who had died of the disease had worked at the track, just like her friend, who also contracted CJD. She then doggedly traced twelve others who had been infected and died. However, there are those (the beef industry among them) who insist this is a freak statistical coincidence, especially as none of the cases appear to involve new variant CJD. An investigation by the New Jersey Department of Health maintained that these deaths were examples of 'spontaneous' CJD. Janet Skarbek, who now claims there are sixteen victims, remains unconvinced. At the time of writing CJD is not a notifiable disease in the USA, although it has been in Canada since 2000.

For some of the psychology behind both Monroe and Piper's actions (particularly the latter's obsessing on the former), I would refer you to the article 'Psychiatric problems following bereavement by murder or manslaughter' by C.M. Parkes (London Hospital Medical College) in the *British Journal of Psychiatry*, 162: 49–54 (1993).

Finally, *Steel Rain* made it due to the support of David Miller and the enthusiasm and hard work of Martin Fletcher. My heartfelt thanks to both of them.

Tom Neale, London